（中英文双语对照）

孙大雨 译

【英】威廉·莎士比亚 著

李尔王

上海三联书店

KING LEAR.

DRAMATIS PERSONAE

Lear, King of Britain
King of France
Duke of Burgundy
Duke of Cornwall
Duke of Albany
Earl of Kent
Earl of Gloucester
Edgar, Son to Gloucester
Edmund, Bastard Son to Gloucester
Fool.
Curan, a Courtier
Old Man, Tenant to Gloucester
Oswald, steward to Goneril
Physician
An Officer employed by Edmund
Gentleman, attendant on Cordelia
A Herald
Servants to Cornwall
Goneril, daughter to Lear
Regan, daughter to Lear
Cordelia, daughter to Lear

剧 中 人 物

李尔,不列颠国王

法兰西国王

淳庚岱公爵

康华公爵

亚尔白尼公爵

铿德伯爵

葛洛斯忒伯爵

蔼特加,葛洛斯忒之子

蔼特孟,葛洛斯忒之野生子

傻子

居任,廷臣

老人,葛洛斯忒之佃户

奥士伐,刚瑙烈之管家

医师

蔼特孟所雇之队长一人

考黛莲之近侍一人

传令官一人

康华之仆从数人

刚瑙烈 ⎫

雷耿 ⎬ 李尔之女

考黛莲 ⎭

Knights attending on the King, Officers, Messengers, Soldiers, and Attendants

SCENE: Britain

李尔之随从武卫数人,军官数人,信使数人,军士多
人,侍从数人

剧景:不列颠

ACT I.

SCENE I. *King Lear's Palace.*

[*Enter* Kent, Gloucester, *and* Edmund.]

Kent I thought the King had more affected the Duke of Albany than Cornwall.

Gloucester It did always seem so to us; but now, in the division of the kingdom, it appears not which of the Dukes he values most; for equalities are so weighed that curiosity in neither can make choice of either's moiety.

Kent Is not this your son, my lord?

Gloucester His breeding, sir, hath been at my charge; I have so often blush'd to acknowledge him that now I am braz'd to't.

Kent I cannot conceive you.

Gloucester Sir, this young fellow's mother could: whereupon she grew round-wombed, and had indeed, sir, a son for her cradle ere she had a husband for her bed. Do you smell a fault?

Kent I cannot wish the fault undone, the issue of it being so proper.

Gloucester But I have a son, sir, by order of law, some year elder than this, who yet is no dearer in my account; though this knave came something saucily into the world before he was sent for, yet was his mother fair; there was good sport at his making, and the whoreson must be

第 一 幕

第 一 景

［李尔王宫中。］

［铿德，葛洛斯忒与蔼特孟上。

铿　　德　我以为国王对亚尔白尼要比对康华公爵更心爱些。

葛洛斯忒　我们总是这么样看法；不过在现今划分国土这件事上，却瞧不出他更看重的是那一位公爵；因为两份土地的好坏分配得那么均匀，所以即使最细心的端详也分辨不出彼此有什么厚薄。

铿　　德　这一位不是令郎吗，伯爵？

葛洛斯忒　将他抚养成人是由我担负的，伯爵；我红着脸承认他的回数多了，也就脸皮老了。

铿　　德　我不明白你的意思。

葛洛斯忒　伯爵，这少年人的母亲可明白；因此上她就鼓起肚子，床上还不曾有丈夫，摇篮里倒先有了孩子了。你觉得是个过错吗？

铿　　德　我却不能愿意你没有那过错，你看这果子结的多么漂亮体面。

葛洛斯忒　不过我还有个嫡出的儿子，比这个要大上一岁光景，但并不比他更在我心上；虽然这小子不招自来，出世得有些莽撞，他母亲可长得真俏，造他出来的那时节真好玩儿，所以这小杂种是少不了要承认的。——

acknowledged. — Do you know this noble gentleman, Edmund?

Edmund   No, my lord.

Gloucester   My Lord of Kent. remember him hereafter as my honourable friend.

Edmund   My services to your lordship.

Kent   I must love you, and sue to know you better.

Edmund   Sir, I shall study deserving.

Gloucester   He hath been out nine years, and away he shall again. — The king is coming.

[*Sennet within.*]

[*Sennet Enter one bearing a coronet*, King Lear, Cornwall, Albany, Goneril, Regan, Cordelia, *and* Attendants.]

Lear   Attend the lords of France and Burgundy, Gloucester.

Gloucester   I shall, my liege.

[*Exeunt* Gloucester *and* Edmund.]

Lear   Meantime we shall express our darker purpose. —
Give me the map there. — Know that we have divided
In three our kingdom; and 'tis our fast intent
To shake all cares and business from our age;
Conferring them on younger strengths, while we
Unburden'd crawl toward death. — Our son of Cornwall, —
And you, our no less loving son of Albany,
We have this hour a constant will to publish
Our daughters' several dowers, that future strife
May be prevented now. The princes, France and Burgundy,
Great rivals in our youngest daughter's love,
Long in our court have made their amorous sojourn,
And here are to be answer'd. — Tell me, my daughters,
Since now we will divest us both of rule,
Interest of territory, cares of state,
Which of you shall we say doth love us most?

蔼特孟，你认识这位贵人吗？

蔼 特 孟	不认识，父亲。
葛 洛 斯 忒	铿德伯爵。往后记住了他是我的高贵的朋友。
蔼 特 孟	愿替伯爵奔走。
铿 德	我准会心爱你，请让我多多地结识你一些。
蔼 特 孟	伯爵，我决不辜负您那番好意。
葛 洛 斯 忒	他出门了九年，如今又要走了。〔幕后号角声起〕国
	王在来了。

〔号角鸣奏。一人捧小王冠前导，李尔王，康华，亚尔白尼，刚瑙烈，雷耿，考黛莲与众侍从上。〕

李 尔	葛洛斯忒，去陪侍法兰西和浮庚岱的君主。
葛 洛 斯 忒	遵命，王上。　　　　〔葛洛斯忒与蔼特孟同下。
李 尔	同时我们要公布一个尚未经

宣明的计划。——给我那张地图。——
要知道我们把国土已分成了三份；
而且决意从衰老的残躯上卸除
一切焦劳和政务的纷烦，付与
力壮的年轻人，好让我们释去了
负担，从容爬进老死的境域。——
我们的儿婿康华，——还有你，我们
同样心爱的亚尔白尼儿婿，
这如今我们决意要公布女儿们
各别的妆奁，好永免将来的争执。
法兰西君王，浮庚岱公爵，争着
向我们小公主求情的敌手，在我们
宫廷上已留得有不少求凰的时候，
如今便得给他们一声回答。——
女儿们，说我听，如今我们既然要
解除政柄，捐弃国疆的宗主权，
消泯从政的烦忧，你们三人中
那一个对我最存亲爱？如果谁
爱亲的天性最合该消受亲恩，

That we our largest bounty may extend
Where nature doth with merit challenge. —Goneril,
Our eldest-born, speak first.

Goneril   Sir, I love you more than words can wield the
matter,
Dearer than eyesight, space, and liberty;
Beyond what can be valu'd, rich or rare;
No less than life, with grace, health, beauty, honour,
As much as child e'er lov'd, or father found;
A love that makes breath poor and speech unable;
Beyond all manner of so much I love you.

Cordelia   [*Aside.*] What shall Cordelia speak? Love, and
be silent.

Lear   Of all these bounds, even from this line to this,
With shadowy forests and with champains rich'd,
With plenteous rivers and wide-skirted meads,
We make thee lady: to thine and Albany's issue
Be this perpetual. —What says our second daughter,
Our dearest Regan, wife to Cornwall?

Regan   I am made of that self metal as my sister,
And prize me at her worth. In my true heart
I find she names my very deed of love;
Only she comes too short: that I profess
Myself an enemy to all other joys
Which the most precious square of sense possesses,
And find I am alone felicitate
In your dear highness' love.

Cordelia   [*Aside.*] Then poor Cordelia!
And yet not so; since I am sure, my love's
More richer than my tongue.

Lear   To thee and thine hereditary ever,
Remain this ample third of our fair kingdom;
No less in space, validity, and pleasure,

　　　　　那么,我自会给与她最大的恩赐。
　　　　　刚瑙烈我们的长女,你先说。

刚　瑙　烈　父亲,我爱你不能用言语形容,
　　　　　要胜过我爱目力与空间与自由
　　　　　胜过一切富丽和珍奇的有价品;
　　　　　我爱你不差似爱一个温雅,健康,
　　　　　美丽,和荣誉的生命;自来儿女
　　　　　爱父亲至多不过如此,父亲
　　　　　也从未见过更多的爱亲心;这爱啊,
　　　　　只嫌语言太薄弱,言语不灵通;
　　　　　我这爱没有边沿,漫无止境。

考　黛　莲　[旁白]考黛莲有什么话说? 只是爱,不说话。

李　　　尔　这一方地土,从这条界线到那条,
　　　　　里边有的是森林和肥沃的平原,
　　　　　丰盛的江河,辽阔的草坪,我们
　　　　　赐与你,让你和亚尔白尼的后人
　　　　　世代承继。我们的次女雷耿,
　　　　　康华的妻子,你有什么话?

雷　　　耿　我和大姊赋得有相同的品性,
　　　　　我自忖和她同样地堪当受赐。
　　　　　我抚心自问,但觉她正道出了
　　　　　我欲言未道的衷忱;只是她尚有
　　　　　未尽:我自承我仇视官能锐敏到
　　　　　登峰造极时感到的那一切的欢愉,
　　　　　我认定唯有你为父的慈情真能
　　　　　使我幸福。

考　黛　莲　[旁白]然后是贫乏的考黛莲!
　　　　　可是并不然;我确信我的爱,沉重
　　　　　要赛过嘴上的夸张。

李　　　尔　我们把三份国境中这整整的一份
　　　　　付与你和你世代的子孙后世;
　　　　　这地土的大小,价值,和给人的欢愉,

Than that conferr'd on Goneril. —Now, our joy,
Although our last and least, to whose young love
The vines of France and milk of Burgundy
Strive to be interess'd; what can you say to draw
A third more opulent than your sisters? Speak.
Cordelia   Nothing, my lord.
Lear   Nothing?
Cordelia   Nothing.
Lear   Nothing will come of nothing. speak again.
Cordelia   Unhappy that I am, I cannot heave
My heart into my mouth: I love your majesty
According to my bond; no more nor less.
Lear   How, how, Cordelia? mend your speech a little,
Lest you may mar your fortunes.
Cordelia   Good my lord,
You have begot me, bred me, lov'd me: I
Return those duties back as are right fit,
Obey you, love you, and most honour you.
Why have my sisters husbands if they say
They love you all? Haply, when I shall wed,
That lord whose hand must take my plight shall carry
Half my love with him, half my care and duty.
Sure I shall never marry like my sisters,
To love my father all.
Lear   But goes thy heart with this?
Cordelia   Ay, good my lord.
Lear   So young, and so untender?
Cordelia   So young, my lord, and true.
Lear   Let it be so; thy truth then be thy dower;
For, by the sacred radiance of the sun,
The mysteries of Hecate, and the night;

比我给刚瑙烈的那一份并不差池。——
现在轮到了我们的宝贝，虽然
最年轻也最娇小，为要得到她
垂青，葡萄遍地的法兰西和盛产
牛乳的浡庚岱在互相争竞；我问你，
你有什么话说我听，好取得一份
比你姊姊们的更富饶的国境？你说。

李　　尔 ... 没有话说？

考　黛　莲 我没有什么话说，父亲。

考　黛　莲 没有话说。

李　　尔 没有话说就没有东西。再说过。

考　黛　莲 不幸得很，可是我的心我不能
把它放在嘴上。我爱父亲
按着做女儿的本份不多也不少。

李　　尔 怎么的，怎么的，考黛莲？改正你的话；
不然，你会弄坏你自己的运道。

考　黛　莲 你对我有生身，鞠育，和慈爱的亲恩，
好父亲；我自有当然的责任相报答：
我对你该随顺，爱敬，十二分尊重。
两位姊姊都说她们只爱你，
为什么她们都有丈夫？也许
有一天我嫁了夫君，那夫君受了我
白首相终的信誓，也得取去我
一半的爱心，一半的关怀和本份。
我千万不能和她们一般，结了婚
还全然只爱着父亲。

李　　尔 你可是真心说话？

考　黛　莲 　　　　　　　　　哎，好父亲。

李　　尔 这么样年轻，难道这么样不温柔？

考　黛　莲 这么样年轻，父亲，又这么样真心。

李　　尔 就是那么样；你就把真心作嫁奁。
我把太阳的圣光赫盖脱的魔法，

By all the operation of the orbs
From whom we do exist and cease to be;
Here I disclaim all my paternal care,
Propinquity, and property of blood,
And as a stranger to my heart and me
Hold thee from this for ever. The barbarous Scythian,
Or he that makes his generation messes
To gorge his appetite, shall to my bosom
Be as well neighbour'd, pitied, and reliev'd,
As thou my sometime daughter.

Kent   Good my liege, —

Lear   Peace, Kent!
Come not between the dragon and his wrath.
I lov'd her most, and thought to set my rest
On her kind nursery. — Hence, and avoid my sight! —

                              [*To* Cordelia.]

So be my grave my peace, as here I give
Her father's heart from her. — Call France. who stirs?
Call Burgundy. — Cornwall and Albany,
With my two daughters' dowers digest this third:
Let pride, which she calls plainness, marry her.
I do invest you jointly in my power,
Pre-eminence and all the large effects
That troop with majesty. Ourself, by monthly course,
With reservation of an hundred knights
By you to be sustain'd, shall our abode
Make with you by due turns. Only we still retain
The name, and all the additions to a king;
The sway, revenue, execution of the rest,

黑夜和主宰人死生的星辰间的气运，
起一个誓言：我从此对你打消
我一切为父的关怀，父女间的亲挚，
和血统的相连与合一，我从此
永远将你当作一个陌路人看待。
雪席安蛮邦的野番，那些个杀子
佐肴专为果自己口腹的狠心人，
他们在我这心头会和你，我这个
从前的女儿，同样地亲切，得到
相同的怜爱和温存。

铿　德　德　　　　　　　　　我的好主人，——

李　　尔　静着，铿德！
别来到怒龙面前拦住去路。
我爱她最深，本想把所余的孤注
一掷地全给她作为抚养的恩金。——
［对考黛莲］走开别在我面前！——［自语］如今我
　　　对她
取消了做父亲的慈爱，但愿我能在
死后安心无悔！——去叫法兰西
君王。谁去？去叫浡庚岱公爵。——
康华和亚尔白尼，你们到手了
我两个女儿的妆奁，如今再把那
第三份去平分。让傲慢，她自己却叫做
平淡无华，为她找一位夫君。
我叫你们合享我原有的威权，
我原先那权位的出众超群，和跟着
君王的一切外表的光荣。我自己，
还留着百名须你们负担的武士，
一月一迁游，更替着和你们同住。
可是我们依然要保存着国王
这名号，和君主所有的表面的尊荣；
至于职掌大权，司国家的赋税，

Beloved sons, be yours; which to confirm,
This coronet part betwixt you.

[Giving the crown.]

Kent   Royal Lear,
Whom I have ever honour'd as my king,
Lov'd as my father, as my master follow'd,
As my great patron thought on in my prayers. —
Lear   The bow is bent and drawn; make from the shaft.
Kent   Let it fall rather, though the fork invade
The region of my heart! be Kent unmannerly
When Lear is mad. What wouldst thou do, old man?
Think'st thou that duty shall have dread to speak
When power to flattery bows? To plainness honour's
      bound
When majesty falls to folly. Reverse thy state,
And in thy best consideration check
This hideous rashness. answer my life my judgment,
Thy youngest daughter does not love thee least;
Nor are those empty-hearted whose low sound
Reverbs no hollowness.
Lear   Kent, on thy life, no more!
Kent   My life I never held but as a pawn
To wage against thine enemies, nor fear to lose it,
Thy safety being the motive.
Lear   Out of my sight!
Kent   See better, Lear; and let me still remain
The true blank of thine eye.
Lear   Now, by Apollo, —

　　　　　和其余一切的发号施政，爱婿们，
　　　　　都听凭你们去措置；为取信我这话，
　　　　　你们把这顶小王冠取去分用。　　　〔给予王冠〕

铿　德　圣主李尔，我素常将你当作
　　　　　君王相尊崇，父亲一般地敬爱，
　　　　　主子似的相从，祈祷时又当作
　　　　　大恩人去想念，——

李　尔　　　　　　　　　　　弓已经引满，
　　　　　弦丝已经绷紧；快躲开这支箭。

铿　德　宁愿让它离弦，即使那箭锋
　　　　　会刺透这心口！李尔发了疯，铿德
　　　　　就该当无礼。你要做什么，老人？
　　　　　你以为威权在谄媚面前低了头，
　　　　　责任便跟着骇怕得噤口无声吗？
　　　　　你丢了堂堂君主的尊严甘心
　　　　　堕入愚顽，我自顾忠诚便不能
　　　　　不直言不讳。留下你大好的君权，
　　　　　去从长计较后，控制这骇人的鲁莽。
　　　　　让我冒死主张我这番判断，
　　　　　你那个小女爱你得并不最轻微；
　　　　　有些人，他们那不善逢迎的低声里
　　　　　虽不露内在的空虚，却并非真正
　　　　　寡情无义。

李　尔　　　　　　铿德，凭你的性命，
　　　　　不准再说！

铿　德　　　　　　　我只把自己的性命
　　　　　当作和你的仇人们打赌的注子，
　　　　　为你的安全，我不怕将它输掉。

李　尔　去你的！

铿　德　　　　　　看得清楚些，李尔，让我
　　　　　常为你作一方鉴戒的明镜。

李　尔　咄，我对太阳神亚波罗起个誓——

Kent   Now by Apollo, king,
Thou swear'st thy gods in vain.
Lear   O vassal! miscreant!
                    [*Laying his hand on his sword.*]
Albany and Cornwall Dear sir, forbear.
Kent Kill thy physician, and the fee bestow
Upon the foul disease. Revoke thy gift,
Or, whilst I can vent clamour from my throat,
I'll tell thee thou dost evil.
Lear   Hear me, recreant!
On thine allegiance, hear me! —
That thou hast sought to make us break our vow, —
Which we durst never yet, — and with strain'd pride
To come between our sentence and our power,
Which nor our nature nor our place can bear,
Our potency made good, take thy reward.
Five days we do allot thee for provision
To shield thee from diseases of the world,
And on the sixth to turn thy hated back
Upon our kingdom. if on the tenth day following
Thy banish'd trunk be found in our dominions,
The moment is thy death. Away! by Jupiter,
This shall not be revok'd.
Kent Fare thee well, king: sith thus thou wilt appear,
Freedom lives hence, and banishment is here. —
[*To* Cordelia.] The gods to their dear shelter take thee,
      maid,
That justly think'st and hast most rightly said!

铿　　德	咄，我也对太阳神亚波罗起誓，	
	国王，你空对你的天神们赌咒。	
李　　尔	嗯，你这奴才！无耻的贱人！	［手握剑把］
亚尔白尼 康　　华	亲爱的父亲，不要这样。	
铿　　德	宰掉我这个良医，去酬谢那恶病。	
	快收回你那些恩赐，要是不然，	
	只要我喉舌间还能发一声叫喊，	
	我总会告诉你你铸成了大错，贻下	
	无穷的祸患。	
李　　尔	听我说，下流的东西！	
	我把君臣间的道义心责你静听！	
	你想叫我们毁坏我们从不敢	
	毁坏的誓约，你想凭你那匹夫	
	诞妄的骄横拦阻我们的权能，	
	不叫施行生效，——这样的情势，	
	不论是我们的性情或地位，都不堪	
	忍受，——既然你冒渎了君威，如今	
	便得去接受那多事生非的酬报，	
	好叫我们也恢复威仪的旧观。	
	我们给你五天期限，免了你	
	遭受琐屑的纠纷与窘迫，第六天	
	你就得离开我们这厌弃你的国境。	
	如果在十天之后，你那个放逐到	
	国外去的正身依旧在境内找得，	
	顿时就将你处死。滚出去！我对	
	天皇巨璧德起个誓言，这事情	
	决不收回成命。	
铿　　德	拜辞了，王上：	
	既然你如此，定要我远离你左右；	
	我在此遭放逐，去国外便有了自由——	
	［对考黛莲］小公主，你心地诚实，言语也大方，	

[*To* Regan *and* Goneril.]

And your large speeches may your deeds approve,

That good effects may spring from words of love. —

Thus Kent, O princes, bids you all adieu;

He'll shape his old course in a country new.

[*Exit.*]

[*Flourish. Re-enter* Gloucester, *with*

France, Burgundy, *and* Attendants.]

Gloucester   Here's France and Burgundy, my noble lord.

Lear   My Lord of Burgundy,

We first address toward you, who with this king

Hath rivall'd for our daughter: what in the least

Will you require in present dower with her,

Or cease your quest of love?

Burgundy   Most royal majesty,

I crave no more than hath your highness offer'd,

Nor will you tender less.

Lear   Right noble Burgundy,

When she was dear to us, we did hold her so;

But now her price is fall'n. Sir, there she stands.

If aught within that little seeming substance,

Or all of it, with our displeasure piec'd,

And nothing more, may fitly like your grace,

She's there, and she is yours.

Burgundy   I know no answer.

Lear   Will you, with those infirmities she owes,

Unfriended, new-adopted to our hate,

Dower'd with our curse, and stranger'd with our oath,

我指望天神们护佑你安全无恙！——
［对刚瑙烈及雷耿］愿你们用行为去征信你们的
浮夸，
使亲爱的言辞能有优良的显化。——
我铿德，公侯们，向你们说一声再见；
他将在新去的国中度他的老年。　　　　　　［下。
［号声大作。葛洛斯忒重入，同来者法兰西王，淳庚
岱公爵，与众随从。

葛 洛 斯 忒　　大王，法兰西和淳庚岱君主们来了。

李　　　尔　　淳庚岱大公爵，
你同这位国王已争求了许多时
我们的小女，如今我们先对你
开谈：至少你要多少现给作
陪嫁的妆奁，再少了你便会停止
你的追求？

淳　庚　岱　　　　　　　　　最尊贵的大王陛下，
我企求的不会超过你自愿给的弘恩，
你也不会少给。

李　　　尔　　　　　　　　　　淳庚岱贵爵，
当先我们宝爱她那时节确然是
如此，但现今她已经贬低了价值。
你瞧，她站在那边。那短小的身肢里
不论她有什么，或是那短小的身肢
全部，加上了我们的不欢，（此外
却并无什么妆奁作陪嫁），如果
这么样便能叫你称心如意，
那么，她就在那边，就归你所有。

淳　庚　岱　　我不知怎么样回答。

李　　　尔　　　　　　　　　　她有了那种种
缺陷，孤零得亲友全无，新遭
我们的痛恨，把我们的咒骂作妆奁，
我们又赌誓将她当作陌路人

Take her, or leave her?

Burgundy   Pardon me, royal sir;

Election makes not up in such conditions.

Lear Then leave her, sir; for, by the power that made me,

I tell you all her wealth. — [*To* France] For you, great
  king,

I would not from your love make such a stray

To match you where I hate; therefore beseech you

To avert your liking a more worthier way

Than on a wretch whom nature is asham'd

Almost to acknowledge hers.

France   This is most strange,

That she, who even but now was your best object,

The argument of your praise, balm of your age,

Most best, most dearest, should in this trice of time

Commit a thing so monstrous, to dismantle

So many folds of favour. Sure her offence

Must be of such unnatural degree

That monsters it, or your fore-vouch'd affection

Fall'n into taint; which to believe of her

Must be a faith that reason without miracle

Should never plant in me.

Cordelia   I yet beseech your majesty,

(If for I want that glib and oily art

To speak and purpose not; since what I well intend,

I'll do't before I speak,) that you make known

It is no vicious blot, murder, or foulness,

No unchaste action or dishonour'd step,

That hath depriv'd me of your grace and favour;

相待，这么样你还要她不要？

浡　庚　岱　请恕我，大王；我不能在这样的情形下
　　　　　定我的取舍。

李　　　尔　　　　　　　那么，让她去吧；
　　　　　因为我敢对赋予我生命的造化神
　　　　　起誓，我已告诉你她全部的资财。——
　　　　　［对法兰西王］对于你，大王，我不愿那样辜负
　　　　　你殷勤的厚意，将自己痛恨的来和你
　　　　　相配；因此，请你把爱慕心掉离这
　　　　　便是亲情也羞于承认的小贱人
　　　　　身上，转移到更值你青眼的他方。

法　兰　西　这事情太过离奇，只不久以前
　　　　　她是你眼中的珍宝，称赞的主题，
　　　　　你老年的慰藉，最好也最亲爱，
　　　　　难道这么一瞬间竟许会闯下
　　　　　骇人的大祸，褪掉你一层层的爱宠。
　　　　　她那个过错定必是荒唐得真叫人
　　　　　诧骇，要不然那先前你自承的钟爱
　　　　　也不能完全不受谤毁；可是
　　　　　若要我信她闯下了那样的大祸，
　　　　　只凭我理智的力量，没有奇迹
　　　　　降临，那是万万地不能。

考　黛　莲　　　　　　　　　　我求
　　　　　父王陛下（假如为了我没有
　　　　　那油滑的本领，满口花言巧语，
　　　　　内里却绝无一丝半缕的存心；
　　　　　因为我有了善良的用意，总要在
　　　　　宣说之前做到），我求你申明
　　　　　我并无恶劣的污点，或其他的邪恶，
　　　　　并未有不贞的举动，失足伤名，
　　　　　致使你把对我的恩宠和钟爱
　　　　　剥夺得不留分毫的余剩。我求你

But even for want of that for which I am richer, —
A still-soliciting eye, and such a tongue
That I am glad I have not, though not to have it
Hath lost me in your liking.

Lear   Better thou
Hadst not been born than not to have pleas'd me better.

France Is it but this? a tardiness in nature
Which often leaves the history unspoke
That it intends to do? — My lord of Burgundy,
What say you to the lady? Love's not love
When it is mingled with regards that stands
Aloof from the entire point. Will you have her?
She is herself a dowry.

Burgundy   Royal king,
Give but that portion which yourself propos'd,
And here I take Cordelia by the hand,
Duchess of Burgundy.

Lear Nothing. I have sworn; I am firm.

Burgundy I am sorry, then, you have so lost a father
That you must lose a husband.

Cordelia   Peace be with Burgundy!
Since that respects of fortune are his love,
I shall not be his wife.

France Fairest Cordelia, that art most rich, being poor,
Most choice, forsaken; and most lov'd, despis'd,
Thee and thy virtues here I seize upon.
Be it lawful I take up what's cast away.
Gods, gods! 'tis strange that from their cold'st neglect
My love should kindle to inflam'd respect. —
Thy dowerless daughter, king, thrown to my chance,

申明我所以失宠乃因缺少了
（这缺少反使我感觉到自己的富有）
一双时时切盼着恩赐的眼睛，
一个没有它我反自欣幸的巧舌，
虽然没有它害我失掉了你的爱。

李　　尔　　与其你不能得我的欢心，不如我
不曾生你好些。

法　兰　西　　　　　　　　　就只那么样吗？
只是生性稍慢些，不曾把心中
想做的事情预先向你申诉？——
浡庚岱公爵，你对小公主怎么说？
爱情要是混和了与主题不生
关系的利害的权衡，便不是爱情。
你要娶她吗？她本身便是份妆奁。

浡　庚　岱　　圣君李尔，你只须给她你自己
倡言要给的那妆奁，我自会接受
考黛莲作我们浡庚岱的公爵夫人。

李　　尔　　没有。我发了誓言；决不能翻改。

浡　庚　岱　　真可惜你把父亲的爱心毁伤得
那么样不堪，甚至连丈夫也因而
丧失。

考　黛　莲　　　　　　　浡庚岱，不用说话！既然
他的爱专在计较财富的有无，
我不能做他的妻子。

法　兰　西　　最秀丽的考黛莲，贫穷但也最富有，
孤独无依，但最是无双地美妙，
被人所贱视，可是最受我珍爱，
如果取人家遗弃的可称合法，
我如今便取得你和你的那种种美德。
天神们，天神们！奇怪的是他们那么样
冷淡，我的爱却燃烧成融融的敬仰。——
国王，你这位没有妆奁的小女儿，

Is queen of us, of ours, and our fair France.
Not all the dukes of waterish Burgundy
Can buy this unpriz'd precious maid of me. —
Bid them farewell, Cordelia, though unkind
Thou losest here, a better where to find.
Lear Thou hast her, France: let her be thine; for we
Have no such daughter, nor shall ever see
That face of hers again. — Therefore be gone
Without our grace, our love, our benison. —
Come, noble Burgundy.
　　　　　[*Flourish. Exeunt all but France*, Goneril,
　　　　　　　　　Regan, and Cordelia.]
France Bid farewell to your sisters.
Cordelia The jewels of our father, with wash'd eyes
Cordelia leaves you. I know you what you are;
And, like a sister, am most loath to call
Your faults as they are nam'd. Love well our father.
To your professed bosoms I commit him;
But yet, alas, stood I within his grace,
I would prefer him to a better place.
So, farewell to you both.
Regan Prescribe not us our duties.
Goneril　　　　　　　　　　　　Let your study
Be to content your lord, who hath receiv'd you
At fortune's alms. You have obedience scanted,
And well are worth the want that you have wanted.
Cordelia Time shall unfold what plighted cunning hides;

> ——我如今有幸——正好做我们自己，
> 臣民们，和锦绣山河的法兰西的王后。
> 任它水浸的淳庚岱有多少位公侯，
> 也休想有我这珍奇无价的闺秀
> 作夫人。——考黛莲，向他们说声再会去，
> 虽然你失掉这恩义断绝的无情界，
> 但也找得了一处更美满的好所在。

李　　尔　法兰西，你就有了她。就让她归了你；
　　　　　我们不认有这样的女儿，从此
　　　　　也不想再见她的脸。——你就这样走；
　　　　　我们的恩宠，慈爱，和祝福你全没有。——
　　　　　来，尊贵的淳庚岱。

　　　　　[号声大作。人众尽退，只留法兰西，刚瑙烈，雷耿与
　　　　　考黛莲四人在场。

法　兰　西　向你两位姐姐作别。

考　黛　莲　你们这两颗父亲心目中的珍宝，
　　　　　考黛莲潮润着眼睛和你们分手。
　　　　　你们的本性如何我全都明白；
　　　　　只是为妹的不愿敞口言明
　　　　　你们的过错。好好地爱着父亲。
　　　　　我将他付托给你们所自承的敬爱；
　　　　　但是啊，如果我不曾失掉那恩宠，
　　　　　我愿将他付托给较好的所在。
　　　　　跟你们再会了。

雷　　耿　我们的本份不用你来吩咐。

刚　瑙　烈　你快去学习些抚慰夫君的妇道，
　　　　　他肯收受你也算是命运舍慈悲。
　　　　　对父亲的顺从你用得太过刻齿，
　　　　　那么你不肯给人正合该人家
　　　　　给你也照样地不肯。

考　黛　莲　凭百褶千层的奸诈隐藏得多么巧，
　　　　　时间自会显露她本来的真面貌；

Who cover faults, at last shame them derides.
Well may you prosper!

France　　　　Come, my fair Cordelia.

　　　　　　　[*Exeunt* France *and* Cordelia.]

Goneril　Sister, it is not little I have to say of what most nearly appertains to us both. I think our father will hence to-night.

Regan　That's most certain, and with you; next month with us.

Goneril　You see how full of changes his age is; the observation we have made of it hath not been little; he always loved our sister most; and with what poor judgment he hath now cast her off appears too grossly.

Regan　'Tis the infirmity of his age; yet he hath ever but slenderly known himself.

Goneril　The best and soundest of his time hath been but rash; then must we look to receive from his age, not alone the imperfections of long-ingraffed condition, but therewithal the unruly waywardness that infirm and choleric years bring with them.

Regan　Such unconstant starts are we like to have from him as this of Kent's banishment.

Goneril　There is further compliment of leave-taking between France and him. Pray you let us hit together; if our father carry authority with such dispositions as he bears, this last surrender of his will but offend us.

Regan　We shall further think of it.

Goneril　We must do something, and i' th' heat.

　　　　　　　[*Exeunt.*]

SCENE II. The Earl *of* Gloucester's *Castle.*

　　　　[*Enter* Edmund *with a letter.*]

Edmund　Thou, nature, art my goddess; to thy law
My services are bound. Wherefore should I

遮掩着罪恶的人们最后总难免
羞辱到来把他们嘲笑的那一天。
祝你们亨通如意!

法　兰　西　来吧,我的明艳的考黛莲。

　　　　　　　　　　　　　　　　　　[法兰西与考黛莲同下。

刚　瑙　烈　妹子,关于可说是跟我们两人都有份的事情我还有不少话说呢。我想今晚上父亲就要离开这儿了。

雷　　耿　那当然是,且是跟你们走;下个月就轮到我们。

刚　瑙　烈　你瞧,他岁数大了,多么变化不定;我们过去的观察只怕还不很到家呢;他向来最爱妹妹,如今下的多么坏的判断丢掉了她,是不用说得也谁都知道的。

雷　　耿　那是因为他年纪大了,人就懵懂了起来;可是他素来做事,总是连自己也莫名其妙的。

刚　瑙　烈　他最好最健全的年头上也只是鲁莽罢了;那么,岁数一大,我们指望着要生受他的不光是习惯成了自然的短处,还得吃他老来糊涂和刚愎任性的亏呢,那才不容易办。

雷　　耿　就说赶掉铿德那一类的任性乱来,我们大概也得受领些吧。

刚　瑙　烈　法兰西还在跟他行作别的礼。我劝你让我们合在一起;要是父亲还揽着权任着他的老性子干下去,他刚才把君权交出来只会闹得跟我们过不去。

雷　　耿　我们再想一下。

刚　瑙　烈　我们一定得有个办法,而且得赶快。

第　二　景

　　[葛洛斯忒伯爵堡邸中。
　　[蔼特孟上场,手执信一封。

蔼　特　孟　你啊,天性,你是我敬奉的女神;
我对你的大道尽忠乃是理所当然。

Stand in the plague of custom, and permit
The curiosity of nations to deprive me,
For that I am some twelve or fourteen moonshines
Lag of a brother? Why bastard? wherefore base?
When my dimensions are as well compact,
My mind as generous and my shape as true,
As honest madam's issue? Why brand they us
With base? with baseness? bastardy? base, base?
Who, in the lusty stealth of nature, take
More composition and fierce quality
Than doth, within a dull, stale, tired bed,
Go to the creating a whole tribe of fops,
Got 'tween asleep and wake? — Well then,
Legitimate Edgar, I must have your land.
Our father's love is to the bastard Edmund
As to the legitimate; fine word — legitimate!
Well, my *legitimate*, if this letter speed,
And my invention thrive, Edmund the base
Shall top the *legitimate*. I grow; I prosper. —
Now, gods, stand up for bastards!
                    [*Enter* Gloucester.]
Gloucester   Kent banish'd thus? and France in choler
    parted?
And the king gone to-night? subscrib''d his pow'r?
Confin'd to exhibition? All this done
Upon the gad! — Edmund, how now! What news?

只因我比那长兄晚生了十二回，
十四回月色的盈亏，为什么我便该
生受那瘟人的习俗摧残，让苛细
刻薄的世人剥削我应有的权益？
为什么是野种？ 凭什么叫做低微？
我这副身肢和人家一般地构造，
内心的高贵和外表的端方比得上
任何淑妇贞妻的后代。为什么
他们总苦苦地将人污辱，说是
低微？ 微贱？ 野种？ 低微，低微？
我们才真是天性的骄子，偷趁
父母间元神蓬勃的须臾，取得了
浑厚的成分和锐不可当的质素；
我们比较他们，——在迟钝不灵，
平凡陈腐，和困顿厌倦的床褥间，
半醒和半睡中，产生的那一群蠢才，——
他们怎能和我们相比？ 好吧，
合法的蔼特加，我定要得你的地土。
我们的父亲爱他的野种蔼特孟
和爱他的嫡子一样。好字眼，"嫡子"！
不错，嫡子，如果这封信成了功，
这计划进行得顺遂，低微的蔼特孟
准会占据那嫡子的上风。我发扬
长大，顺利亨通；如今，天神们，
我求你们护佑我们野种！

　　　　　〔葛洛斯忒上。

葛 洛 斯 忒　铿德便这么被他流放到国外？
法兰西又是含怒而别？ 再加上
国王自己今晚上要离开此地？
让掉了大权，只靠一点儿支应？
这都是心血来潮时的妄动轻举！ ——
蔼特孟，怎么了！ 有什么消息没有？

Edmund So please your lordship, none.

[Putting up the letter.]

Gloucester Why so earnestly seek you to put up that letter?

Edmund I know no news, my lord.

Gloucester What paper were you reading?

Edmund Nothing, my lord.

Gloucester No? What needed, then, that terrible dispatch of it into your pocket? the quality of nothing hath not such need to hide itself. Let's see. Come, if it be nothing, I shall not need spectacles.

Edmund I beseech you, sir, pardon me. It is a letter from my brother that I have not all o'er-read; and for so much as I have perus'd, I find it not fit for your o'erlooking.

Gloucester Give me the letter, sir.

Edmund I shall offend, either to detain or give it. The contents, as in part I understand them, are to blame.

Gloucester Let's see, let's see.

Edmund I hope, for my brother's justification, he wrote this but as an essay or taste of my virtue.

Gloucester *[Reads.]* *'This policy and reverence of age makes the world bitter to the best of our times; keeps our fortunes from us till our oldness cannot relish them. I begin to find an idle and fond bondage in the oppression of aged tyranny; who sways, not as it hath power, but as it is suffered. Come to me, that of this I may speak more. If our father would sleep till I waked him, you should enjoy half his revenue for ever, and live the beloved of your brother,* ED-GAR. Hum! Conspiracy?—*Sleep till I waked him,—you should enjoy half his revenue.* —My son Edgar! Had he a hand to write this? a heart and brain to breed it in? When came this to you? who brought it?

Edmund It was not brought me, my lord, there's the cunning of it; I found it thrown in at the casement of my closet.

蔼　特　孟	禀告父亲，没有消息。	［藏信。］
葛洛斯忒	为什么赶忙把那封信藏起来？	
蔼　特　孟	我不晓得什么消息，父亲。	
葛洛斯忒	你在看那张什么纸头？	
蔼　特　孟	没有什么，父亲。	
葛洛斯忒	没有。那么，用得到那样慌慌张张塞在口袋里做什么？要没有什么便用不到这样藏起来。给我看来，要真的没有什么，我便不用戴眼镜了。	
蔼　特　孟	求您宽容，父亲；这封信是哥哥写给我的，我还没有把它看完；可是我所看到的，我觉得给您看不合式。	
葛洛斯忒	把信给我，你这家伙。	
蔼　特　孟	不论我留着或是交出来都得开罪您老人家。可是怪不了我，只怪这里边我所知道的那一部分的内容。	
葛洛斯忒	等我们看吧，等我们看吧。	
蔼　特　孟	为哥哥剖白罪名起见，我希望他写这封信只为要试探我的德性怎么样。	
葛洛斯忒	［读信］"我们做人一世，正当在大好年华的时节，这个敬惜老年的政策便来把世界变成了苦涩无味的东西，我们好好的财富都给留难了起来，直等到我们也老了，不再能享乐，才算完事。我开始感觉到一个又柔弱又愚昧的老人的专制势力在那里束缚我，压迫我；但那个势力所以能那样当权，并非为了它本身有什么力量，却只因我们尽它去横行。你来看我一下，我再和你细谈。要是父亲在我弄醒他之前一直睡着，你可以永远享得他收入的一半，而且永远是你哥哥的爱弟。蔼特加。"哼！是阴谋？——"在我弄醒他之前一直睡着，你可以享得他收入的一半！"——我的儿子蔼特加！他居然有写得出这话的手？想得出这话的心肠？——这是什么时候到你手里来的？是谁带给你的？	
蔼　特　孟	不是带给我的，父亲；刁就刁在这里；是扔在我房里窗槛前面给我捡到的。	

Gloucester You know the character to be your brother's?

Edmund If the matter were good, my lord, I durst swear it were his; but in respect of that, I would fain think it were not.

Gloucester It is his.

Edmund It is his hand, my lord; but I hope his heart is not in the contents.

Gloucester Has he never before sounded you in this business?

Edmund Never, my lord; but I have heard him oft maintain it to be fit that, sons at perfect age, and fathers declined, the father should be as ward to the son, and the son manage his revenue.

Gloucester O villain, villain! His very opinion in the letter! Abhorred villain! Unnatural, detested, brutish villain! worse than brutish! — Go, sirrah, seek him; I'll apprehend him. Abominable villain!—Where is he?

Edmund I do not well know, my lord. If it shall please you to suspend your indignation against my brother till you can derive from him better testimony of his intent, you should run a certain course; where, if you violently proceed against him, mistaking his purpose, it would make a great gap in your own honour, and shake in pieces the heart of his obedience. I dare pawn down my life for him that he hath writ this to feel my affection to your honour, and to no other pretence of danger.

Gloucester Think you so?

Edmund If your honour judge it meet, I will place you where you shall hear us confer of this, and by an auricular assurance have your satisfaction; and that without any further delay than this very evening.

Gloucester He cannot be such a monster.

Edmund Nor is not, sure.

Gloucester To his father, that so tenderly and entirely loves him. Heaven and earth! Edmund, seek him out; wind me into him, I pray you: frame the business after your own wisdom. I would unstate myself, to be in a due resolution.

葛洛斯忒　　你知道这是你哥哥的笔迹吗？

蔼　特　孟　　写的要是好话，父亲，我敢发誓那是他的笔迹，可是如今这样子，我但愿不是他的。

葛洛斯忒　　是他的。

蔼　特　孟　　是他的笔迹，父亲；不过我希望这话里没有他的真心。

葛洛斯忒　　关于这件事，他可从来不曾探问过你吗？

蔼　特　孟　　不曾有过，父亲；但我常听他主张，儿子在成年以后，父亲已衰老了，那时候，最合式的办法是父亲让儿子去保护他，儿子经管着父亲的收入。

葛洛斯忒　　啊，坏蛋，坏蛋！他信里就是这个主张！骇人听闻的坏蛋！这逆伦的该死的坏蛋，和禽兽没有分别！比禽兽还坏！——去，小子，找他去；我要把他逮起来；这可恶透顶的坏蛋！他在那儿？

蔼　特　孟　　我不很知道，父亲。要是父亲按捺一下子，等到从他身上得到了可靠些的凭证，知道他真意怎样，然后才对他发怒，那样才是一条实在的正路；可是您若先就对他暴躁了起来，误会了他的用意，便会把您自己的尊严弄得扫地，而且把他的顺从心也打破了。我敢将自己的生命作抵，他写这封信只为试探我对大人的敬爱如何，此外却没有危害的用意。

葛洛斯忒　　你以为这样吗？

蔼　特　孟　　要是大人觉得合式，在听得见我们谈论这事的地方我把您藏了起来，那时候您亲自耳闻了证据，便可以完全知道；这事不用耽搁时间，就在今晚上可以做到。

葛洛斯忒　　他不会是这样一个怪物似的——

蔼　特　孟　　当然不会。

葛洛斯忒　　对待他的父亲；我爱他得那么温存；那么全心全力地爱他。我对天地赌咒！蔼特孟，找他出来；我要你去替我弄清楚他的底细；你自己去见机行事好了。为解决这个疑难，我宁愿把地位财产全都不要。

Edmund   I will seek him, sir, presently, convey the business as I shall find means, and acquaint you withal.

Gloucester   These late eclipses in the sun and moon portend no good to us; though the wisdom of nature can reason it thus and thus, yet nature finds itself scourged by the sequent effects: love cools, friendship falls off, brothers divide: in cities, mutinies; in countries, discord; in palaces, treason; and the bond cracked 'twixt son and father. This villain of mine comes under the prediction; there's son against father; the king falls from bias of nature; there's father against child. We have seen the best of our time; machinations, hollowness, treachery, and all ruinous disorders follow us disquietly to our graves. Find out this villain, Edmund; it shall lose thee nothing; do it carefully. And the noble and true-hearted Kent banished! his offence, honesty! 'Tis strange.   [*Exit.*]

Edmund   This is the excellent foppery of the world, that, when we are sick in fortune, — often the surfeit of our own behaviour, — we make guilty of our disasters the sun, the moon, and the stars; as if we were villains on necessity, fools by heavenly compulsion, knaves, thieves, and treachers by spherical pre-dominance, drunkards, liars, and adulterers, by an enforced obedience of planetary influence; and all that we are evil in, by a divine thrusting on. an admirable evasion of whoremaster man, to lay his goatish disposition to the charge of a star! My father compounded with my mother under the dragon's tail, and my nativity was under ursa major; so that it follows I am rough and lecherous. Tut! I should have been that I am, had the maidenliest star in the firmament twinkled on my bastardizing. Edgar —

[*Enter Edgar.*]

And pat he comes like the catastrophe of the old comedy. my cue is villainous melancholy, with a sigh like Tom o' Bedlam. O, these eclipses do portend these divisions! fa, sol, la, mi.

Edgar   How now, brother Edmund! what serious contem-

蔼　特　孟　我就去寻他，父亲，随机应变地去办事，再来让您
　　　　　　知道。

葛洛斯忒　近来这些日食月食不是好兆；虽然格致学上可以如
　　　　　　此这般地解释，可是到头来我们大家还是遭了它们
　　　　　　的殃；爱情冷了，友谊中断了，兄弟间失了和睦；城
　　　　　　里有兵变；乡下有扰乱；宫中有叛逆；而父子间的关
　　　　　　系破裂掉。我的这个坏蛋就中了这兆头；这是儿子
　　　　　　跟父亲过不去；国王违反了他本性的慈爱；那是父
　　　　　　亲对孩子不好。最好的日子我们见过了；如今是阴
　　　　　　谋，虚伪，叛逆和一切有破坏性的骚扰很不安静地
　　　　　　送我们去世。把这个坏蛋找出来，蔼特孟；那不会
　　　　　　叫你吃亏的；跟我小心着去干吧。还有那性情高贵
　　　　　　心地真实的铿德给流放了出去！他的罪过只是诚
　　　　　　实！真奇怪。　　　　　　　　　　　　　　　〔下。

蔼　特　孟　这世界真叫做活该上当，我们要是遇到了运气不
　　　　　　好，——那往往是我们自己的行为不检点，——我们
　　　　　　便会把晦气往太阳，月亮，和星子身上一推；仿佛我
　　　　　　们是命里注定了的坏蛋，天意叫我们做傻瓜，交了做
　　　　　　恶人，偷儿，和反贼的星宿，星命气数间逃不掉要成
　　　　　　醉鬼，要撒谎，要奸淫；所有一切只要我们有不好的
　　　　　　地方，都怪天命。人那个王八羔子真会推掉责任，不
　　　　　　说自己性子淫，倒去责备一颗星！我母亲同父亲在
　　　　　　龙星尾巴下结了我的胎，我的生日又归算在大熊星
　　　　　　底下；因此我便得又粗鲁，又淫荡。呸，即使天上最
　　　　　　贞洁不过的星子照在我给他们私生的时辰上，我还
　　　　　　是跟我现在一个样。蔼特加——
　　　　　　　　　　　〔蔼特加上。
　　　　　　他来得正好，活像旧式喜剧里快要收场时那紧张的
　　　　　　情节一样。我出场扮演的模样是愁眉苦脸，还得像
　　　　　　疯叫花汤姆似的长吁短叹着。唉，这些日食月食便
　　　　　　是这些东崩西裂的预兆！ fa, sol, la, mi.

蔼　特　加　怎么了，蔼特孟兄弟！你这么一本正经在冥想些

plation are you in?

Edmund   I am thinking, brother, of a prediction I read this other day, what should follow these eclipses.

Edgar   Do you busy yourself with that?

Edmund   I promise you, the effects he writes of succeed unhappily; as of unnaturalness between the child and the parent; death, dearth, dissolutions of ancient amities; divisions in state, menaces and maledictions against king and nobles; needless diffidences, banishment of friends, dissipation of cohorts, nuptial breaches, and I know not what.

Edgar   How long have you been a sectary astronomical?

Edmund   Come, come, when saw you my father last?

Edgar   The night gone by.

Edmund   Spake you with him?

Edgar   Ay, two hours together.

Edmund   Parted you in good terms? Found you no displeasure in him by word or countenance?

Edgar   None at all.

Edmund   Bethink yourself wherein you may have offended him; and at my entreaty forbear his presence until some little time hath qualified the heat of his displeasure, which at this instant so rageth in him that with the mischief of your person it would scarcely allay.

Edgar   Some villain hath done me wrong.

Edmund   That's my fear. I pray you have a continent forbearance till the speed of his rage goes slower; and, as I say, retire with me to my lodging, from whence I will fitly bring you to hear my lord speak; pray you, go; there's my key. —If you do stir abroad, go armed.

Edgar   Armed, brother!

Edmund   Brother, I advise you to the best; I am no honest man if there be any good meaning toward you, I have told you what I have seen and heard; but faintly, nothing like the image and horror of it: pray you, away!

什么?

蔼　特　孟　我正想起了前儿念到的一个预言,说是这些日食月食就主有什么事情要跟着来。

蔼　特　加　你可是在这件事上用功夫吗?

蔼　特　孟　让我告诉你,他预言的那些结局不幸都应验了;比如说,亲子间反常的变故;死亡,饥荒,旧交的中断;国家的分裂,对国王贵族们的威吓和毁谤,用不到的猜疑,亲人被流放,军队给解散,婚姻被破坏,和诸如此类的事变。

蔼　特　加　你变成一个占星的术士有多久了?

蔼　特　孟　得了,得了,你最近看见父亲是什么时候?

蔼　特　加　昨天晚上。

蔼　特　孟　跟他说了话没有?

蔼　特　加　说的,连说了有两个钟点。

蔼　特　孟　是好好分手的吗? 他说话里头和脸上不见有什么不高兴吗?

蔼　特　加　一点也没有。

蔼　特　孟　你想一下有什么事许是得罪了他,我劝你暂且别到他跟前去,过些时候等他的气渐渐平了下去再说,眼前他真是一团火,就是害了你的性命也不能叫他息怒。

蔼　特　加　有坏蛋捉狭了我。

蔼　特　孟　我也怕是这样。我劝你耐着点性子,等他把恼怒放平静些再理会,并且依我说,你还是到我那里躲一下好,机会巧我可以到那边领你去听到父亲亲自说的话。我劝你就去;钥匙在这儿。你要是出去,还得带着武器。

蔼　特　加　带着武器,兄弟?

蔼　特　孟　哥哥,我劝你都是为你好;你得带着武器;要是他对你有什么好意,我就不是老实人。我把见到听到的告诉了你;可是只约略告诉了你一点,实在的情景可怕到怎样还没有说呢;我劝你就走。

Edgar   Shall I hear from you anon?

Edmund   I do serve you in this business. —

[*Exit* Edgar.]

A credulous father, and a brother noble,

Whose nature is so far from doing harms

That he suspects none; on whose foolish honesty

My practices ride easy. I see the business.

Let me, if not by birth, have lands by wit;

All with me's meet that I can fashion fit.

[*Exit.*]

SCENE III.   *The Duke of* Albany's *Palace.*

[*Enter* Goneril *and* Oswald.]

Goneril   Did my father strike my gentleman for chiding of
his fool?

Oswald   Ay, madam.

Goneril   By day and night, he wrongs me; every hour

He flashes into one gross crime or other,

That sets us all at odds. I'll not endure it.

His knights grow riotous, and himself upbraids us

On every trifle. When he returns from hunting,

I will not speak with him; say I am sick.

If you come slack of former services,

You shall do well; the fault of it I'll answer.

Oswald   He's coming, madam; I hear him.

[*Horns within.*]

Goneril   Put on what weary negligence you please,

You and your fellows; I'd have it come to question.

蔼　特　加	我能马上听你的信息吗?	
蔼　特　孟	这个我会替你办。——	［蔼特加下。

一个轻易听信人言的父亲，
加上了一个心地高贵的哥哥。
他天性绝不会伤人，因此他对人
也毫无疑忌；他那么愚蠢的诚实
正好让我使权谋去从容摆布。
我知道怎样办了。我生来既没有
地土，就让我施展些智谋，用些计；
只要调度得合式，什么都可以。　　　　　［下。

第　三　景

［亚尔白尼公爵府邸中。］
［刚瑙烈与管家奥士伐上。］

刚　瑙　烈	我父亲动武打我的家臣，可是为说了一下他是傻子吗?
奥　士　伐	正是的，夫人。
刚　瑙　烈	不论在白天在夜晚，他总欺侮我； 每一点钟里不是闯下这样， 便得闯下那样一场大祸， 真把我们搅扰得颠倒了乾坤。 这样我可不能再忍受。他那班 侍从的武士荒淫暴乱，他自己 为一点小事便破口将我们叱责。 他打猎回来时我不愿同他说话； 只说我病了。假若你不如以前 那么样恭敬从命，倒是很好； 那不恭的过错自有我来担负。
奥　士　伐	他在来了，夫人；我听得见他。　　［幕后号角声起。］
刚　瑙　烈	你同你的伙伴们尽自去装出 厌倦的要理不理的神情对他；

If he distaste it, let him to our sister,
Whose mind and mine, I know, in that are one,
Not to be overruled. Idle old man,
That still would manage those authorities
That he hath given away! Now, by my life,
Old fools are babes again; and must be us'd
With checks as flatteries, when they are seen abus'd.
Remember what I have said.

Oswald   Very well, madam.

Goneril   And let his knights have colder looks among you;
What grows of it, no matter; advise your fellows so.
I would breed from hence occasions, and I shall,
That I may speak. I'll write straight to my sister,
To hold my very course. Prepare for dinner.

[Exeunt.]

SCENE IV. *A Hall in Albany's Palace.*

[Enter Kent, disguised.]

Kent   If but as well I other accents borrow,
That can my speech defuse, my good intent
May carry through itself to that full issue
For which I rais'd my likeness. Now, banish'd Kent,
If thou canst serve where thou dost stand condemn'd,
So may it come, thy master, whom thou lov'st,
Shall find thee full of labours.

[Horns within. Enter King Lear,
Knights, *and* Attendants.]*

Lear   Let me not stay a jot for dinner; go get it ready.

[Exit an Attendant.]*

　　　　　　　　我故意要把这件事跟他较量。
　　　　　　　　要是那么样不合他那副脾胃,
　　　　　　　　让他去到妹子那边,她和我,
　　　　　　　　我知道,对于那一层却同心合意,
　　　　　　　　不能让他作主。痴愚的老人,
　　　　　　　　他还想掌握他已经给掉的权威!
　　　　　　　　我将性命来打赌,年老的傻瓜
　　　　　　　　乃是童稚的再始,遇到了他们
　　　　　　　　不受抬举时,便当用责骂去对付。
　　　　　　　　你得记住我的话。

奥 士 伐　　　　　　　　　　　　正是,夫人。

刚 瑙 烈　给他的武士们更多看些你们的冷淡;
　　　　　　　　结果怎么样,不要紧;去知照管事们。
　　　　　　　　我愿在这里边孵化出一些个机会,
　　　　　　　　我要那么做,然后我才好说话。
　　　　　　　　我马上写信给妹子,叫她和我走
　　　　　　　　同一条道路。去预备开饭去吧。　　　　　〔同下。

第 四 景

　　　　　　　　〔亚尔白尼公爵府内的大厅。〕
　　　　　　　　〔铿德乔装上。

铿 德　只要我换上一副异样的口齿,
　　　　　　　　掩住了本来的言辞,我这片挚忱
　　　　　　　　便能功圆事竟地完成那个
　　　　　　　　我这般乔装所要成就的事功。
　　　　　　　　被放逐的铿德,如今你在论罪后
　　　　　　　　既然还能这么样为他效忠,
　　　　　　　　此后你那位爱戴的主上有的是
　　　　　　　　要你为他披肝沥胆时。
　　　　　　　　〔幕后号角声起。李尔与卫士及随从同上。

李 尔　别让我等一忽儿的饭:去,就去端整着来。〔一侍从退。

How now! what art thou?

Kent A man, sir.

Lear What dost thou profess? What wouldst thou with us?

Kent I do profess to be no less than I seem; to serve him truly that will put me in trust; to love him that is honest; to converse with him that is wise and says little; to fear judgment; to fight when I cannot choose; and to eat no fish.

Lear What art thou?

Kent A very honest-hearted fellow, and as poor as the king.

Lear If thou be'st as poor for a subject as he's for a king, thou art poor enough. What wouldst thou?

Kent Service.

Lear Who wouldst thou serve?

Kent You.

Lear Dost thou know me, fellow?

Kent No, sir; but you have that in your countenance which I would fain call master.

Lear What's that?

Kent Authority.

Lear What services canst thou do?

Kent I can keep honest counsel, ride, run, mar a curious tale in telling it, and deliver a plain message bluntly. That which ordinary men are fit for, I am qualified in, and the best of me is diligence.

Lear How old art thou?

Kent Not so young, sir, to love a woman for singing; nor so old to dote on her for anything; I have years on my back forty-eight.

Lear Follow me; thou shalt serve me. If I like thee no worse after dinner, I will not part from thee yet. — Dinner, ho, dinner! Where's my knave? my fool? —

喂！你是什么？

铿	德	我是一个人，大人。

李　　尔　你是干什么的？找我们有什么事？

铿　　德　我敢说我实质上不差似外表，能忠心侍候一个要我担干纪的人；爱诚实的君子，好跟聪明和少说话的人来往；怕世界末日的大审判；到了非打架不成时也能动武；并且不吃鱼。

李　　尔　你是什么人？

铿　　德　一个心地诚实透了的人，和国王一般可怜。

李　　尔　假使你在小百姓里头跟李尔在国王里头一样地可怜，也就够可怜的了。你要做什么？

铿　　德　要侍候人。

李　　尔　你要侍候谁？

铿　　德　您。

李　　尔　你认识我吗，人儿？

铿　　德　不，大人；但是您脸上那神色，我见了不由得不叫您主子。

李　　尔　那是什么神色？

铿　　德　威仪。

李　　尔　你能做什么事？

铿　　德　我能守得住正经的秘密，骑得马，跑得路，把一个文雅细致的故事能一说就坏，送一个明白的口信送得干脆；普通人能做的事情我都来得，我的好处是勤谨。

李　　尔　你有多大年纪？

铿　　德　不瞒您说，大人，若说年轻，还不会为一个婆娘会唱歌儿，便看中她；若说年纪大吧，还说不上老来糊涂，不管女人三七二十一，见了就着迷；我这背上驮得有春秋四十八。

李　　尔　你跟着我，侍候我就是：等我吃了饭还觉得你不错的话，就算留定了你。——开饭，喂，开饭！那小子上哪儿去了？我那傻子呢？——你去，去叫

Go you and call my fool hither. —
[*Exit an* attendant.]
[*Enter* Oswald.]
You, you, sirrah, where's my daughter?

Oswald So please you, —   [*Exit.*]

Lear What says the fellow there? Call the clotpoll
back. — [*Exit a* Knight.]Where's my fool, ho? — I
think the world's asleep. [*Re-enter* Knight.] How
now! where's that mongrel?

Knight He says, my lord, your daughter is not well.

Lear Why came not the slave back to me when I
called him?

Knight Sir, he answered me in the roundest manner, he
would not.

Lear *He would not* !

Knight My lord, I know not what the matter is; but to
my judgment your highness is not entertained with
that ceremonious affection as you were wont; there's
a great abatement of kindness appears as well in the
general dependants as in the duke himself also and
your daughter.

Lear Ha! say'st thou so?

Knight I beseech you pardon me, my lord, if I be mistak-
en; for my duty cannot be silent when I think your
highness wronged.

Lear Thou but rememberest me of mine own conception.
I have perceived a most faint neglect of late; which I
have rather blamed as mine own jealous curiosity than
as a very pretence and purpose of unkindness. I will
look further into't. But where's my fool? I have not
seen him this two days.

Knight Since my young lady's going into France, sir, the
fool hath much pined away.

Lear No more of that; I have noted it well. —Go you and
tell my daughter I would speak with her. —
[*Exit* Attendant.]
Go you, call hither my fool.   [*Exit another* Attendant.]
[*Re-enter Oswald.*]
O, you, sir, you, come you hither, sir. who am I, sir?

Oswald My lady's father.

Lear *My lady's father* ! my lord's knave. you whoreson

他来。——

　　　　　　　　　　　　　　　　　　　［一侍从下。
　　　　　　　　　　　　［奥士伐上。
呸,呸,奴才,我女儿在哪儿?

奥　士　伐　对不起,——

李　　　尔　那东西说什么? 把那蠢才叫回来。——［一卫士下。]我那傻子呢,喂? 大概这世界全都睡了觉。——［卫士返。]怎么样! 那狗子生的野杂种上哪儿去了?

卫　　　士　他说,禀王上,他说公主身体不舒服。

李　　　尔　那奴才我叫了他怎么不回来?

卫　　　士　禀王上,他回话说得很干脆,他说他不回来。

李　　　尔　他不回来!

卫　　　士　大人,不知是怎么回事;但是小的觉得他们款待王上近来比不上往常那么敬爱有礼了;公爵和公主连同他们那班下人都显得怠慢多了。

李　　　尔　哼! 你这么说吗?

卫　　　士　要是小的说错了,求王上宽恩恕罪;小的责任在身,觉得王上受了委曲,不能不说。

李　　　尔　你只提醒了我自己的猜疑。我近来觉得受了一点点疏忽;我总怪自己太多疑,太细心,不以为他们有意怠慢我。我得看一下究竟怎么样。可是我那傻子呢? 我这两天就没有瞧见他。

卫　　　士　王上,自从小公主上法国去后,傻子伤心得怎么似的。

李　　　尔　不准再提了,我很知道。——你去告诉我女儿,我要跟她谈话。
　　　　　　　　　　　　　　　　　　　［一侍从下。
　　　　你去叫我的傻子来。　　　　　　　［又一侍从下。
　　　　　　　　　　［奥士伐重上。
嗄,你来了,你,跑过来,大爷。你说吧,我是谁?

奥　士　伐　公爵夫人的父亲。

李　　　尔　"公爵夫人的父亲"! 好一个主子的奴才。你这婊子

dog! you slave! you cur!

Oswald I am none of these, my lord; I beseech your pardon.

Lear Do you bandy looks with me, you rascal?

[*Striking him.*]

Oswald I'll not be struck, my lord.

Kent Nor tripp'd neither, you base football player.

[*Tripping up his heels.*]

Lear I thank thee, fellow; thou servest me, and I'll love thee.

Kent Come, sir, arise, away! I'll teach you differences: away, away! If you will measure your lubber's length again, tarry; but away! go to; have you wisdom? so.

[*Pushes* Oswald *out.*]

Lear Now, my friendly knave, I thank thee: there's earnest of thy service. [*Giving* Kent *money.*]

[*Enter* Fool.]

Fool Let me hire him too. — here's my coxcomb.

[*Giving* Kent *his cap.*]

Lear How now, my pretty knave! how dost thou?

Fool Sirrah, you were best take my coxcomb.

Kent Why, fool?

Fool Why, for taking one's part that's out of favour. Nay, an thou canst not smile as the wind sits, thou'lt catch cold shortly. there, take my coxcomb; why, this fellow hath banish'd two on's daughters, and did the third a blessing against his will; if thou follow him, thou must needs wear my coxcomb. — How now, nuncle! Would I had two coxcombs and two daughters!

Lear Why, my boy?

Fool If I gave them all my living, I'd keep my coxcombs myself. There's mine; beg another of thy daughters.

Lear Take heed, sirrah, — the whip.

Fool Truth's a dog must to kennel; he must be whipped out, when the lady, the brach, may stand by the fire and stink.

养的狗！你这贱奴才，狗畜生！

李　　尔　　对不起，大人，我不是这些。

李　　尔　　坏蛋，你敢对我瞋眼？　　　　　　　　　　　〔打他。

奥　士　伐　　大人，我不能让人随便打。

铿　　德　　踢脚球的贱货，你也不要绊倒吧。

　　　　　　　　　　　　　　　　　　　〔将奥士伐绊倒地下。

李　　尔　　多谢你，人儿，你侍候我，我自会喜欢你。

铿　　德　　得了吧，起来，滚出去！让我教会你学学什么叫做尊
　　　　　卑上下：滚出去，滚开！你再要摔个觔斗就待着；滚
　　　　　蛋！滚你的；你有灵性没有？得。

　　　　　　　　　　　　　　　　　　　　〔将奥士伐推出。

李　　尔　　好仆人，谢你：先给你一点侍候我的定金。

　　　　　　　　　　　　　　　　　　　　〔给钱与铿德。

　　　　　　　　　〔傻子上。

傻　　子　　让我也雇了他。——我给你这顶鸡冠帽。

　　　　　　　　　　　　　　　　　　　　〔授帽与铿德。

李　　尔　　怎么样，我的好小子！你好不好？

傻　　子　　小子，你最好接了我这顶鸡冠帽。

铿　　德　　为什么，傻子？

傻　　子　　为什么？为的是你跑到倒霉的这一边来。哼，若是
　　　　　你不会顺风转舵保管不久就倒遭殃。拿去，接下我
　　　　　这顶鸡冠帽；哎，这老人赶走了两个大女儿，又倒反
　　　　　心不由己的祝福了一个小女儿；你若要跟他，非得戴
　　　　　上我这顶鸡冠帽不成。——你怎么样，老伯伯？我
　　　　　但愿有两顶鸡冠帽和两个女儿。

李　　尔　　为什么，小子？

傻　　子　　假使我把财产都给了她们，自己还得留着帽子戴。
　　　　　现在我的给了你吧：你再向你两个女儿要一顶。

李　　尔　　混小子，胡说八道，小心鞭子。

傻　　子　　真话是条公狗，它得耽在狗窠里；我们得使鞭子把它
　　　　　赶出屋外去，但不妨容假话那条母狗在里边，让它在
　　　　　火炉前面烤烤火，发点儿臭味。

Lear A pestilent gall to me!

Fool Sirrah, I'll teach thee a speech.

Lear Do.

Fool Mark it, nuncle: —

> Have more than thou showest,
> Speak less than thou knowest,
> Lend less than thou owest,
> Ride more than thou goest,
> Learn more than thou trowest,
> Set less than thou throwest;
> Leave thy drink and thy whore,
> And keep in-a-door,
> And thou shalt have more
> Than two tens to a score.

Kent This is nothing, fool.

Fool Then 'tis like the breath of an unfee'd lawyer, you gave me nothing for't. — Can you make no use of *nothing*, nuncle?

Lear Why, no, boy; *nothing* can be made out of nothing.

Fool [*to* Kent] Pr'ythee tell him, so much the rent of his land comes to; he will not believe a fool.

Lear A bitter fool!

Fool Dost thou know the difference, my boy, between a bitter fool and a sweet one?

Lear No, lad ; teach me.

Fool
> That lord that counsell'd thee
>> To give away thy land,
> Come place him here by me, —
>> Do thou for him stand:
> The sweet and bitter fool
>> Will presently appear;
> The one in motley here,

李	尔	这话苦得懊恼死人!
傻	子	[对铿德]小子,我教你一篇话来。
李	尔	你说吧。
傻	子	听着,伯伯:

有得多咧显得少
懂得多咧说得少,
多多有着出借少,
多多骑马走路少,
学得多咧信得少,
赢得多咧下得少
不喝酒咧也不嫖,
关上大门多睡觉;
老是这样我敢保,
没有错儿呱呱叫。

铿	德	你这一车的话没有说出什么来,傻子。
傻	子	那么,便好比一个义务律师替你辩护一样,因为你没有给我什么。——伯伯,"没有什么"可没有什么用处吗?
李	尔	不错,小子;"没有什么"里弄不出什么花样来。
傻	子	[对铿德]劳你驾告诉他,他偌大一块国土的钱粮就这么样了;你跟他说吧,他不会听信一个傻子说的话。
李	尔	好一个苦愤的傻子!
傻	子	你知道吗,小子,苦傻子和甜傻子的分别在哪儿?
李	尔	不知道,小子,告诉我。
傻	子	

有个人啊劝过你
  送掉那一片好江山,
那个人啊你代他
  在我这身边站一站:
就此甜傻子和苦傻子
  顷刻之间很分明;
这个穿着花花衣,

The other found out there.

Lear Dost thou call me fool, boy?

Fool All thy other titles thou hast given away; that thou wast born with.

Kent This is not altogether fool, my lord.

Fool No, faith, lords and great men will not let me; if I had a monopoly out, they would have part on't; and loads too, they will not let me have all the fool to myself; they'll be snatching. Nuncle, give me an egg, and I'll give thee two crowns.

Lear What two crowns shall they be?

Fool Why, after I have cut the egg i' the middle and eat up the meat, the two crowns of the egg. When thou clovest thy crown i' the middle and gav'st away both parts, thou borest thine ass on thy back o'er the dirt; thou hadst little wit in thy bald crown when thou gavest thy golden one away. If I speak like myself in this, let him be whipped that first finds it so.

[*Sing.*]

Fools had ne'er less grace in a year;
For wise men are grown foppish,
And know not how their wits to wear,
Their manners are so apish.

Lear When were you wont to be so full of songs, sirrah?

Fool I have used it, nuncle, e'er since thou mad'st thy daughters thy mothers; for when thou gav'st them the rod, and puttest down thine own breeches,

Then they for sudden joy did weep,
And I for sorrow sung,
That such a king should play bo-peep
And go the fools among.

Pr'ythee, nuncle, keep a schoolmaster that can teach thy fool to lie. I would fain learn to lie.

那个在那边不做声。

李　　尔　小子，你叫我傻子吗？

傻　　子　你把一切别的称呼全给掉了；傻子那名称你生来就有，可给不掉。

铿　　德　大人，这傻子并不完全傻。

傻　　子　说老实话，那班大人老爷们不让我独享盛名；若是我去要得了专利权出来，他们便都要分我一杯羹；还有那班贵妇夫人们，她们也不让我独当傻子，总你抢我夺地分些去。老伯伯，你给我一个鸡子儿，我给还你两顶冠冕。

李　　尔　是怎样的两顶冠冕？

傻　　子　哎，我把鸡子儿打中间切开，把里边吃了个精光，便还你两顶蛋壳的冠冕。你把你的王冠分作两半都送给了人，便好比骑驴怕污泥弄脏了驴蹄，把驴子驮在背上走；你把黄金的头盖送人的时候，你那透顶的头盖里准是连一点儿灵性都没有了。要是我这样直说便该捱鞭子的话，那个觉得我说话有理的人便该先来捱一顿。

　　　　　　这年头傻子最不受欢迎，

　　　　　　　　因为乖人都成了大傻瓜；

　　　　　　他们的行径有些像猢狲，

　　　　　　　　空有了聪明不知怎样耍。

李　　尔　混小子，你从什么时候唱起的这接二连三的歌？

傻　　子　老伯伯，你叫公主们做了王太后我才这样的；你把棍子交给了她们，自己褪下了裤子预备捱打，那时节啊，

　　　　　　她们快乐得眼泪双流，

　　　　　　　　我可伤心得把歌儿唱起，

　　　　　　　　这样的国王太过儿戏，

　　　　　　挤到傻子堆里作班头。

　　　　伯伯，我央你请一位老师教你的傻子撒谎。我喜欢学一学撒谎。

Lear An you lie, sirrah, we'll have you whipped.

Fool I marvel what kin thou and thy daughters are;
they'll have me whipped for speaking true, thou'lt
have me whipped for lying, and sometimes I am
whipped for holding my peace. I had rather be any
kind o' thing than a fool; and yet I would not be thee,
nuncle; thou hast pared thy wit o' both sides, and left
nothing i' the middle. here comes one o' the parings.

[*Enter* Goneril.]

Lear How now, daughter? What makes that frontlet on?
Methinks you are too much of late i' the frown.

Fool Thou wast a pretty fellow when thou hadst no need
to care for her frowning; Now thou art an O without a
figure; I am better than thou art; I am a fool, thou
art nothing. — Yes, forsooth, I will hold my tongue.
So your face [*To* Goneril.] bids me, though you say
nothing. Mum, mum,

> He that keeps nor crust nor crum,
> Weary of all, shall want some. —

[*Pointing to* Lear.] That's a shealed peascod.

Goneril Not only, sir, this your all-licens'd fool,
But other of your insolent retinue
Do hourly carp and quarrel; breaking forth
In rank and not-to-be-endured riots. Sir,
I had thought, by making this well known unto you,
To have found a safe redress; but now grow fearful,
By what yourself too late have spoke and done,
That you protect this course, and put it on
By your allowance; which if you should, the fault
Would not scape censure, nor the redresses sleep,

李　　尔　你若撒谎,混小子,给你吃鞭子。

傻　　子　我真诧异你和两位公主是怎么样的一家子;我待
说了真话她们要鞭打,待说了假话你又要鞭打,有
时不说话也得捱一顿鞭子。我想当什么东西都要
比当傻子强些;虽说那样,伯伯,我可不愿做你老
人家;你把你的机灵的两头都削掉了,不曾留得有
一点中间的剩余。你瞧,你削掉的两头里边有一
头来了。

〔刚瑙烈上。

李　　尔　怎么的,女儿? 做什么像是缠了条束额巾子似的,眉
头蹙得那么紧? 我觉得你近来皱眉蹙额的时候太
多了。

傻　　子　原先你不用顾虑到她皱眉不皱眉,那时候好不自在;
可是如今你是个主字少了个王;现在连我都比你强
些,我是个傻子,你是个没有什么,——〔对刚瑙烈〕
是,真是的,我不说话了;虽然您没有说什么,您的脸
色可叫我别做声。吭,吭;

今儿不留些面包的屑和皮,
全讨厌,赶明儿准要闹肚饥。

那是一荚空豆荚。　　　　　　　　　　　〔指李尔。〕

刚　瑙　烈　父亲,非但你这个言动不羁
有特许的傻子,即便是其他你那班
傲慢的侍从们,也总在时时叫骂,
刻刻地吹毛求疵,闹出些叫人
容忍不住的喧嚣扰攘。我本想,
父亲,全告你知道了能得一个
必然的矫正;但近来你自身的言谈
举止,倒使我生怕你庇护着那些
行径,这准许和纵容,更加紧他们
那不存惧惮的骚扰;若真是这样,
那过错便难逃责难,矫正也就
不再会延迟,这匡救虽然通常时

Which, in the tender of a wholesome weal,
Might in their working do you that offence,
Which else were shame, that then necessity
Will call discreet proceeding.

Fool For you know, nuncle,

The hedge-sparrow fed the cuckoo so long
That it had it head bit off by it young.

So out went the candle, and we were left darkling.

Lear Are you our daughter?

Goneril Come, sir,
I would you would make use of that good wisdom
Whereof I know you are fraught, and put away
These dispositions, that of late transform you
From what you rightly are.

Fool May not an ass know when the cart draws the
horse?—*Whoop, Jug! I love thee!*

Lear Doth any here know me? This is not Lear.
Doth Lear walk thus? speak thus? Where are his eyes?
Either his notion weakens, his discernings
Are lethargied.—Ha! waking? 'Tis not so!—
Who is it that can tell me who I am?

Fool Lear's shadow.

Lear I would learn that; for, by the marks of sovereign-
ty, Knowledge, and reason, I should be false persua-
ded I had daughters.

Fool Which they will make an obedient father.

Lear Your name, fair gentlewoman?

Goneril This admiration, sir, is much o' the favour
Of other your new pranks. I do beseech you
To understand my purposes aright;
As you are old and reverend, you should be wise.
Here do you keep a hundred knights and squires;
Men so disorder'd, so debosh'd, and bold,

　　　　　　　对你是冒犯，对我也难免贻羞，
　　　　　　　但为了顾念国家的福利和安全，
　　　　　　　如今便不愧叫作贤明的举措。

傻　　　子　因为你知道，老伯伯，
　　　　　　　　篱雀儿把布谷喂养得那么久，
　　　　　　　　小布谷大了便得咬掉它的头。
　　　　　　　蜡烛熄掉了，我们在黑暗里边。

李　　　尔　你是我们的女儿不是？

刚　瑙　烈　别那样，父亲，
　　　　　　　我愿你运用你富有的那贤明的智慧，
　　　　　　　愿你放弃近日来那使你改换
　　　　　　　本来面目的行为。

傻　　　子　一辆马车拉着一匹马时一个笨蛋他知不知道？啊
　　　　　　　呀，姣，我爱你！

李　　　尔　这儿有人认识我没有？这不是
　　　　　　　李尔。李尔是这样走路的吗？
　　　　　　　这样说话的吗？他眼睛在哪里？
　　　　　　　若不是他的心已经衰颓，他智能
　　　　　　　已变成鲁钝——哈，醒着吗？不能！
　　　　　　　谁能告诉我我是谁？

傻　　　子　李尔的影儿。

李　　　尔　我要知道我是谁；因为假如我要凭我的君权，知识，
　　　　　　　和理智的标记作征信，我便会误认我自己不是本
　　　　　　　人。我曾经有过女儿来的。

傻　　　子　她们要把那影儿变成个孝顺的父亲。

李　　　尔　你芳名叫什么，贵夫人？

刚　瑙　烈　你这番惊愕，父亲，正和你其他
　　　　　　　新开的玩笑一样。我请你要了解
　　　　　　　我意向的所在，如今既然你已是
　　　　　　　年高而可敬，你也就该当明达。
　　　　　　　这里你带着一百名武士与随从；
　　　　　　　那样紊乱，放荡，与莽撞的手下人，

That this our court, infected with their manners,
Shows like a riotous inn; epicurism and lust
Make it more like a tavern or a brothel
Than a grac'd palace. The shame itself doth speak
For instant remedy. be, then, desir'd
By her that else will take the thing she begs,
A little to disquantity your train,
And the remainder, that shall still depend,
To be such men as may besort your age,
Which know themselves, and you.

Lear   Darkness and devils! —
Saddle my horses! call my train together! —
Degenerate bastard! I'll not trouble thee.
Yet have I left a daughter.

Goneril   You strike my people, and your disorder'd rabble
Make servants of their betters.

                    [*Enter* Albany.]

Lear   Woe that too late repents! —
[*To* Albany.] O, sir, are you come?
Is it your will? Speak, sir. — Prepare my horses. —
Ingratitude, thou marble-hearted fiend,
More hideous when thou show'st thee in a child
Than the sea-monster !

Albany   Pray, sir, be patient.

Lear   [*To* Goneril] Detested kite, thou liest!
My train are men of choice and rarest parts,
That all particulars of duty know,
And in the most exact regard support
The worships of their name. — O most small fault,
How ugly didst thou in Cordelia show!
Which, like an engine, wrench'd my frame of nature

我们这宫廷沾染了他们的习气，
便化成下流的客店一般，口腹
和淫欲放纵得不像一个尊严
优雅的宫廷，却浑如酒肆或娼寮。
这耻辱本身要我们立时去改善。
因此请允从我削减从人的愿望，
莫待到后来由我去动手裁减；
至于那编余的人数，依旧作随从，
也还得适合你如许的年龄，知道你
也知道他们自己。

李　　尔　　　　　　　黑暗和魔鬼！——
快套马！召集我的随从侍卫！——
下流的野种！我不再在这里打扰。
我还有一个女儿在。

刚　瑙　烈　你自己打我的仆从，你那群漫无
纪律的暴徒役使着他们的上级。

　　　　　　　　　　　〔亚尔白尼上。

李　　尔　可痛我后悔太迟了。——〔对亚尔白尼〕啊，你来了？
这可是你的主意？你说，你说。——
快备好鞍马。——忘恩负义，你这个
顽石作心肠的魅鬼，在子女身上
显现，要比显现在海怪身上
更可怕！

亚 尔 白 尼　　　　　父亲，请你耐一点心儿。

李　　尔　〔对刚瑙烈〕该杀的恶霸！你撒谎欺人！
我的从人们尽是些上士和奇才，
详知自身的职务，又都万分
谨慎地护持着他们的令誉。——啊，
一点点轻微的小疵，但你在考黛莲
一片完美中便显得何等丑恶！
你好比一具刑讯架，把我的亲情
扭脱了它原来的关节；打从我心里

From the fix'd place; drew from my heart all love,
And added to the gall. O Lear, Lear, Lear!
Beat at this gate that let thy folly in [*Striking his head.*]
And thy dear judgment out!—Go, go, my people.
Albany My lord, I am guiltless, as I am ignorant
Of what hath mov'd you.
Lear It may be so, my lord.
Hear, nature, hear; dear goddess, hear!
Suspend thy purpose, if thou didst intend
To make this creature fruitful;
Into her womb convey sterility;
Dry up in her the organs of increase,
And from her derogate body never spring
A babe to honour her! If she must teem,
Create her child of spleen, that it may live
And be a thwart disnatur'd torment to her.
Let it stamp wrinkles in her brow of youth;
With cadent tears fret channels in her cheeks;
Turn all her mother's pains and benefits
To laughter and contempt; that she may feel
How sharper than a serpent's tooth it is
To have a thankless child!—Away, away!

[*Exit.*]

Albany Now, gods that we adore, whereof comes this?
Goneril Never afflict yourself to know the cause,
But let his disposition have that scope
That dotage gives it.

[*Re-enter* Lear.]

Lear What, fifty of my followers at a clap!
Within a fortnight!
Albany What's the matter, sir?
Lear I'll tell thee.—Life and death!—[*To* Goneril] I am
    asham'd
That thou hast power to shake my manhood thus;
That these hot tears, which break from me perforce,

全盘把慈爱提出来,同苦胆搀和。
啊李尔,李尔,李尔! 你得要
痛打让愚顽进入,[自击头]让可贵的判断
出来的这重门! ——去来,去来,我的人。

亚尔白尼　父王,我没有过错,我不知什么事
　　　　　使你这样恼怒。

李　　尔　　　　　　也许是,公爵。——
听啊,造化,亲爱的女神,请你听!
要是你原想叫这东西有子息,
请拨转念头,使她永不能生产;
毁坏她孕育的器官,别让这逆天
背理的贱身生一个婴孩增光彩!
如果她务必要蕃滋,就赐她个孩儿
要怨毒作心肠,等日后对她成一个
暴戾乖张,不近情的心头奇痛。
那孩儿须在她年轻的额上刻满
愁纹;两颊上使泪流凿出深槽;
将她为母的劬劳与训诲尽化成
人家的嬉笑与轻蔑;然后她方始
能感到,有个无恩义的孩子,怎样　　　　　　[下。
比蛇牙还锋利,还恶毒! ——都走,都走!

亚尔白尼　呀,天神在上,是为了什么?

刚　瑙　烈　切莫去自找烦恼,想明白原由;
由他人老懵懂,去任情怪诞吧。

　　　　　　　[李尔重上。

李　　尔　什么,一下子就是五十名随从?
还不到十四天?

亚尔白尼　　　　怎么一回事,父王?

李　　尔　回头我告你。——[对刚瑙烈]凭我的生和死!
我惭愧,你能使我这七尺的昂藏
震撼得这么不堪;我惭愧我自己,
值得为了你乱下这涔涔的热泪。

Should make thee worth them. Blasts and fogs upon thee!
Th' untented woundings of a father's curse
Pierce every sense about thee! Old fond eyes,
Beweep this cause again, I'll pluck you out
And cast you, with the waters that you lose,
To temper clay. Ha! is it come to this?
Let it be so. I have another daughter,
Who, I am sure, is kind and comfortable.
When she shall hear this of thee, with her nails
She'll flay thy wolvish visage. Thou shalt find
That I'll resume the shape which thou dost think
I have cast off for ever. Thou shalt, I warrant thee.

          [*Exeunt* Lear, Kent, *and* Attendants.]

Goneril   Do you mark that, my lord?

Albany   I cannot be so partial, Goneril,
To the great love I bear you, —

Goneril   Pray you, content. —What, Oswald, ho!
[*To the* Fool] You, sir, more knave than fool, after your
    master.

Fool   Nuncle Lear, nuncle Lear, tarry; take the fool with
    thee. —

    A fox when one has caught her,
    And such a daughter,
    Should sure to the slaughter,
    If my cap would buy a halter.
    So the fool follows after.

                  [*Exit.*]

Goneril   This man hath had good counsel! A hundred
    knights!
'Tis politic and safe to let him keep
At point a hundred knights! yes, that on every dream,
Each buzz, each fancy, each complaint, dislike,
He may enguard his dotage with their powers

天雷打死你天火烧成灰！被亲爹
咒成的那无法医疗的创伤，穿透你
每一个官能！昏愚的老眼，你再要
为这事滴泪，我准会将你挖出来，
连同你淌掉的泪水扔入尘埃。
呃！竟会到这样地步？好吧。
我还有一个女儿在，我信他为人
温良体贴。她听了你这样对我，
便会用指爪撕去你这张狼脸。
你以为我已经永远卸去，但你会，
保你会见我恢复，旧时的形象。

　　　　　　　　　　　　　[李尔，铿德，及从人齐下，

刚　瑙　烈	你看见吗，夫君？
亚尔白尼	我不能为了我们的恩情很深厚， 刚瑙烈，便偏袒——
刚　瑙　烈	请你放心。——在那儿，奥士伐，喂！—— [对傻子]你这大爷，不像个傻子，却真是 学成和主子一丝不差的贱奴才。
傻　　　子	李尔伯伯，李尔伯伯，等一下；带了你的傻子 走。——

　　　　这帽儿能换到绞索子，——
　　　　那我若逮到了狐狸，
　　　　和这样的一个女孩儿，
　　　　我准把她们全绞死。
　　　　傻子便这样的跟主子。　　　　　　　　[下。

刚　瑙　烈	这人计算多好！一百名武士！ 给他留一百名剑利乃明的侍卫， 好一个足智多谋的策略！不错， 只要有一个梦幻，一点点流长 和飞短，一阵子空想，一回的诉苦 或嫌厌，他便会指使他们那暴力 护卫他自身的昏懂，甚至威胁

And hold our lives in mercy. — Oswald, I say!

Albany   Well, you may fear too far.

Goneril   Safer than trust too far:
Let me still take away the harms I fear,
Not fear still to be taken: I know his heart.
What he hath utter'd I have writ my sister;
If she sustain him and his hundred knights,
When I have show'd th' unfitness, —

[Re-enter Oswald.]

How now, Oswald!

What, have you writ that letter to my sister?

Oswald   Ay, madam.

Goneril   Take you some company, and away to horse;
Inform her full of my particular fear,
And thereto add such reasons of your own
As may compact it more. Get you gone;
And hasten your return.

[Exit Oswald.]

No, no, my lord!

This milky gentleness and course of yours
Though I condemn it not, yet, under pardon,
You are much more attask'd for want of wisdom
Than prais'd for harmful mildness.

Albany   How far your eyes may pierce I cannot tell;
Striving to better, oft we mar what's well.

Goneril   Nay then, —

Albany   Well, well; the event.

[Exeunt.]

SCENE V. *Court before the Duke of Albany's Palace.*

[Enter Lear, Kent, and Fool.]

Lear   Go you before to Gloucester with these letters.
acquaint my daughter no further with anything you
know than comes from her demand out of the letter.

我们生命的安全。——奥士伐,在哪儿!

亚尔白尼 不过你也许过虑得太远了吧。

刚　瑙　烈 总要比过分的信任妥当。让我
永远把叫我担惊的祸事去掉。
别使我常怕受那些祸事的灾害。
他的心我知道。他说的我已写信
给妹子知道;我也已表示维持他
和他那一百名武卫的不妥,她如果
还是要,——

　　　　　　　〔奥士伐重上。

　　　　　怎么,奥土伐! 你写了给我
妹子的那封信没有?

奥　士　伐 哎,夫人。

刚　瑙　烈 你带上几个同伴,上马就去;
多多告诉她我私下的惧怕,再添些
你能想得的理由,好叫我的话
分外圆到。去吧,赶早回来。　　　——〔奥士伐下。
不行,不行,夫君,我虽然不责你
你那行径的懦弱无能,可是,
恕我说,只怪你没有智谋深算,
却不得称赞你那遗害种祸的温柔。

亚尔白尼 你眼光射得多么远我可不知道;
但一心想改善,我们把好事常弄糟。

刚　瑙　烈 不,那么——

亚尔白尼 算了,算了,且看后事吧。　　　　　　　〔同下。

第　五　景

〔亚尔白尼公爵府前之庭院。〕
〔李尔,铿德,与傻子上。

李　　尔 你先带着这封信往葛洛斯武去。她看过信有话问你
你才回答,不要把你知道的事情都告诉她。若是你

If your diligence be not speedy, I shall be there afore you.

Kent I will not sleep, my lord, till I have delivered your letter.

                           [*Exit.*]

Fool If a man's brains were in's heels, were't not in danger of kibes?

Lear Ay, boy.

Fool Then I pr'ythee be merry; thy wit shall not go slipshod.

Lear Ha, ha, ha!

Fool Shalt see thy other daughter will use thee kindly; for though she's as like this as a crab's like an apple, yet I can tell what I can tell.

Lear What canst tell, boy?

Fool She'll taste as like this as a crab does to a crab. Thou canst tell why one's nose stands i' the middle on's face?

Lear No.

Fool Why, to keep one's eyes of either side's nose, that what a man cannot smell out, he may spy into.

Lear I did her wrong, —

Fool Canst tell how an oyster makes his shell?

Lear No.

Fool Nor I neither; but I can tell why a snail has a house.

Lear Why?

Fool Why, to put's head in; not to give it away to his daughters, and leave his horns without a case.

Lear I will forget my nature. So kind a father! — Be my horses ready?

Fool Thy asses are gone about 'em. The reason why the seven stars are no more than seven is a pretty reason.

Lear Because they are not eight?

Fool Yes indeed; thou wouldst make a good fool.

差事赶办得不快,我会比你先到那边。

铿	德	主上,我把信送到了才睡觉。　　　　　　　　〔下。
傻	子	一个人脑子生在脚跟里,它有没有生冻疮的危险?
李	尔	有的,小子。
傻	子	那么,我劝你,快乐些吧,你的脑子准不会踢着鞋跟走路的。
李	尔	哈,哈,哈!
傻	子	瞧着吧,你那个女儿跟这个一样会待你得很亲爱的;因为虽然她跟这一个相像得好比山楂子像苹果,可是我能说给你听我能说的话。
李	尔	你能说什么,小子?
傻	子	她跟这个是一样的味儿,好比一只山楂像另一只山楂似的。人的鼻子生在脸盘正中,你可说得出是为什么?
李	尔	说不上来。
傻	子	哎,为的是要把两只眼睛分在鼻子两边;那么,一个人遇到了一件事,鼻子闻不出来就可以用眼睛去瞅。
李	尔	我冤屈了她了。
傻	子	你可说得出牡蛎怎么样造它的壳的?
李	尔	说不上来。
傻	子	我也说不上来,可是我能说为什么蜗牛有房子。
李	尔	为什么?
傻	子	哎,为的是好把它的头缩在里边;不是为拿去送给它的女儿们的,结果倒反弄得自己的角没有一个壳儿装。
李	尔	我不能太讲恩情了。这样慈爱的父亲! 我的马套好了没有?
傻	子	你的那班笨驴去套去了。为什么那七星只是七颗,不多出来,那道理真是妙。
李	尔	是因为它们不是八颗吗?
傻	子	一点不错;你倒可以当一个很好的傻子。

Lear To tak't again perforce! —Monster ingratitude!

Fool If thou wert my fool, nuncle, I'ld have thee beaten
    for being old before thy time.

Lear How's that?

Fool Thou shouldst not have been old till thou hadst been
    wise.

Lear O, let me not be mad, not mad, sweet heaven!
Keep me in temper; I would not be mad! —

[*Enter* Gentleman.]

How now? are the horses ready?

Gent Ready, my lord.

Lear Come, boy.

Fool She that's a maid now, and laughs at my departure,
Shall not be a maid long, unless things be cut shorter.

[*Exeunt.*]

李	尔	用武力都拿回来！妖怪似的忘恩负义！
傻	子	要是你当了我的傻子，老伯伯，你没有到时候先老，我就打你。
李	尔	那是怎么的？
傻	子	你不曾变得聪明就不该老。
李	尔	啊，让我别发疯，别发疯，仁蔼的天！叫我耐着性子；我不要发疯呀！——［近侍上。］怎么样了！马备好了没有？
近	侍	备好了，主上。
李	尔	来，小子。
傻	子	若有个闺女取笑我空自去奔跑， 她不久就破身，除非事情会变好。　　　　［同下。

ACT II.

SCENE I. *The Castle of the* Earl *of* Gloucester.

[*Enter* Edmund *and* Curan, *meeting.*]

Edmund   Save thee, Curan.

Curan   And you, sir. I have been with your father, and given him notice that the Duke of Cornwall and Regan, his duchess will be here with him this night.

Edmund   How comes that?

Curan   Nay, I know not. — You have heard of the news a-broad, I mean the whispered ones, for they are yet but ear-kissing arguments?

Edmund   Not I. pray you, what are they?

Curan   Have you heard of no likely wars toward, 'twixt the two dukes of Cornwall and Albany?

Edmund   Not a word.

Curan   You may do, then, in time. Fare you well, sir.

[*Exit.*]

Edmund   The Duke be here to-night? The better! best!
This weaves itself perforce into my business.
My father hath set guard to take my brother;
And I have one thing, of a queasy question,
Which I must act: — briefness and fortune work!

第 二 幕

第 一 景

[葛洛斯忒伯爵堡邸中。]

[蔼特孟与居任同上。

蔼 特 孟　上帝保佑你，居任。

居　　任　也保佑您阁下。我才见过了令尊，告诉他康华公爵
　　　　　和爵夫人雷耿今晚上要到他这儿来。

蔼 特 孟　做什么？

居　　任　那我可不知道。您听到外边的风声吗，我是说那些
　　　　　私下里的传闻，因为那还只是些咬耳朵偷说的谣
　　　　　言呢？

蔼 特 孟　我没有听到。请问是什么风声？

居　　任　您没有听说康华和亚尔白尼两位公爵许就要打
　　　　　仗吗？

蔼 特 孟　一点都没有。

居　　任　那就请听吧，这正是时候了。再会，阁下。

　　　　　　　　　　　　　　　　　　　　　　　　［下。

蔼 特 孟　今晚上公爵要来？那更好！最妙了！
　　　　　这一来准会和我的事攀上了藤蔓。
　　　　　父亲已然安排好要逮住哥哥；
　　　　　我还有件妙事应付得要小心着意，
　　　　　我一定得做：要做得爽利做得快，

Brother, a word! descend! brother, I say!

[*Enter* Edgar.]

My father watches! sir, fly this place;
Intelligence is given where you are hid!
You have now the good advantage of the night.
Have you not spoken 'gainst the Duke of Cornwall?
He's coming hither; now, i' the night, i' the haste,
And Regan with him; have you nothing said
Upon his party 'gainst the Duke of Albany?
Advise yourself.

Edgar   I am sure on't, not a word.

Edmund   I hear my father coming! pardon me;
In cunning I must draw my sword upon you.
Draw; seem to defend yourself; now quit you well.
Yield! come before my father! — Light, ho, here! —
Fly, brother. — Torches, torches! — So farewell.

[*Exit* Edgar.]

Some blood drawn on me would beget opinion
Of my more fierce endeavour.   [*Wounds his arm.*]

                  I have seen drunkards
Do more than this in sport. — Father, father! —
Stop, stop! No help?

[*Enter* Gloucester, *and* Servants *with torches.*]

Gloucester   Now, Edmund, where's the villain?

Edmund   Here stood he in the dark, his sharp sword out,
Mumbling of wicked charms, conjuring the moon
To stand auspicious mistress.

Gloucester   But where is he?

Edmund   Look, sir, I bleed!

Gloucester   Where is the villain, Edmund?

Edmund   Fled this way, sir. When by no means he could, —

另外也得靠命运帮我的忙！——
哥哥，说句话；下来！哥哥，我说啊！

〔蔼特加上。

父亲警戒着，要逮你！快逃开这里！
你躲在这里有人向他告了密！
你现在有黑夜替你庇护着安全。
你说了康华公爵的坏话没有？
他赶着这夜晚，说话就到，忙着来，
雷耿和他同来；你在他这边
没说过亚尔白尼公爵的坏话吗？
你自己想一下。

| 蔼　特　加 | 　　　　　　我真的没有说过。 |

蔼　特　孟　我听见父亲在来了！请你原谅；
我一定得假装向着你拔剑相斗。
快拔出剑来；装着自卫的模样；
好好地和我对剑。赶快认了输！
到父亲跟前来！——拿火来，喂，这儿来！——
快逃，哥哥！——火把，火把！〔蔼特加下。〕——
　再会。
身上刺出一点血，会叫人信我　　　　　〔自刺臂上。
追他得分外急切。我见过醉汉
刺着玩比这样还要凶。——父亲，父亲！——
住手，住手！——没有人来救吗？

〔葛洛斯忒上，仆从持火把随上。

葛　洛　斯　忒　蔼特孟，那坏蛋在哪儿？
蔼　特　孟　他站在这暗中，握一把利剑，咕噜着
邪魔的咒语，在那里召遣月亮
做他的卫护女神。

葛　洛　斯　忒　　　　　　可是他在那儿？
蔼　特　孟　您看，父亲，我流血！
葛　洛　斯　忒　　　　　那坏蛋呢，蔼特孟？
蔼　特　孟　往这边逃走的，父亲，他见他不能——

Gloucester   Pursue him, ho! — Go after. —

                                     [Exeunt Servants.*]*

                                    By no means what?

Edmund   Persuade me to the murder of your lordship;
But that I told him the revenging gods
'Gainst parricides did all their thunders bend,
Spoke with how manifold and strong a bond
The child was bound to the father; sir, in fine,
Seeing how loathly opposite I stood
To his unnatural purpose, in fell motion
With his prepared sword, he charges home
My unprovided body, lanc'd mine arm;
But when he saw my best alarum'd spirits
Bold in the quarrel's right, rous'd to the encounter,
Or whether gasted by the noise I made,
Full suddenly he fled.

Gloucester   Let him fly far;
Not in this land shall he remain uncaught;
And found — dispatch'd. The noble duke my master,
My worthy arch and patron, comes to-night;
By his authority I will proclaim it,
That he which finds him shall deserve our thanks,
Bringing the murderous coward to the stake;
He that conceals him, death.

Edmund   When I dissuaded him from his intent
And found him pight to do it, with curst speech
I threaten'd to discover him; he replied:
'Thou unpossessing bastard! dost thou think,
If I would stand against thee, would the reposal
Of any trust, virtue, or worth in thee
Make thy words faith'd? No; what I should deny, —
As this I would; ay, though thou didst produce
My very character, — I'd turn it all
To thy suggestion, plot, and damned practice;

葛洛斯忒 追他去,喂!赶着他。〔数仆从下。〕"不能"怎么样?

蔼　特　孟 劝诱我将您谋害,可是我告他
罚罪的天神们对杀害尊亲的大恶
不惜用他们所有的雷火来惩处,
我又向他说孩儿对父亲有多少
地厚天高的情义;总之,父亲
他见我怎样跟他那不近情的意向
狠狠地敌对,他便使用他那柄
有备的佩剑,忍着心向我一击,
击中我无备的身躯,刺伤这臂膀;
但或许他眼见我已激发得性起,
并不甘多让,贾着勇要跟他周旋,
或许是我大声的叫嚷使他惊心,
他就蓦然逃去。

葛洛斯忒 　　　　　　尽他去远走
高飞,在这境地里可不会逮不住;
逮住了——就得死! 公爵,我那位主上,
我的尊贵的首领与恩公,今晚来;
我要请准他,用他的权能宣示:
谁若找到了这谋杀亲尊的懦夫,
引他上焚身的刑柱,便该受我们
酬谢;谁要是将他窝藏着,就得死。

蔼　特　孟 我劝他放弃他那番不轨的图谋,
他厉声疾色,回报我他用心的坚决;
我便恐吓他要宣布案情,他回答道:
"你这传不到遗产的野种! 你想,
我要是跟你作对,既无人信你
有什么优良的德性和高贵的身份,
还有谁信你吐露的乃是真情?
不;我所否认的,——这我得否认;
哎,即使你取出我亲手的笔迹,——
我会推说那都是你一人的蛊惑,

And thou must make a dullard of the world,
If they not thought the profits of my death
Were very pregnant and potential spurs
To make thee seek it.

Gloucester   O, strong and fast'ned villain!
Would he deny his letter? I never got him.

> [*Trumpets within.*]

Hark, the duke's trumpets! I know not why he comes.
All ports I'll bar; the villain shall not scape;
The duke must grant me that. besides, his picture
I will send far and near, that all the kingdom
May have due note of him; and of my land,
Loyal and natural boy, I'll work the means
To make thee capable.

> [*Enter* Cornwall, Regan, *and* Attendants.]

Cornwall   How now, my noble friend! since I came hither,
Which I can call but now, I have heard strange news.

Regan   If it be true, all vengeance comes too short
Which can pursue the offender. How dost, my lord?

Gloucester   O madam, my old heart is crack'd, —
it's crack'd!

Regan   What, did my father's godson seek your life?
He whom my father nam'd? your Edgar?

Gloucester   O lady, lady, shame would have it hid!

Regan   Was he not companion with the riotous knights
That tend upon my father?

Gloucester   I know not, madam: It is too bad, too bad.

Edmund   Yes, madam, he was of that consort.

Regan   No marvel then though he were ill affected;

狡谋,和罪大恶极的毒计所酿成;
若要人不信,你所以要伤我的生命
都因我死后的好处对你蕴蓄着
太多有力量的激刺,你便非得将
世人都变成了呆子,万无指望。"

葛 洛 斯 忒　啊,这坏透了的恶棍真骇人听闻!
他能不承认那信吗?那坏种决不是
我亲生的儿子。　　　　　〔幕后号声作进行曲。〕
　　　　　　　那是公爵的号声,
你听! 我不知为什么他到这里来。
我要把所有的口岸完全封锁住;
那坏蛋逃不掉;公爵得准我这件事。
另外我还要把他的图像不拘
远近地分送,使全国都对他注目;
至于我那些地土,私生的爱儿,
你忠诚出于天性,我自会设法
叫你有承袭的权能。

　　　　　　〔康华、雷耿与从人们上。

康　　华　你好,尊贵的朋友! 我虽是才来,
但已闻见了一个惊人的消息。
雷　　耿　如果是实事,把严刑酷罚全用尽
也不够惩治这罪犯。你好,伯爵?
葛 洛 斯 忒　唉,夫人,这衰老的心儿碎了,——
碎了!
雷　　耿　　　　　什么,我父亲的教子谋害你?
他还是我父亲提的名? 你的蔼特加?
葛 洛 斯 忒　唉,夫人,夫人,我没有脸说话!
雷　　耿　他可是就同侍候我父亲的那班
荒淫暴乱的武士们作伴的吗?
葛 洛 斯 忒　那我不知道,夫人。——太坏了,太坏了。
蔼 特 孟　正是的,夫人,他交的是那些伙伴。
雷　　耿　那么,无怪他存心变得那样坏;

'Tis they have put him on the old man's death,
To have the expense and waste of his revenues.
I have this present evening from my sister
Been well inform'd of them; and with such cautions
That if they come to sojourn at my house,
I'll not be there.

Cornwall   Nor I, assure thee, Regan. —
Edmund, I hear that you have shown your father
A childlike office.

Edmund   'Twas my duty, sir.

Gloucester   He did bewray his practice, and receiv'd
This hurt you see, striving to apprehend him.

Cornwall   Is he pursu'd?

Gloucester   Ay, my good lord.

Cornwall   If he be taken, he shall never more
Be fear'd of doing harm. make your own purpose,
How in my strength you please. —For you, Edmund,
Whose virtue and obedience doth this instant
So much commend itself, you shall be ours.
Natures of such deep trust we shall much need;
You we first seize on.

Edmund   I shall serve you, sir,
Truly, however else.

Gloucester   For him I thank your grace.

Cornwall   You know not why we came to visit you?

Regan   Thus out of season, threading dark-ey'd night;
Occasions, noble Gloucester, of some poise,
Wherein we must have use of your advice.
Our father he hath writ, so hath our sister,
Of differences, which I best thought it fit
To answer from our home; the several messengers

　　　　　　那都因他们鼓动他谋害了这老人，
　　　　　　好合伙朋分，花掉他身后的进款。
　　　　　　就在今晚上我从我大姐那边
　　　　　　得知了他们的详细，她又警告我
　　　　　　他们若是去到我家中留驻，
　　　　　　我莫要收留。

康　　华　　　　　　　我也不收留，雷耿。
　　　　　　蔼特孟，我听说你对你父亲却很尽
　　　　　　为儿的爱敬。

蔼　特　孟　　　　　　　是我的本份，爵爷。
葛洛斯忒　他把那败种的阴谋揭破，要逮他，
　　　　　　因此便受了你见的这一处创伤。

康　　华　有人追他吗？

葛洛斯忒　　　　　　有的，善良的主上。

康　　华　逮到了他时，他便休想再叫人
　　　　　　怕他作恶。定下你自己的算计，
　　　　　　你能尽我们的权威，任意去处置。——
　　　　　　至于你，蔼特孟，你那顺从的德行
　　　　　　如今显得你这样优良中正，
　　　　　　我们要将你重用。我们正需人
　　　　　　有这般可靠的禀性，就最先得到你。

蔼　特　孟　不论怎样的事，我都愿替公爵
　　　　　　奔走。

葛洛斯忒　　　　　我为他感谢爵爷的恩典。

康　　华　你可不知道为什么我们来这里吗？

雷　　耿　这样不合时，引线似的穿过黑夜
　　　　　　这难穿的针眼；尊贵的葛洛斯忒，
　　　　　　我们有要事要向你征询主意。
　　　　　　我们的父亲和姐姐都写信来申诉
　　　　　　他们父女间的争执，我忖度情形
　　　　　　最好还是离了家到外边来回答；
　　　　　　故此两方的信使从家里跟了来

From hence attend despatch. Our good old friend,
Lay comforts to your bosom; and bestow
Your needful counsel to our business,
Which craves the instant use.

Gloucester   I serve you, madam. —
Your graces are right welcome.

[*Flourish. Exeunt.*]

SCENE II. *Before Gloucester's Castle.*

[*Enter* Kent *and* Oswald, *severally.*]

Oswald   Good dawning to thee, friend; art of this house?

Kent   Ay.

Oswald   Where may we set our horses?

Kent   I' the mire.

Oswald   Pr'ythee, if thou lov'st me, tell me.

Kent   I love thee not.

Oswald   Why then, I care not for thee.

Kent   If I had thee in Lipsbury pinfold, I would make thee
care for me.

Oswald   Why dost thou use me thus? I know thee not.

Kent   Fellow, I know thee.

Oswald   What dost thou know me for?

Kent   A knave; a rascal; an eater of broken meats; a
base, proud, shallow, beggarly, three-suited, hun-
dred-pound, filthy, worsted-stocking knave; a lily-
livered, action-taking, whoreson, glass-gazing, su-
perserviceable, finical rogue; one-trunk-inheriting
slave; one that wouldst be a bawd in way of good service, and art nothing but the composition of a knave,

正等着我们差他们回去报信。

我们的老友，你且放平了心绪，

为我们这事情贡献一点我们

正迫切待用的意见。

葛洛斯忒 遵命，夫人。——

极欢迎你们两位大人来恩幸。〔号声作。人众同下。

第 二 景

〔葛洛斯忒堡邸前。〕

〔铿德与奥士伐先后上。

奥 士 伐 快天亮了，朋友，你好；你可是这家里的人吗？

铿 德 哎。

奥 士 伐 我们把马儿歇在哪儿？

铿 德 歇到泥洼里去。

奥 士 伐 劳你驾，要是你乐意我的话，告我一声。

铿 德 我不乐意你。

奥 士 伐 那么我也不理会你。

铿 德 若是我在列士白莱豢牲园里碰见了你，准叫你理
会我。

奥 士 伐 为什么你这样子对我？我并不认识你。

铿 德 我可认识你这家伙。

奥 士 伐 你认得我是什么人？

铿 德 我认得你是个坏蛋，是个混混儿；吃残羹冷饭的东
西，一副贱骨头，神气十足，呆头呆脑的，叫花的胚；
给了你常年三套衣服穿，就买得你叫不完的老爷太
太；只有一百镑钱的绅士；卑鄙下贱，穿不起丝袜子
的坏蛋；芝麻大的胆，挨了打骂不敢自己动手，却只
会递状子仰仗官府来出头的东西；婊子养的，尽自
对着镜子发呆，手忙脚乱地瞎讨好，打扮得整整齐
齐的痞棍，整份儿家私只一只箱子的奴才；为侍
候人愿意去当娼妓；我看你只是坏蛋，要饭的，耗子

        beggar, coward, pander, and the son and heir of a mongrel bitch; one whom I will beat into clamorous whining, if thou denyest the least syllable of thy addition.

Oswald   Why, what a monstrous fellow art thou, thus to rail on one that's neither known of thee nor knows thee!

Kent   What a brazen-faced varlet art thou, to deny thou knowest me! Is it two days ago since I beat thee and tripped up thy heels before the king? Draw, you rogue! for, though it be night, yet the moon shines; I'll make a sop o' the moonshine of you, you whoreson cullionly barbermonger, draw!

[Drawing his sword.]

Oswald   Away! I have nothing to do with thee.

Kent   Draw, you rascal. you come with letters against the king. and take vanity the puppet's part against the royalty of her father. draw, you rogue, or I'll so carbonado your shanks! draw, you rascal; come your ways.

Oswald   Help, ho! murder! help!

Kent   Strike, you slave! stand, rogue, stand; you neat slave, strike!

[Beating him.]

Oswald   Help, ho! murder! murder!

[Enter Edmund, with his rapier drawn.]

Edmund   How now! What's the matter?

[Parting them.]

Kent   With you, goodman boy, an you please: come, I'll flesh you; come on, young master.

[Enter Cornwall, Regan, Gloucester, and Servants .]

Gloucester   Weapons! arms! What's the matter here?

Cornwall   Keep peace, upon your lives!

He dies that strikes again! What is the matter?

Regan   The messengers from our sister and the king?

Cornwall   What is your difference? speak.

Oswald   I am scarce in breath, my lord.

Kent   No marvel, you have so bestirr'd your valour. You cowardly rascal, nature disclaims in thee; a tailor made thee.

胆,王八羔子,杂种的狗这几件东西的混账:我给了你这些个外号你若道半个"不"字,准打得你拉长了嗓子直叫。

奥 士 伐　啊,你这家伙真是个怪物,你不认识人家人家也不认识你,却这么乱骂人!

铿　　德　你不认识我,好一个铜打铁铸的厚脸皮,你这臭蛋!我在国王面前摔了你的觔斗,又打你,可不是只两天前的事吗? 拔出剑来打,你这痞棍! 这时候虽是在晚上,月亮却照得很亮,我定把你戳成一团豆蔻香油煎满月,你这婊子养的蠢才,跟人剃头刮脸的下作货,拔出剑来打。　　　　　　　　　　〔拔剑欲击。〕

奥 士 伐　去你的! 我不来理会你。

铿　　德　拔出剑来,你这坏蛋! 你带于国王不利的信来,甘心做那玩意儿的帮凶,跟她的父亲王上作对。拔出剑来,你这痞棍,不然我就横剁你的脚胫! 拔出剑来,你这坏蛋;来呀。

奥 士 伐　救命啊! 杀人! 救命!

铿　　德　使你的剑,奴才! 站住,混混儿,站住,你这真正的奴才,使你的剑来!　　　　　　　　　　　　　　〔击打他〕

奥 士 伐　救命啊! 杀人! 杀人!
　　　　　　　　　　〔蔼特孟执剑上。

蔼 特 孟　怎么的! 为什么事?　　　　　　〔分开他们。〕

铿　　德　跟您来,好角色,要是您高兴的话,来,我教您开剑,来吧,小主人。
　　　　　　　　　〔康华、雷耿、葛洛斯忒与仆从上。

葛 洛 斯 忒　使刀弄剑的这是怎么回事?

康　　华　快停住,我把你们的生命打赌!
　　　谁再动了剑就得死! 怎么一回事?

雷　　耿　可是大姐和国王差来的使者们?

康　　华　你们争吵些什么? 说呀。

奥 士 伐　我回不过气来,大人。

铿　　德　怪不得,原来你已使足了你的胆。你这卑懦的坏蛋,没有人性的东西;是一个裁衣匠把你缝出来的。

Cornwall   Thou art a strange fellow; a tailor make a man?

Kent   Ay, a tailor, sir; a stonecutter or a painter could not have made him so ill, though he had been but two hours at the trade.

Cornwall   Speak yet, how grew your quarrel?

Oswald   This ancient ruffian, sir, whose life I have spared at suit of his grey beard, —

Kent   Thou whoreson zed! thou unnecessary letter! —My lord, if you'll give me leave, I will tread this unbolted villain into mortar and daub the walls of a jakes with him. —Spare my grey beard, you wagtail?

Cornwall   Peace, sirrah! —
You beastly knave, know you no reverence?

Kent   Yes, sir; but anger hath a privilege.

Cornwall   Why art thou angry?

Kent   That such a slave as this should wear a sword,
Who wears no honesty. Such smiling rogues as these,
Like rats, oft bite the holy cords a-twain
Which are too intrinse t' unloose; smooth every passion
That in the natures of their lords rebel;
Bring oil to fire, snow to their colder moods;
Renege, affirm, and turn their halcyon beaks
With every gale and vary of their masters,
Knowing naught, like dogs, but following.
A plague upon your epileptic visage!
Smile you my speeches, as I were a fool?
Goose, an I had you upon Sarum plain,
I'd drive ye cackling home to Camelot.

Cornwall   What, art thou mad, old fellow?

Gloucester   How fell you out? Say that.

康	华	你这人好怪,裁衣匠怎么缝得出人来?
铿	德	不错,是裁衣匠缝的,爵爷;石刻师或画师做他出来 不能这样坏,即使他们只学了两点钟的手艺。
康	华	可是说出来,你们怎样吵起的架?
奥 士 伐		爵爷,这老流氓我看他的灰白胡子,饶了他的命,——
铿	德	你这婊子养的,只当你是个屁! ——爵爷,要是你准 许的话,我把这不成材的坏蛋踹成了灰泥,把他涂在 茅厕的墙上。——饶我的灰白胡子,你这摇尾巴 的鸟?
康	华	不许说话,贱货! —— 你这畜生似的坏东西,懂不懂规矩?
铿	德	是,爵爷,但是一个人在盛怒之下自有一点特别的权 利,他来不及顾到礼貌了。
康	华	你为什么盛怒?
铿	德	为的是这样的奴才也居然佩着剑, 内里却不曾佩得有分毫的高贵。 这一类谄笑的痞棍跟耗子一般, 常把紧得放不松的神圣的绳缒 咬作了两截;他们主子的天性里 只要起了点反常逆变的波澜, 他们便无有不从旁掀风作浪; 火上添油,冷些的心情上洒雪; 说是道非,转动钓鱼郎似的鸟喙, 全跟着主人风色的变幻而定向; 狗一般什么也不懂,只晓得追随。 瘟死你这羊癫风上身的嘴脸! 你可是笑我说话好比个傻子吗? 笨鹅我若在舍剌谟平原上碰见你, 准把你呷呷呷的赶回你老家开米洛。
康	华	什么,你发了疯吗,老头儿?
葛 洛 斯 忒		你们怎样吵起架来的? 你说吧。

Kent   No contraries hold more antipathy
Than I and such a knave.

Cornwall   Why dost thou call him *knave*? What is his
fault?

Kent   His countenance likes me not.

Cornwall   No more perchance does mine, or his, or hers.

Kent   Sir, 'tis my occupation to be plain.
I have seen better faces in my time
Than stands on any shoulder that I see
Before me at this instant .

Cornwall   This is some fellow
Who, having been prais'd for bluntness, doth affect
A saucy roughness, and constrains the garb
Quite from his nature; he cannot flatter, he, —
An honest mind and plain, — he must speak truth!
An they will take it, so; if not, he's plain.
These kind of knaves I know which in this plainness
Harbour more craft and more corrupter ends
Than twenty silly-ducking observants
That stretch their duties nicely.

Kent   Sir, in good faith, in sincere verity,
Under the allowance of your great aspect,
Whose influence, like the wreath of radiant fire
On flickering Phoebus' front, —

Cornwall   What mean'st by this?

Kent   To go out of my dialect, which you discommend so
much. I know, sir, I am no flatterer: he that beguiled
you in a plain accent was a plain knave; which, for
my part, I will not be, though I should win your displeasure to entreat me to't.

Cornwall   What was the offence you gave him?

Oswald   I never gave him any.

铿	德	天下再无两件相反的东西，
		比较我和他这么个恶棍之间，
		含得有更多不相容的敌忾。
康	华	为什么你叫他恶棍？他恶在哪里？
铿	德	他这嘴脸我不喜欢。
康	华	你也许不喜欢我的脸，或他的，她的。
铿	德	公爵，我说话一辈子只知道坦白。
		自来我却见过了比在我眼前
		架在这些肩上的任是那一副
		都好些的嘴脸。
康	华	这是个那样的家伙，
		给人赞了他率直无华，便故意
		装出那莽撞的粗暴，把外表做作得
		和本性截然相反，他不能奉承，——
		只有他那副诚实坦白的心肠，——
		他定得说实话！他们若听他，就罢；
		假如不然，他是在那里坦白。
		这一类坏货，我知道在这些坦白里，
		包藏的奸刁和恶意，要多过二十个
		折背伛腰，礼数周全的随侍们。
铿	德	公爵，我来说真话，我来说实话，
		请准您伟大的光座，你放出的运数
		便好比炜伯氏闪耀的额前那轮
		辉煌的火环，——
康	华	这是什么意思？
铿	德	这是不说我自己的话，因为我的话您那么不赞成。
		公爵，我知道我不是拍马屁的能手；谁假装着说话坦
		白来哄骗您，谁就是个十足的坏蛋；拿我自己来说
		吧，即使您央我当那么个东西，我不肯当会使您生
		气，我还是不愿意当的。
康	华	你是怎么样冲撞他的？
奥 士 伐		我从没有冲撞过他。

It pleas'd the king his master very late
To strike at me, upon his misconstruction;
When he, compact, and flattering his displeasure,
Tripp'd me behind; being down, insulted, rail'd,
And put upon him such a deal of man,
That worthied him, got praises of the king
For him attempting who was self-subdu'd;
And in the fleshment of this dread exploit
Drew on me here again.

Kent None of these rogues and cowards
But Ajax is their fool.

Cornwall Fetch forth the stocks! —
You stubborn ancient knave, you reverent braggart,
We'll teach you, —

Kent Sir, I am too old to learn;
Call not your stocks for me. I serve the king,
On whose employment I was sent to you.
You shall do small respect, show too bold malice
Against the grace and person of my master,
Stocking his messenger.

Cornwall Fetch forth the stocks! — As I have
life and honour, there shall he sit till noon.

Regan *Till noon*! Till night, my lord; and all night too!

Kent Why, madam, if I were your father's dog,
You should not use me so.

Regan Sir, being his knave, I will.

Cornwall This is a fellow of the self-same colour
Our sister speaks of. — Come, bring away the stocks!

[*Stocks brought out.*]

Gloucester Let me beseech your grace not to do so;
His fault is much, and the good king his master

最近国王,他那位主子,只因
他自己一时的误解,动手打了我;
他便在旁帮同他,曲意去逢迎
他那阵恼怒,将我在背后绊倒;
我倒了,他就使足了男儿的气焰,
咒骂,凌辱,显得他是位好汉;
那样能对自行克制的人逞强,
他便博得了国王称赞他勇武;
他见这荒谬的行径初试得成功,
所以又复在这里拔剑挑衅。

铿　　德　若跟这些坏蛋懦夫们对比,
　　　　　夸口的蔼杰士只能当他们的傻子。

康　　华　拿出脚枷来!——你这倔强的老坏蛋,
　　　　　夸口的老贼,我们得教你——

铿　　德　　　　　　　　　　　　公爵,
　　　　　叫我学,我年纪太老了;别对我用脚枷。
　　　　　我侍候国王,是他差我来这里的;
　　　　　你枷了他派来的信使,对他太不敬,
　　　　　对我主人的尊严显得太毒辣。

康　　华　拿出脚枷来!我还有生命和荣誉在,
　　　　　他便得在那里枷坐到午上。

雷　　耿　　　　　　　　　　"到午上!"
　　　　　到晚上,我的夫君,还得整晚上!

铿　　德　啊呀,夫人,我若是您父亲的狗,

　　　　　　　　　　　　　　　　〔脚枷自幕后抬出。〕

　　　　　你也不该这么样待我。

雷　　耿　　　　　　　　　　大爷,
　　　　　你是他的奴才,我就要这么办。

康　　华　这就跟我们大姐说起的那人
　　　　　一般模样。——来,把脚枷抬过来!

葛洛斯忒　让我恳求爵爷不要这样做;
　　　　　他过错很大,好王上他主子自会

Will check him for't. your purpos'd low correction
Is such as basest and contemned'st wretches
For pilferings and most common trespasses
Are punish'd with; the king must take it ill,
That he, so slightly valu'd in his messenger,
Should have him thus restrain'd.

Cornwall   I'll answer that.

Regan   My sister may receive it much more worse,
To have her gentleman abus'd, assaulted,
For following her affairs. —Put in his legs.

                        [Kent *is put in the stocks.*]

Cornwall   Come, my good lord, away.

                [*Exeunt all but* Gloucester *and* Kent.]

Gloucester   I am sorry for thee, friend; 'tis the duke's
    pleasure,
Whose disposition, all the world well knows,
Will not be rubb'd nor stopp'd. I'll entreat for thee.

Kent   Pray do not, sir: I have watch'd, and travell'd
    hard;
Some time I shall sleep out, the rest I'll whistle.
A good man's fortune may grow out at heels;
Give you good morrow!

Gloucester   [*Aside.*]The duke's to blame in this; 'twill be
    ill taken.

                             [*Exit.*]

Kent   Good king, that must approve the common saw,
Thou out of heaven's benediction com'st
To the warm sun!
Approach, thou beacon to this under globe,
That by thy comfortable beams I may
Peruse this letter! Nothing almost sees miracles
But misery. I know 'tis from Cordelia,
Who hath most fortunately been inform'd
Of my obscured course; and shall find time
From this enormous state, seeking to give
Losses their remedies. All weary and o'erwatch'd,
Take vantage, heavy eyes, not to behold

　　　　　将他去责骂。您想用的这低微的惩处；
　　　　　只是对那班卑鄙下流的犯小偷
　　　　　和通常小罪的贱人们施行的刑罚；
　　　　　君王见了他这么样坐罪受禁，
　　　　　您把他遣来的信使轻看到如此，
　　　　　准会因而失欢。

康　　华　　　　　　　　　　我自有应付。

雷　　耿　大姐知道了她家臣为奉行使命，
　　　　　无端受侮辱与凶掀，更要失欢。——
　　　　　把他腿子装进去。　　　　　〔铿德枷上脚枷。〕

康　　华　来，伯爵，进去吧。　　　〔除葛洛斯忒与铿德外，
　　　　　　　　　　　　　　　　　人众尽下。

葛 洛 斯 忒　朋友，我替你很伤心，可是公爵
　　　　　要这样，他的性情，满天下都知道，
　　　　　不容人反对或阻挡。我替你去求情。

铿　　德　请不用，大人。我赶路没有睡，累得很；
　　　　　待我睡掉一些时候，其余的
　　　　　用口哨来消磨。一个好人的命运
　　　　　也会在上枷的脚上长得很好；
　　　　　祝福你早安！

葛 洛 斯 忒　〔旁白〕这要怪公爵，国王准会生气。　　　　〔下。

铿　　德　好君王，你定得经验到这句老话，
　　　　　舍弃了天赐的宏恩来晒暖太阳。
　　　　　到来啊，你这指迷下界的灯塔，
　　　　　凭你那慰人的光线我好拆看
　　　　　一封信！若非身处着悲惨，简直
　　　　　可说决无人能见到奇迹的来临。
　　　　　我知道这是考黛莲的信，多亏她　　　〔拆信〕
　　　　　得报了我低贱的生涯。〔读信〕——"将在这混乱
　　　　　非常的局势里寻找到时机——设法
　　　　　把损失弥补回来。"——又累又倦，
　　　　　我一双睡眼啊，借此正好不见

This shameful lodging.
Fortune, good night; smile once more; turn thy wheel!

[He sleeps.]

SCENE III. *The same.*

[Enter Edgar.*]*

Edgar   I heard myself proclaim'd;
And by the happy hollow of a tree
Escap'd the hunt. No port is free; no place,
That guard and most unusual vigilance
Does not attend my taking. While I may scape
I will preserve myself; and am bethought
To take the basest and most poorest shape
That ever penury in contempt of man
Brought near to beast; my face I'll grime with filth,
Blanket my loins, elf all my hair in knots,
And with presented nakedness outface
The winds and persecutions of the sky.
The country gives me proof and precedent
Of Bedlam beggars, who with roaring voices
Strike in their numb'd and mortified bare arms
Pins, wooden pricks, nails, sprigs of rosemary;
And with this horrible object, from low farms,
Poor pelting villages, sheep-cotes and mills,
Sometime with lunatic bans, sometime with prayers,
Enforce their charity. *Poor Turlygod! poor Tom!*
That's something yet; Edgar I nothing am.

[Exit.]

SCENE IV. *The same.*

[Enter Lear, Fool, *and* Gentleman.*]*

这张可耻的床。

再会了,命运;再笑笑;转动着轮子! 　　　　　〔睡去。

第　三　景

〔布景同前。〕

〔蔼特加上。

蔼　特　加　我听到缉捕我自己的告示;

幸喜有一棵空树施援才逃掉

这追拿。没有一个安全的口岸,

没有一处所在没有守卫

和异常的警备要把我擒拿。能逃时

总得保全着自己;我已经决心

装一副贫困糟蹋人,把他逼近了

畜道的那绝顶卑微和可怜的外观;

我要用泥污涂面,用毡毯裹腰,

使头发缠绕扭结,用自愿的裸露

去凌冒风威和天降的种种虐待。

这境内疯叫化汤姆的实证和先例

我见过不少,他们号叫着,把一些

铁针,木刺,钉子,迷迭香的小枝,

刺进他们那麻木无知的裸臂;

他们装扮着这般可怕的模样,

向隘陋的田庄,贫贱的村落,羊栏和

磨坊里,有时狂咒,有时祈求,

强化他们的布施。可怜的抖累古!

苦汤姆! 如今还有他,我蔼特加没有了。 　　〔下。

第　四　景

〔布景同前。〕

〔李尔、傻子及近侍上。

Lear 'Tis strange that they should so depart from home,
And not send back my messenger.

Gent   As I learn'd,
The night before there was no purpose in them
Of this remove.

Kent   Hail to thee, noble master!

Lear Ha!
Mak'st thou this shame thy pastime?

Kent   No, my lord.

Fool Ha, ha! he wears cruel garters. Horses are tied by
          the head, dogs and bears by the neck, monkeys by
          the loins, and men by the legs; when a man is over-
          lusty at legs, then he wears wooden nether-stocks.

Lear What's he that hath so much thy place mistook
To set thee here?

Kent   It is both he and she,
Your son and daughter.

Lear No.

Kent Yes.

Lear No, I say.

Kent I say, yea.

Lear No, no, they would not.

Kent Yes, they have.

Lear By Jupiter, I swear no!

Kent By Juno, I swear ay!

Lear   They durst not do't;
They would not, could not do't; 'tis worse than murder,
To do upon respect such violent outrage;
Resolve me, with all modest haste, which way
Thou mightst deserve, or they impose, this usage,
Coming from us.

Kent   My lord, when at their home
I did commend your highness' letters to them,
Ere I was risen from the place that show'd
My duty kneeling, came there a reeking post,

李	尔	奇怪,他们竟会这样出了门,
		不叫我差去的信使回来。
近	侍	据我
		听说,他们昨晚上还没有决意
		要离家外出。
铿	德	您来了,尊贵的主上!
李	尔	吓?
		你把这羞辱当好玩吗?
铿	德	不,大人。
傻	子	哈哈!他绑着一副无情的吊袜带。系马系住头,绑
		狗绑熊绑着脖子,猴儿要捆着腰,人得扎住了两条
		腿;一个人跑腿跑得太忙了,就得穿上一副木头做的
		长袜子。
李	尔	什么人把你这样地错认了高低,
		枷锁在这里?
铿	德	他们俩:您女儿和女婿。
李	尔	不是。
铿	德	是的。
李	尔	我说不是。
铿	德	我说是的。
李	尔	不是,不是,他们不会。
铿	德	是的,是他们干的。
李	尔	我对天皇巨璧德发誓,那不是!
铿	德	我对天后巨诺发誓,那是的!
李	尔	他们不敢这样做,他们不能,
		不会这样做;这简直比杀人还凶,
		故意施这样的狂暴;你要快些说,
		可又得从容让我知道个周详,
		我派你出来,你是怎么样才该受,
		他们才该罚你受,这样的遭际。
铿	德	大人,我正在他们府里边晋呈
		给他们您大人的书信,循礼在下跪,

Stew'd in his haste, half breathless, panting forth
From Goneril his mistress salutations;
Deliver'd letters, spite of intermission,
Which presently they read; on whose contents
They summon'd up their meiny, straight took horse;
Commanded me to follow and attend
The leisure of their answer; gave me cold looks.
And meeting here the other messenger,
Whose welcome I perceiv'd had poison'd mine, —
Being the very fellow which of late
Display'd so saucily against your highness, —
Having more man than wit about me, drew;
He rais'd the house with loud and coward cries.
Your son and daughter found this trespass worth
The shame which here it suffers.

Fool Winter's not gone yet, if the wild geese fly that way.

> Fathers that wear rags
>> Do make their children blind.
> But fathers that bear bags
>> Shall see their children kind.
> Fortune, that arrant whore,
>> Ne'er turns the key to th' poor. —

But for all this, thou shalt have as many dolours for thy
daughters as thou canst tell in a year.

Lear O, how this mother swells up toward my heart!
Hysterica passio, — down, thou climbing sorrow,
Thy element's below! — Where is this daughter?

Kent With the earl, sir, here within.

Lear Follow me not; Stay here.

[*Exit.*]

Gent Made you no more offence but what you speak of?

还不曾起身，突然来到了一名
在急忙里煎熬得汗气蒸腾的信使，
差些儿回不过气来，喘出他主妇
刚瑙烈对他们的问候；他不顾我在先，
他在后，把信递上，他们顿时
就看，这一看就匆匆召集了随从，
马上上马；他们吩咐我跟着，
等有空再给回音；还给我看白眼。
在这里我又碰见了那名信使，
都为欢迎他，我才遭他们的冷淡——
就是近来常在您大人跟前
胆大妄为的那东西——一时恼怒
上来，我就奋不顾利害的轻重，
拔剑向他挑衅；哪知他一叠连
懦怯的叫喊，惊动了这邸中上下。
您女儿女婿就派我这番过误
该当受这般羞辱。

傻　　　子　要是野鹅往那边飞，冬天还没有过咧。

衣衫破烂的父亲们
　　把女儿变成了瞎子。
背负钱袋的父亲们
　　享尽儿女们的孝思。
命运是个滥贱的娼家
　　从不跟穷酸眼笑眉花。——

可是，因此上你为女儿们所受的熬煎要同你数上一
年的洋钱那么多呢。

李　　　尔　啊，一阵子昏愦涌上心来！
"歇司替厉亚"，往下退；上升的悲痛啊，
下边是你的境界！——这女儿在哪里？

铿　　　德　跟伯爵在一起，大人，就在这里边。

李　　　尔　别跟我来；待在这儿。　　　　　　　〔下。

近　　　侍　除了你说的，你没有干过错事吗？

Kent None. —

How chance the king comes with so small a number?

Fool An thou hadst been set i' the stocks for that question, thou hadst well deserved it.

Kent Why, fool?

Fool We'll set thee to school to an ant, to teach thee there's no labouring in the winter. All that follow their noses are led by their eyes but blind men; and there's not a nose among twenty but can smell him that's stinking. Let go thy hold when a great wheel runs down a hill, lest it break thy neck with following it. but the great one that goes up the hill, let him draw thee after. When a wise man gives thee better counsel, give me mine again; I would have none but knaves follow it, since a fool gives it.

> That sir which serves and seeks for gain,
> > And follows but for form,
> Will pack when it begins to rain,
> > And leave thee in the storm.
> But I will tarry; the fool will stay,
> > And let the wise man fly;
> The knave turns fool that runs away;
> > The fool no knave, perdy.

Kent Where learn'd you this, fool?

Fool Not i' the stocks, fool!

> [*Re-enter* Lear, *with* Gloucester.]

Lear Deny to speak with me? They are sick? they are weary?

They have travell'd all the night? Mere fetches,

The images of revolt and flying off.

Fetch me a better answer.

Gloucester   My dear lord,

You know the fiery quality of the duke;

How unremovable and fix'd he is

In his own course.

铿	德	没有。——
		怎么国王的随从带来得这样少？
傻	子	要是你戴上脚枷因为问了那句话，那倒是活该你受
		的罪。
铿	德	为什么，傻子？
傻	子	我们要叫你去拜一只蚂蚁作老师，让它教你大冷天

别去工作。我们跟着鼻子走路的人，除非是瞎子，都
会用眼睛；可是就在二十个瞎子中间，也没有一个的
鼻子闻不出他那阵臭味儿来的。一个大轮子滚下山
来时你得撒手；不然，你若跟着它下来，准把你的脑
袋瓜儿打烂。可是一个大轮子滚上山去时，你尽管
让它拉着你走。有聪明人给你出得更聪明的主意
时，把咱们这主意还给咱们；这是个傻子出的主意，
除了坏蛋，咱们不劝旁人去听信。

> 眼巴巴只为好处的先生，
>> 他当差不过是装模作样，
> 老天一下雨他就得飞奔，
>> 留你在风雨中间去乘凉。
> 让聪明人拔出腿子跑吧，
>> 但我要待着，傻子可不走；
> 傻瓜一走掉便是个坏蛋；
>> 傻子可不是坏蛋，我赌咒。

| 铿 | 德 | 这是你从哪儿学来的，傻子？ |
| 傻 | 子 | 不是戴着脚枷学来的，傻瓜！ |

[李尔重上，葛洛斯忒同来。

李	尔	不跟我说话？他们不舒服？累了？
		昨晚上赶了整夜的路？只是些推托，
		一片抗上叛乱的形景。给我去
		要个好些的回音来。
葛 洛 斯 忒		亲爱的王上，
		你知道公爵的性情何等暴躁，
		他定下了主见，怎样也不能动摇。

Lear Vengeance! plague! death! confusion!

Fiery? What *quality*? why, Gloucester, Gloucester,

I'd speak with the Duke of Cornwall and his wife.

Gloucester Well, my good lord, I have inform'd them so.

Lear *In form'd them*? Dost thou understand me, man?

Gloucester Ay, my good lord.

Lear The King would speak with Cornwall. the dear father

Would with his daughter speak, commands her service.

Are they *inform'd* of this? My breath and blood!

Fiery? *the fiery duke*? Tell the hot duke that—

No, but not yet; may be he is not well;

Infirmity doth still neglect all office

Whereto our health is bound; we are not ourselves

When nature, being oppress'd, commands the mind

To suffer with the body. I'll forbear;

And am fallen out with my more headier will,

To take the indispos'd and sickly fit

For the sound man. —Death on my state! Wherefore

[Looking on Kent.]

Should he sit here? This act persuades me

That this remotion of the duke and her

Is practice only. Give me my servant forth.

Go tell the duke and's wife I'd speak with them,

Now, presently; bid them come forth and hear me,

Or at their chamber door I'll beat the drum

Till it cry Sleep to death.

Gloucester I would have all well betwixt you.

[Exit.]

Lear O me, my heart, my rising heart! but down!

Fool Cry to it, nuncle, as the cockney did to the eels
      when she put em i the paste alive; she knapped em o
      the coxcombs with a stick and cried *Down, wantons,*

李　　　尔		灾殃！疫疠！死！摧残倒坏！
		"暴躁"？你说是什么"性情"？喂，
		葛洛斯忒，葛洛斯忒，我要跟
		康华公爵和他的妻子说话。
葛 洛 斯 忒		是，王上，我已经通报过他们了。
李　　　尔		"通报过"他们？你懂得我没有，你？
葛 洛 斯 忒		哎，不错的，我的好王上。
李　　　尔		国王要跟公爵康华说话。
		亲爱的父亲要跟他女儿说话，
		着她来侍候。把这个"通报过"他们吗？
		我这条老命！"暴躁！""暴躁的公爵？"
		你去告诉那冒火的公爵，说是——
		不，还不要，也许他当真不很好；
		病痛常使我们忽略健康时
		一应的名份；有时躯壳上的安宁，
		受到了病痛的压迫，使精神也陪同
		形骸受苦，就不由我们去自主。
		我要耐着心；如今自己太使性，
		便把抱病人当作无病人去准绳。——
		〔望着铿德〕不如死！为什么他要枷坐在此？
		这件事使我信他们故意不露脸
		只是个奸计。放下我的仆人来！
		去告诉公爵和他的妻子，说我要
		跟他们说话，就在此刻，马上；
		叫他们出来听话，不然我要在
		他们卧室门前一声声地捶鼓，
		捶破他们的梦魂。
葛 洛 斯 忒		我但愿你们大家和气。　　　　　　〔下。
李　　　尔		天啊，我的心，向上升的心！下去！
傻　　　子		喝它下去，老伯伯，好比厨娘把活跳的鳗鱼放进热面
		糊里去时一样；她手里拿着棍儿，向它们呆脑袋上几
		下一敲，喝道"下去，贱东西，下去！"那厨娘的兄弟却

        down! 'Twas her brother that, in pure kindness to his
        horse, buttered his hay.

[*Re-enter* Gloucester, *with* Cornwall, Regan, *and Servants*.]

Lear   Good-morrow to you both.

Cornwall   Hail to your grace!

                        [Kent *is set at liberty*.]

Regan   I am glad to see your highness.

Lear   Regan, I think you are; I know what reason
I have to think so; if thou shouldst not be glad,
I would divorce me from thy mother's tomb,
Sepulchring an adultress. —[*To* Kent] O, are you free?
Some other time for that. —Beloved Regan,
Thy sister's naught. O Regan, she hath tied
Sharp—tooth'd unkindness, like a vulture, here, —

                      [*Points to his heart*.]

I can scarce speak to thee; thou'lt not believe
With how deprav'd a quality—O Regan!

Regan   I pray you, sir, take patience. I have hope
You less know how to value her desert
Than she to scant her duty.

Lear   Say, how is that?

Regan   I cannot think my sister in the least
Would fail her obligation. if, sir, perchance
She have restrain'd the riots of your followers,
'Tis on such ground, and to such wholesome end
As clears her from all blame

Lear   My curses on her!

Regan   O, sir, you are old;
Nature in you stands on the very verge
Of her confine. you should be rul'd and led
By some discretion, that discerns your state

　　　　对他的马非凡爱惜,草料上都涂上奶油。

　　　　　　　　　〔葛洛斯忒重上,康华、雷耿及仆从同来。

李　　尔　愿你们两个早安。

康　　华　　　　　　　　祝福您老人家!　　　〔铿德被释。〕

雷　　耿　看见父王,我很高兴。

李　　尔　雷耿,我想你不致不高兴见我;
　　　　我知道什么缘由我得这么想;
　　　　若是你不高兴,我要跟你那位
　　　　地下的母亲离婚,让她在墓中
　　　　还担个通奸的罪名。——啊,放了你吗?

　　　　　　　　　　　　　　　　〔对铿德〕

　　　　那件事以后再说。——心爱的雷耿,
　　　　你大姐真是个坏货。喔,雷耿,
　　　　她把她尖牙的狠毒,像一只兀鹰,　　　〔指心〕
　　　　钉住在这儿! 我几乎不能向你说;
　　　　你不能相信她用多卑劣的行径——
　　　　喔,雷耿。

雷　　耿　　　　　　　　父王,我劝你要镇静。
　　　　我怕并非她疏忽了为儿的本份,
　　　　却是你不能赏识她品性的优良。

李　　尔　哦,怎么说?

雷　　耿　　　　　　　我不信在本份上大姐
　　　　会有一点儿的差池。可是,父王,
　　　　假如她约束了你那班随从的暴乱,
　　　　那无非是为了种种的原因,为了
　　　　归根结局的安全,在她却并无
　　　　丝毫的不是。

李　　尔　我咒她!

雷　　耿　　　　　　　啊,父王,你已经老了;
　　　　你所有的生机命脉已到了尽头
　　　　边上。你得让慎重明达的旁人
　　　　约束指引你,旁人看你要比

Better than you yourself. Therefore, I pray you
That to our sister you do make return;
Say you have wrong'd her, sir.

Lear   Ask her forgiveness?
Do you but mark how this becomes the house:
Dear daughter, I confess that I am old;

[Kneeling.]

Age is unnecessary. on my knees I beg
That you'll vouchsafe me raiment, bed, and food.

Regan   Good sir, no more; These are unsightly tricks.
Return you to my sister.

Lear   [*Rising.*]   Never, Regan,
She hath abated me of half my train;
Look'd black upon me; struck me with her tongue,
Most serpent-like, upon the very heart.
All the stor'd vengeances of heaven fall
On her ingrateful top! Strike her young bones,
You taking airs, with lameness!

Cornwall   Fie, sir, fie!

Lear   You nimble lightnings, dart your blinding flames
Into her scornful eyes! Infect her beauty,
You fen-suck'd fogs, drawn by the powerful sun,
To fall and blast her pride!

Regan   O the blest gods!
So will you wish on me when the rash mood is on.

Lear   No, Regan, thou shalt never have my curse;
Thy tender-hefted nature shall not give
Thee o'er to harshness. her eyes are fierce; but thine
Do comfort, and not burn. 'Tis not in thee
To grudge my pleasures, to cut off my train,
To bandy hasty words, to scant my sizes,
And, in conclusion, to oppose the bolt
Against my coming in; thou better know'st

你自己清楚得多。因此我劝你
还是回到大姐那边去;说一声
你委屈了她,父王。

李　　尔　　　　　　　　向她请罪?　　　　　　　　　　　　〔下跪〕
你看这样于尊卑的伦次如何:
"亲爱的女儿,我承认我已经年老;
老年乃是个累赘。我特为跪下,
求你恩赏给我衣食和居处。"

雷　　耿　父王,别再那样了;多难看的把戏。
回大姐那里去吧。

李　　尔　　　　　　　　雷耿,我决不。　　　　　　　　　　　〔起立〕
她裁了我半数的侍卫;用白眼对我;
毒蛇般用她的长舌戳痛我这心。
上天千年万年来郁积的天谴
一起倾泻在她那颗忘恩的头上!
凶邪的大气,使她腹中的胎儿
四肢残废!

康　　华　　　　　　　算了,父王,别瞎说!

李　　尔　急电的乱刀,把你们疾闪的锋芒
插进她那双睥睨不认人的眼睛!
洼湿间蛰伏的浓雾,被太阳的光威
吸引出来的毒雾啊,快去损坏
她年轻的美貌,摧毁她倔强的骄傲!

雷　　耿　啊,神圣的天神们! 你暴性一发,
也会同样地咒我。

李　　尔　不会,雷耿,你决不会被我诅咒;
你温柔的本性不会变成悍暴。
她眼中放射着凶焰,但你的目光
和煦温人而不加灼痛。你不会
对我的所好嫉忌,裁我的随从,
向我申申地诟骂,削我的支应,
总之,闭关下闩地摈我在门外;

The offices of nature, bond of childhood,
Effects of courtesy, dues of gratitude;
Thy half o' the kingdom hast thou not forgot,
Wherein I thee endow'd.

Regan   Good sir, to the purpose.

Lear Who put my man i' the stocks?

                              [*Tucket within.*]

Cornwall   What trumpet's that?

Regan I know't — my sister's. this approves her letter,
That she would soon be here.

                    [*Enter* Oswald.]

                         Is your lady come?

Lear This is a slave, whose easy-borrowed pride
Dwells in the fickle grace of her he follows. —
Out, varlet, from my sight!

Cornwall   What means your grace?

Lear Who stock'd my servant? Regan, I have good hope
Thou didst not know on't. — Who comes here? O heavens!

                    [*Enter* Goneril.]

If you do love old men, if your sweet sway
Allow obedience, if yourselves are old,
Make it your cause; send down, and take my part! —
[*To* Goneril.] Art not asham'd to look upon this beard? —
O Regan, wilt thou take her by the hand?

Goneril Why not by the hand, sir? How have I offended?
All's not offence that indiscretion finds
And dotage terms so.

Lear   O sides, you are too tough;
Will you yet hold? — How came my man i' the stocks?

你多懂些亲子间的义理，儿女的本责，
和蔼的言行，和领受了深恩的铭感；
我给你的那半份江山你不曾忘掉。

雷　耿	父王，有事快说。
李　尔	谁枷我这信使的？

　　　　　　　　　　　　　　[幕后号声作进行曲。]

康　华	那是什么号报？
雷　耿	我知道，——大姐的。

这正合她来信说就到。——[奥士伐上。]你主妇
　　来了？

李　尔　这气焰好来得容易的奴才，全仗他
那恩宠无常的主妇替他撑腰。——
滚开，臭蛋，不要到我眼前来！

康　华　父王你什么意思？

李　尔　　　　　　　谁把我仆人
上的枷？——雷耿，我但愿你不曾知道。——
谁来了？

　　　　　　[刚瑙烈上。
　　　　啊，天神们，如果你们
还爱惜老年人，如果你们那统治
寰宇的仁善还容许敬顺耄耋，
如果你们自己也已经老了，
就得替我来主持；快派遣神使
下来帮我！——[对刚瑙烈]你对着这胡须不
　　羞吗？
喔，雷耿，你会牵着她的手？

刚　瑙　烈　为什么不牵手？我怎样做错了事？
被莽撞乱认作过错，老来的懵懂
强派的，并非真正是过错。

李　尔　　　　　　　　　啊，
肚子，你太韧，太结实了；你还受得住？——
我仆人怎么上了枷？

Cornwall I set him there, sir; but his own disorders
Deserv'd much less advancement.

Lear   You? did you?

Regan I pray you, father, being weak, seem so.
If, till the expiration of your month,
You will return and sojourn with my sister,
Dismissing half your train, come then to me;
I am now from home, and out of that provision
Which shall be needful for your entertainment.

Lear Return to her, and fifty men dismiss'd?
No, rather I abjure all roofs, and choose
To wage against the enmity o' the air.
To be a comrade with the wolf, and howl
Necessity's sharp pinch! Return with her?
Why, the hot-blooded France, that dowerless took
Our youngest born, I could as well be brought
To knee his throne, and, squire—like, pension beg
To keep base life afoot. Return with her?
Persuade me rather to be slave and sumpter
To this detested groom.

                              [*Pointing to* Oswald.]

Goneril   At your choice, sir.

Lear I pr'ythee, daughter, do not make me mad.
I will not trouble thee, my child; farewell.
We'll no more meet, no more see one another.
But yet thou art my flesh, my blood, my daughter;
Or rather a disease that's in my flesh,
Which I must needs call mine; thou art a boil,
A plague sore, an embossed carbuncle,
In my corrupted blood. But I'll not chide thee;
Let shame come when it will, I do not call it;
I do not bid the thunder-bearer shoot,
Nor tell tales of thee to high-judging Jove.

康　华　　　　　　　　　　是我叫上的；
　　　　　　可是他自己的胡作非为该受
　　　　　　更重的惩创。

李　尔　　　　　　　　你！原来是你？

雷　耿　　我劝你，父亲，衰老了，就莫再逞强。
　　　　　　你且回去，裁掉你侍从的半数，
　　　　　　寄寓在大姐那边，等一月期满，
　　　　　　然后再来找我；我现在离了家，
　　　　　　又没有那相当的存聚作你的供应。

李　尔　　回到她那里？裁掉了五十名侍从？
　　　　　　不，我宁愿弃绝了屋椽的掩蔽，
　　　　　　在野外跟敌意的风寒激战，我宁愿
　　　　　　作豺狼的伴侣，为饥寒所痛捩而悲嗥！
　　　　　　跟她回去？吓，那热情的法兰西，
　　　　　　他未得妆奁，娶了我们的幼女，
　　　　　　我不如跪在他座前，像侍仆一般，
　　　　　　求赐些年金，养活这低微的老命。
　　　　　　跟她回去？不如劝我当这个
　　　　　　可鄙的奴才的第二重奴仆。　　　　　　　［指奥士伐。

刚瑙烈　　　　　　　　　　随你便。

李　尔　　女儿，我求你不要逼我发狂。
　　　　　　我不再给你麻烦，孩子；别了。
　　　　　　我们从此后决不会再相见面。
　　　　　　可是你还是我亲生的女儿骨肉；
　　　　　　不如说你是我肉里的一堆病毒，
　　　　　　我怎样也得要自认；你是我毒血
　　　　　　凝成的一个疔疮，一个痈疡，
　　　　　　一个隆肿的脓痈。我不再骂你了；
　　　　　　要有羞辱来时让它自己来，
　　　　　　我并不呼它来作你的责罚；我不向
　　　　　　居高行审的雅荷说你的坏话，
　　　　　　不求司霹雳的帝神施放巨雷。

Mend when thou canst; be better at thy leisure.
I can be patient; I can stay with Regan,
I and my hundred knights.

Regan   Not altogether so;
I look'd not for you yet, nor am provided
For your fit welcome. Give ear, sir, to my sister;
For those that mingle reason with your passion
Must be content to think you old, and so—
But she knows what she does.

Lear   Is this well spoken?

Regan   I dare avouch it, sir; what, fifty followers?
Is it not well? What should you need of more?
Yea, or so many, sith that both charge and danger
Speak 'gainst so great a number? How in one house
Should many people under two commands
Hold amity? 'Tis hard; almost impossible.

Goneril   Why might not you, my lord, receive attendance
From those that she calls servants, or from mine?

Regan   Why not, my lord? If then they chanc'd to slack
   you,
We could control them. If you will come to me,
For now I spy a danger, I entreat you
To bring but five-and-twenty; to no more
Will I give place or notice.

Lear   I gave you all, —

Regan   And in good time you gave it.

Lear   —Made you my guardians, my depositaries;
But kept a reservation to be follow'd
With such a number. What, must I come to you
With five-and-twenty? Regan, said you so?

Regan   And speak't again my lord; no more with me.

　　　　　　　　　你能改就改；听凭你慢慢去从善。
　　　　　　　　　我能静待着；我能带领了武士
　　　　　　　　　百名，和雷耿同住。

雷　　耿　　　　　　　　　　　不准是那样吧；
　　　　　　　　　我还不期待你来，也不曾预备得
　　　　　　　　　任何供应，能对你作相宜的迎迓。
　　　　　　　　　你得听大姐的话；理解你这番
　　　　　　　　　暴怒的人们不能不以为你老了，
　　　　　　　　　因此——可是她自有她做事的分寸。

李　　尔　　你说实话吗？

雷　　耿　　　　　　　　　我敢担保没有错。
　　　　　　　　　什么，五十名侍从？还嫌不够？
　　　　　　　　　为什么你还多要？嗳，为什么
　　　　　　　　　你要那么多，既然危险和虚靡
　　　　　　　　　都不容这么多的人数？一家有二主，
　　　　　　　　　那么许多人怎么能相安无事？
　　　　　　　　　那太难；简直不能。

刚　瑙　烈　　　　　　　　　为什么你不能
　　　　　　　　　让二妹或是我手下的仆从们侍奉？

雷　　耿　　为什么不那样，父亲？那时候他们
　　　　　　　　　若对你有疏慢，我们便能控制。
　　　　　　　　　要是你来我这里，我如今发现了
　　　　　　　　　一个危险，我请你只带廿五名；
　　　　　　　　　多来了不承认，也不给他们住处。

李　　尔　　我一切都给了你们——

雷　　耿　　　　　　　　　你给得正及时。

李　　尔　　——叫你们作我国土的护持人，信托人；
　　　　　　　　　但是还保留着那么多名的随侍。
　　　　　　　　　什么，只能有廿五名来你这里？
　　　　　　　　　雷耿，你可是这样说？

雷　　耿　　　　　　　　　我再说一遍；
　　　　　　　　　我不容你多带。

Lear Those wicked creatures yet do look well-favour'd,
When others are more wicked; not being the worst
Stands in some rank of praise. —
           [*To* Goneril.] I'll go with thee.
Thy fifty yet doth double five-and-twenty,
And thou art twice her love.

Goneril   Hear, me, my lord:
What need you five-and-twenty, ten, or five,
To follow in a house where twice so many
Have a command to tend you?

Regan   What need one?

Lear O, reason not the need: our basest beggars
Are in the poorest thing superfluous.
Allow not nature more than nature needs,
Man's life is cheap as beast's. thou art a lady;
If only to go warm were gorgeous,
Why, nature needs not what thou gorgeous wear'st,
Which scarcely keeps thee warm. But, for true need, —
You heavens, give me that patience, patience I need!
You see me here, you gods, a poor old man,
As full of grief as age; wretched in both.
If it be you that stirs these daughters' hearts
Against their father, fool me not so much
To bear it tamely; touch me with noble anger,
And let not women's weapons, water-drops,
Stain my man's cheeks! — No, you unnatural hags,
I will have such revenges on you both
That all the world shall, — I will do such things, —

李　　尔　　　　　　　　　　　这些恶虫显得
姿容还端好，却还有更恶的东西在；
不恶到尽头还有些微的可取。——
〔对刚瑙烈〕我跟你回去。五十比廿五加倍，
你比她有两倍的爱。

刚　瑙　烈　　　　　　　　　　　听我说，父亲：
为什么你要廿五，十名，乃至
五名，我们有的是两倍多的随从，
奉了命供你去差遣？

雷　　耿　　　　　　　　　　就是一名
也有何需要？

李　　尔　　　　　　　　唉，不要讲需要；
最贱的东西，对于最穷的乞丐，
也多少带几分富裕。若不容生命
越过它最低的需要，人命只抵得
蚁命一般地贱。你是个贵妇人；
假如穿暖了衣裳已算是华贵，
你的命就不需这样华贵的衣裳，
因为这不能给你多少暖意。
至于那真正的需要，——啊，天哪，
给我那镇定，镇定是我的需要！
你们见我在这里，诸位天神们，
一个可怜的老人，悲痛和风霜
岁月一般深，都是莫奈何地惨怛。
倘使是你们鼓动了这两个女儿
跟她们父亲作对，别把我愚弄得
吞声忍受；用威严的盛怒点燃我，
别让女人的武器，那一双泪眼，
沾湿这大丈夫的脸！——不，不会，
你们这两个灭绝人性的母夜叉，
我要向你们那么样报仇，会叫
全世界都要——我准得做那样的事，——

What they are yet, I know not; but they shall be
The terrors of the earth. You think I'll weep;
No, I'll not weep.   *[Storm and tempest.]*
I have full cause of weeping; but this heart
Shall break into a hundred thousand flaws,
Or ere I'll weep. — O fool, I shall go mad!
      [Exeunt Lear, Gloucester, Kent, *and* Fool.
      Storm heard at a distance.]

Cornwall   Let us withdraw; 'twill be a storm.

Regan   This house is little; the old man and his people
Cannot be well bestow'd.

Goneril   'Tis his own blame; hath put himself from rest,
And must needs taste his folly.

Regan   For his particular, I'll receive him gladly,
But not one follower.

Goneril   So am I purpos'd. —
Where is my lord of Gloucester?

Cornwall   Followed the old man forth; he is return'd.
      [Re-enter Gloucester.]

Gloucester   The king is in high rage.

Cornwall   Whither is he going?

Gloucester   He calls to horse; but will I know not whither.

Cornwall   'Tis best to give him way; he leads himself.

Goneril   My lord, entreat him by no means to stay.

Gloucester   Alack! the night comes on, and the high winds
Do sorely ruffle; for many miles about
There's scarce a bush.

Regan   O, sir, to wilful men
The injuries that they themselves procure
Must be their schoolmasters. Shut up your doors.
He is attended with a desperate train;
And what they may incense him to, being apt
To have his ear abus'd, wisdom bids fear.

什么事还没有知道；可是全世界
都要骇怕得发抖。你们想我要哭了；
不，我不哭。　　　　　　　　　　　［疾风暴雨至。］
我很该哭了；可是要等这颗心——
裂成了十万粒星星，我方始会哭。——
啊，傻子，我要发疯了！
　　　　　　　　　　［李尔、葛洛斯忒、铿德与傻子同下。

康　　华	让我们退去吧；大风暴来了。
雷　　耿	这屋子太小；容不下那个老人 和他的人马来宿歇。
刚　瑙　烈	只怪他自己；他自己不要安顿， 就得去吃他自己荒唐的亏。
雷　　耿	光是他本人我倒很愿意接待， 但不能有一个随从。
刚　瑙　烈	我也这样想。—— 葛洛斯忒伯爵到哪里去了？
康　　华	跟着那老人出去的；他回来了。 　　　　　　［葛洛斯忒重上。
葛洛斯忒	国王在那里大怒。
康　　华	他往哪里去？
葛洛斯忒	他叫着要上马，哪里去我可不知道。
康　　华	还是让他去他的；他自己做主。
刚　瑙　烈	伯爵，你可别把他在这里留下。
葛洛斯忒	哎呀！夜晚上来了，暴风刮得紧； 附近好多哩路程没有一丝儿 半点的树影。
雷　　耿	喔，伯爵，那些 刚愎自用的人自招来的苦楚， 正该作他们的教训。把门关上。 他带着一群强梁无赖的随从； 他们惯会哄骗他，如今不知要 耸动他干什么，你还得担心提防。

Cornwall   Shut up your doors, my lord; 'tis a wild night;
My Regan counsels well. come out o' the storm.

[Exeunt.]

康　　　华　关上门，伯爵，这夜晚来得险恶；
　　　　　　我们的雷耿说得对。躲开这风暴。　　　　　　〔同下。

ACT III.

SCENE I. *A Heath*.

[*A storm with thunder and lightning.*
Enter Kent *and a* Gentleman, *severally.*]

Kent   Who's there, besides foul weather?

Gent   One minded like the weather, most unquietly.

Kent   I know you. Where's the king?

Gent   Contending with the fretful elements;
Bids the wind blow the earth into the sea,
Or swell the curled waters 'bove the main,
That things might change or cease; tears his white hair,
Which the impetuous blasts, with eyeless rage,
Catch in their fury and make nothing of;
Strives in his little world of man to outscorn
The to-and-fro-conflicting wind and rain.
This night, wherein the cub-drawn bear would couch,
The lion and the belly-pinched wolf
Keep their fur dry, unbonneted he runs,
And bids what will take all.

Kent   But who is with him?

Gent   None but the fool, who labours to out-jest

第 三 幕

第 一 景

［一片荒原。］

［风狂雨骤，雷电交作。铿德与一近侍各自上。

铿　德	除了这坏天气，还有那个是谁。
近　侍	一个心里跟天气一般不安静的人。
铿　德	我认识你的。国王在哪里？
近　侍	在跟恼怒的暴雨疾风们厮吵；
	他在叫大风把陆地吹进海洋，
	或把卷峰的海浪涨到岸上来，
	好叫世间的一切都变过或完结；
	他撕着白发，那盲怒的狂飙便顺势
	一把把地揪住，视同无物一般；
	他在他渺小的生命世界里挣扎，
	想赛过往来鏖战的风雨们的淫威，
	这夜晚，便是干了奶的母熊也伏着
	不敢去寻食，狮子和腹痛的饿狼
	都保着毛干，他却光着头呼号
	奔走地要叫一切都同归于尽。
铿　德	可是有谁跟着他？
近　侍	只有那傻子，
	从旁极力地开着玩笑，想辟开

His heart-struck injuries.

Kent   Sir, I do know you;
And dare, upon the warrant of my note,
Commend a dear thing to you. There is division,
Although as yet the face of it be cover'd
With mutual cunning, 'twixt Albany and Cornwall;
Who have, — as who have not, that their great stars
Throne and set high? — servants, who seem no less,
Which are to France the spies and speculations
Intelligent of our state. what hath been seen,
Either in snuffs and packings of the dukes,
Or the hard rein which both of them have borne
Against the old kind king; or something deeper,
Whereof, perchance, these are but furnishings;
But, true it is, from France there comes a power
Into this scatter'd kingdom; who already,
Wise in our negligence, have secret feet
In some of our best ports, and are at point
To show their open banner. Now to you;
If on my credit you dare build so far
To make your speed to Dover, you shall find
Some that will thank you, making just report
Of how unnatural and bemadding sorrow
The king hath cause to plain.
I am a gentleman of blood and breeding,
And from some knowledge and assurance offer
This office to you.

Gent   I will talk further with you.

Kent   No, do not.
For confirmation that I am much more
Than my out wall, open this purse, and take
What it contains. If you shall see Cordelia, —
As fear not but you shall, — show her this ring,

他痛心的患难。

铿　　　德　　　　　　　　　　阁下，我的确认识你；
敢凭我的观察寄托你一件要事。
亚尔白尼和康华之间，双方
虽在表面上互相用奸计遮掩，
我知道已起了分裂；他们有些个——
权星高照的，那一个没有？——属僚们，
外形像属僚，暗中却为法兰西
当间谍和探报，私传着我邦的内情。
看得见的，比如二位公爵间的忿恨
和彼此的暗算，或者两人都对
年高恩重的国王严酷无情，
再不然就有更深的隐事，以上
那种种许只是遮盖这隐事的虚饰；
可是法兰西确已有一军人马
混进了这分崩的王国；他们觑准了
我们的漫不经心，已在几处
我们最优良的港口偷偷登了岸，
准备露他们的旗纛。现在跟你说；
你若敢信赖我，就赶快去多浮，那边
自会有人谢你，你只须据真情
去报告，何等没情理与逼疯人的悲痛
是国王怨愤的原由。
我是个出身贵胄名门的上流人，
为的是知道得清楚可靠，才把
这重任交与你阁下。

近　　　侍　　　　我还得跟你谈谈。

铿　　　德　　　　不，不要。
你想证实我绝对不仅是这片
外表，只把这钱袋解开，拿着
这里边的东西。你若面见到考黛莲，——
放心你准会，——给她看这一只戒指，

And she will tell you who your fellow is
That yet you do not know. Fie on this storm!
I will go seek the king.

Gent Give me your hand; have you no more to say?

Kent Few words, but, to effect, more than all yet;
That when we have found the king, — in which your pain
That way, I'll this, — he that first lights on him
Holla the other.

[*Exeunt severally.*]

SCENE II. *Another part of the heath.*
Storm continues.

[*Enter* Lear *and* Fool.]

Lear Blow, winds, and crack your cheeks! rage! blow!
You cataracts and hurricanoes, spout
Till you have drench'd our steeples, drown'd the cocks!
You sulphurous and thought-executing fires,
Vaunt couriers to oak-cleaving thunderbolts,
Singe my white head! And thou, all-shaking thunder,
Strike flat the thick rotundity o' the world!
Crack nature's moulds, all germens spill at once
That make ingrateful man!

Fool O nuncle, court holy water in a dry house is better
than this rain water out o' door. Good nuncle, in; and
ask thy daughters blessing; here's a night pities nether wise men nor fools.

Lear Rumble thy bellyful! Spit, fire! spout, rain!
Nor rain, wind, thunder, fire are my daughters.
I tax not you, you elements, with unkindness;
I never gave you kingdom, call'd you children,

她就会告你,你现在不认识的同伴
是谁。这风暴真可恶! 我要寻国王去。

近　侍　我们来握手再会;你还有话说吗?

铿　德　只一句,可是,论轻重,比什么都重要;
　　　　若是我们找到了国王,——寻他去你往
　　　　那边走,我向这边,——谁先见到他
　　　　就招呼那一个。　　　　　　　　　[各自下。

第　二　景

[荒原的另一部分。风雨猖狂如故。]
[李尔与傻子上。

李　尔　刮啊,大风,刮出你们的狂怒来!
　　　　把你们的头颅面目刮成个稀烂!
　　　　奔湍的大瀑和疾扫的飞蛟,倒出
　　　　你们那狂暴,打透一处处的塔尖,
　　　　淹尽那所有屋脊上的报风信号!
　　　　硫磺触鼻,闪眼杀死人的天火,
　　　　替劈树的弘雷报警飞金的急电,
　　　　快来快来,来烧焦这一头白发!
　　　　还有你,你这个震骇万物的雷霆,
　　　　锤你的,锤扁这冥顽的浑圆的世界!
　　　　捣破造化的模型,把传续这寡义
　　　　负恩的人类的种子顿时捣散!

傻　子　唉,老伯伯,在屋子里说好话要比在这外边淋雨好得
　　　　多呢。好伯伯,里边去;对你的女儿们求一声情;这
　　　　样的夜晚是不可怜聪明人也不可怜傻瓜的。

李　尔　吼畅你满腹的淫威! 大雨同闪电,
　　　　倒你们的怒涛,烧你们的天火出来!
　　　　你们风雨雷电不是我的女儿,
　　　　我不怪你们怎样地给我白眼;
　　　　我从未给过你们疆土,叫你们

You owe me no subscription; then let fall
Your horrible pleasure; here I stand, your slave,
A poor, infirm, weak, and despis'd old man
But yet I call you servile ministers,
That will with two pernicious daughters join
Your high-engender'd battles 'gainst a head
So old and white as this! O! O! 'tis foul!

Fool He that has a house to put 's head in has a good
head-piece.

> The *codpiece* that will house
> Before the head has any,
> The head and he shall louse;
> So beggars marry many.
> The man that makes his toe
> What he his heart should make
> Shall of a corn cry woe,
> And turn his sleep to wake.

— for there was never yet fair woman but she made
mouths in a glass.

Lear No, I will be the pattern of all patience; I will say
nothing.

[Enter Kent.]

Kent Who's there?

Fool Marry, here's grace and a *codpiece*; that's a wise
man and a fool.

Kent Alas, sir, are you here? Things that love night
Love not such nights as these; the wrathful skies
Gallow the very wanderers of the dark,
And make them keep their caves; since I was man,
Such sheets of fire, such bursts of horrid thunder,

作孩儿，你们不该我顺从和爱敬；
尽管倾倒出你们那骇人的兴采；
我站在这里，你们的奴隶，一个
又可怜，又衰颓，又残弱，给人糟蹋
透了的老人。可是我说，你们啊，
你们是一群下贱卑鄙的鹰狗，
勾连了两个狠毒的女儿，凭高
来痛打一个这般老这般白的头。
唉唉！恶毒啊！

傻　　子　谁头上有屋子遮着头的就有个好遮头。

脑袋还不曾有屋子时，
　"遮阳"若先有了地方住，
它们俩便都会生虮子，
　花子们就这么娶媳妇。
谁要是乱糟蹋脚趾头，
　好比他乱糟蹋他的心，
那痛鸡眼就够他去受，
　好睡里要呜呜地哭醒。

因为从来的美妇人总是要对着镜子做鬼脸的。

李　　尔　不，我要做绝对镇静的典型，
不说一句话。

　　　　　　　　〔铿德上。

铿　　德　谁在那里？

傻　　子　妈妈的，王上和一块"遮阳"在此，咱们俩一个是聪明
人，一个是傻瓜。

铿　　德　啊呀，大人，你在这里吗？夜晚
到了这样，就是爱夜晚的生物
也不再爱它；就是那些素常
夜游的走兽，也被这暴怒的天空
吓住，一起在巢穴之中藏身；
记得我成年以来，就不曾有过
这样大片的电火，这样爆炸得

Such groans of roaring wind and rain I never
Remember to have heard. man's nature cannot carry
Th' affliction nor the fear.

Lear   Let the great gods,
That keep this dreadful pother o'er our heads,
Find out their enemies now. Tremble, thou wretch,
That hast within thee undivulged crimes,
Unwhipp'd of justice. hide thee, thou bloody hand;
Thou perjur'd, and thou simular man of virtue
That art incestuous. caitiff, to pieces shake,
That under covert and convenient seeming
Hast practis'd on man's life. close pent-up guilts,
Rive your concealing continents and cry
These dreadful summoners grace. I am a man
More sinn'd against than sinning.

Kent   Alack, bareheaded!
Gracious my lord, hard by here is a hovel;
Some friendship will it lend you 'gainst the tempest;
Repose you there, whilst I to this hard house, —
More harder than the stones whereof 'tis rais'd;
Which even but now, demanding after you,
Denied me to come in, — return, and force
Their scanted courtesy.

Lear   My wits begin to turn. —
Come on, my boy. how dost, my boy? art cold?
I am cold myself. — Where is this straw, my fellow?
The art of our necessities is strange,
That can make vile things precious. Come, your hovel. —
Poor fool and knave, I have one part in my heart
That's sorry yet for thee.

Fool [*Singing.*]

> *He that has and a little tiny wit* —
> *With hey, ho, the wind and the rain,* —

怕人的响雷，这样咆哮的风号
和雨啸。人的天性受不了这许多
苦难或惊慌。

李　　尔　　　　　　　让上面那片翻江
倒海的老天找出他要找的仇雠。
罪恶不曾露，刑罚未临头的罪犯，
快快去打颤。杀人的凶手，藏起来；
还有破誓的罪人，乱伦的伪善者。
外表堂皇冠冕，私下却谋害过
人命的奸徒，快去抖成千百片。
深藏晦隐的罪戾，赶快去划破
你们的包皮，对这些可怕的传令使
求天恩的赦免。我是个作孽无几
遭孽太深的受屈者。

铿　　德　　　　　　　　唉，光着头？
大人，去这里不远有一间棚屋；
那也许能给你一点友情的庇护，
把这阵风潮避过；你且去歇一下；
待我回这家比石头还硬的人家去，——
他们适才问起你，可不许我进门，——
强他们施铁石的恩情。

李　　尔　　　　　　　　我渐渐觉得
神志紊乱起来了。——小子，跟着来；
怎么样，小子？冷不冷？我自己也冷呢。——
这草堆在那里，朋友？——人逢到急迫时
好不奇怪，滥贱的东西竟会得
变成珍贵。——到你的棚屋里去来，
来吧。——可怜你这个傻子小使，
我心里倒还有些在替你悲伤呢。

傻　　子　［唱］谁要是还有一点神志清，
　　　　　　　哈呀咧啊唷，雨打又风吹，
　　　　　　就是每天都风吹又雨打，

> *Must make content with his fortunes fit,*
> *For the rain it raineth every day.*

Lear   True, boy. —Come, bring us to this hovel.

[Exeunt Lear and Kent.]

Fool   This is a brave night to cool a courtezan. —I'll speak
a prophecy ere I go: —
> When priests are more in word than matter;
> When brewers mar their malt with water;
> When nobles are their tailors' tutors;
> No heretics burn'd, but wenches' suitors;
> When every case in law is right;
> No squire in debt nor no poor knight;
> When slanders do not live in tongues;
> Nor cutpurses come not to throngs;
> When usurers tell their gold i' the field;
> And bawds and whores do churches build;
> Then shall the realm of Albion
> Come to great confusion.
> Then comes the time, who lives to see't,
> That going shall be us'd with feet.

This prophecy Merlin shall make; for I live before his time.

[Exit.]

SCENE III. *A Room in* Gloucester's *Castle.*

[Enter Gloucester and Edmund.]

Gloucester   Alack, alack, Edmund, I like not this unnatural dealing. When I desired their leave that I might
pity him, they took from me the use of mine own
house; charged me on pain of perpetual displeasure,
neither to speak of him, entreat for him, nor any way
sustain him.

Edmund   Most savage and unnatural!

Gloucester   Go to; say you nothing. There is division
betwixt the dukes, and a worse matter than that: I

　　　　　　　　也得满足他的命运。

李　　　尔　　不错，小子。——来吧，领我们到这棚屋里去。

　　　　　　　　　　　　　　　　　　　　　　［李尔与锉德同下。

傻　　　子　　好一个夜晚！——可以弄冷一个婊子的心。我在未
　　　　　　　　去之前要说一阵预言哩：

　　　　　　　　　　　传教师空谈多过了实话时；
　　　　　　　　　　　酿酒的把水搀进了麦芽时；
　　　　　　　　　　　贵人们做了裁衣匠的老师；
　　　　　　　　　　　生大疮的家伙都逛过了窑子；
　　　　　　　　　　　公堂上的案子若件件审明白；
　　　　　　　　　　　穷武士跟他的马弁都不欠债；
　　　　　　　　　　　若是毁谤不在舌尖上生；
　　　　　　　　　　　剪绺的小偷不走进人群；
　　　　　　　　　　　守财奴肯说了他地下的窟藏；
　　　　　　　　　　　窑姐儿同婊子造起了礼拜堂；
　　　　　　　　　　　那时节咱们这英伦的世界
　　　　　　　　　　　准会弄得乱纷纷地倒坏。
　　　　　　　　　　　那时节一来，谁若是还活着，
　　　　　　　　　　　要走路就尽管迈开了大脚。

　　　　　　　　懋琳就得说这一阵预言；因为我比他早生。

　　　　　　　　　　　　　　　　　　　　　　　　　　　　［下。

第　三　景

　　　　　　［葛洛斯忒堡邸中之一室。］
　　　　　　［葛洛斯忒与蔼特孟同上。

葛洛斯忒　唉，唉，蔼特孟，我不喜欢这不近人情的干法。我求
　　　　　　　他们准我去可怜他，他们就不准我使用自己的屋子；
　　　　　　　还命令我不准提起他，替他求情，或是不拘怎样去照
　　　　　　　顾他，不然就要罚我永远失掉他们的恩宠。

蔼　特　孟　真凶蛮无理，真不近人情。

葛洛斯忒　算了；你可别说。两位公爵中间已起了分裂，此外还

have received a letter this night; — 'tis dangerous to
be spoken; — I have locked the letter in my closet;
these injuries the king now bears will be revenged
home; there's part of a power already footed; we
must incline to the king. I will seek him, and privily
relieve him; go you and maintain talk with the duke,
that my charity be not of him perceived; if he ask for
me, I am ill, and gone to bed. If I die for it, as no
less is threatened me, the king my old master must be
relieved. There is some strange thing toward, Edmund; pray you be careful.

[*Exit.*]

Edmund   This courtesy, forbid thee, shall the duke
Instantly know; and of that letter too.
This seems a fair deserving, and must draw me
That which my father loses; no less than all.
The younger rises when the old doth fall.

[*Exit.*]

SCENE IV. *The heath. Before a hovel.*

[*Enter* Lear, Kent, *and* Fool.]

Kent   Here is the place, my lord; good my lord, enter;
The tyranny of the open night's too rough
For nature to endure.   [Storm still.]

Lear   Let me alone.

Kent   Good my lord, enter here.

Lear   Wilt break my heart?

Kent   I had rather break mine own. Good my lord, enter.

Lear   Thou think'st 'tis much that this contentious storm
Invades us to the skin: so 'tis to thee;
But where the greater malady is fix'd,
The lesser is scarce felt. Thou'dst shun a bear,

有件事比这个更糟：今晚上我接到一封信，说出来很
危险；我把信已锁在壁橱里去了；国王如今身受的这
些虐待是会好好地报复的；有一部分军队已经上了
岸；我们得帮着国王这边。我要去找他，私下救他一
救；你去跟公爵说着话，好让我这番善心不给他知
道；他若叫我，只说我不舒服，睡了。就是我为这事
会丧了命，还得要救他；他们确是这么恐吓我的，但
国王是我的老主人。有重大的事变快发生了，蔼特
孟；告诉你，你得小心些。

蔼　特　孟	这一番被禁止的殷勤，连同那封信，
	我得马上让爵爷知道。这是将
	高功去买赏，父亲要失掉的准会
	全归我掌握；那便是他所有的封地。
	年老的倒了，年轻的就乘时兴起。

〔下。

第　四　景

〔荒原上。在一棚屋前。〕
〔李尔，铿德，及傻子上。

铿　　德	就是这地方，大人；好主公，进去吧；
	血肉的人生经不起在夜晚荒野里
	受这样的淫威。

〔风雨猖狂如故。〕

李　　尔	让我一个人在这里。
铿　　德	好主公，里边去。
李　　尔	可要我心碎不成？
铿　　德	我宁愿自己心碎。好主公，进去啊。
李　　尔	你以为这猖狂的风暴侵上了肌肤
	乃是件大事；对你也许是如此；
	可是大患所在处小患就几乎
	不能觉到。你要躲避一只熊，

But if thy flight lay toward the raging sea,
Thou'dst meet the bear i' the mouth. When the mind's
    free,
The body's delicate; the tempest in my mind
Doth from my senses take all feeling else
Save what beats there. — Filial ingratitude!
Is it not as this mouth should tear this hand
For lifting food to't? — But I will punish home.
No, I will weep no more. — In such a night
To shut me out! — Pour on; I will endure.
In such a night as this! O Regan, Goneril! —
Your old kind father, whose frank heart gave all, —
O, that way madness lies; let me shun that;
No more of that.

Kent   Good my lord, enter here.

Lear   Pr'ythee go in thyself; seek thine own ease;
This tempest will not give me leave to ponder
On things would hurt me more. — But I'll go in. —
[*To the* Fool.] In, boy; go first. — You houseless pover-
    ty, —
Nay, get thee in. I'll pray, and then I'll sleep. —

                              [Fool *goes in.*]

Poor naked wretches, wheresoe'er you are,
That bide the pelting of this pitiless storm,
How shall your houseless heads and unfed sides,
Your loop'd and window'd raggedness, defend you
From seasons such as these? O, I have ta'en
Too little care of this! Take physic, pomp;
Expose thyself to feel what wretches feel,
That thou mayst shake the superflux to them
And show the heavens more just.

但若是须向怒号的海上去逃生，
你就宁愿接触那熊的嘴。心宽时
身体才柔弱；如今我心中的风雨
把我感官上一切的知能全去掉，
只除了这心中的捶打。儿女负恩！
是不是好比这张嘴要撕破这只手，
只因它举着食物喂了它？我准得
尽情地责罚。不，我不再哭泣。
这样的夜晚关我在门外？倒下来；
我能忍受。这样的一个夜晚？
啊，雷耿，刚瑙烈！你们的老父，
真慈爱，他慷慨把一切交给了你们，——
啊，那么想就得疯；让我别想；
别再想那个！

铿　　德　　　　　　　　好主公，进这里边去。

李　　尔　你自己进去；去寻求你自己的安适；
这风暴正好不让我有余闲去顾念
更使我痛心的那些事。我还是进去。——
进去，小子；你先走。——无处住的穷人，——
别待着，你进去。我祷告完了就来睡。——
　　　　　　　　　〔傻子入内。
可怜你们那班袒裸的穷人，
不拘你们在那里，都得去身受
这无情风雨的摧残，你们那没有
房檐的头顶，不曾喂饱的肚腹，
还有全身的百孔千穿的褴褛，
怎么能掩护你们度这样的天时？
啊，我太过疏忽了这件事！如今，
盖世的荣华啊，你正好服这剂良药；
暴露你自己，去尝尝赤贫的滋味，
你才会把多余的享受散播给他们，
也显得上天公平些。

Edgar [*Within.*] Fathom and half, fathom and half! Poor Tom! [*The* Fool *runs out from the hovel.*]

Fool Come not in here, nuncle, here's a spirit. Help me, help me!

Kent Give me thy hand. — Who's there?

Fool A spirit, a spirit; he says his name's poor Tom.

Kent What art thou that dost grumble there i' the straw? Come forth.

[*Enter* Edgar, *disguised as a madman.*]

Edgar Away! the foul fiend follows me! —

Through the sharp hawthorn blows the cold wind. —

Hum! go to thy cold bed, and warm thee.

Lear Didst thou give all to thy two daughters? And art thou come to this?

Edgar Who gives anything to poor Tom? whom the foul fiend hath led through fire and through flame, through ford and whirlpool, o'er bog and quagmire; that hath laid knives under his pillow and halters in his pew, set ratsbane by his porridge; made him proud of heart, to ride on a bay trotting horse over four-inched bridges, to course his own shadow for a traitor. — Bless thy five wits! — Tom's a-cold. — O, do de, do de, do de. — Bless thee from whirlwinds, star-blasting, and taking! Do poor Tom some charity, whom the foul fiend vexes. there could I have him now, — and there, and there again, and there.

[*Storm continues.*]

Lear What, have his daughters brought him to this pass? — Couldst thou save nothing? Didst thou give 'em all?

Fool Nay, he reserv'd a blanket, else we had been all shamed.

Lear Now all the plagues that in the pendulous air
Hang fated o'er men's faults light on thy daughters!

Kent He hath no daughters, sir.

Lear Death, traitor! nothing could have subdu'd nature
To such a lowness but his unkind daughters. —
Is it the fashion that discarded fathers
Should have thus little mercy on their flesh?

蔼　特　加　〔在内〕一呼半，一呼半！可怜的汤姆啊！

　　　　　　　　　　　　　〔傻子自棚屋内奔出。

傻　　　子　别进来，伯伯，这儿有个鬼。救命啊，救命！

铿　　　德　牵着我的手。——谁在那里？

傻　　　子　一个鬼，一个鬼，他说他叫可怜的汤姆。

铿　　　德　你是什么人，在那草堆里哼哼地叫苦？走出来。

　　　　　　　　　　　〔蔼特加饰一疯人上。

蔼　特　加　走开，有恶鬼跟着我！"风来吹过多刺的山楂枝。"
　　　　　　呃！上床去暖暖吧。

李　　　尔　你把全份家私都给了你女儿们吗，所以弄成这样？

蔼　特　加　谁把什么东西给苦汤姆？恶鬼领着我穿过了火苗和
　　　　　　火焰，通过了浅水和旋水，跨过了泥沼和泥洼；他把
　　　　　　尖刀放在我枕头下，绞索子放在教堂里我的座上；把
　　　　　　耗子药放在我汤盏边；弄得我心骄气傲，骑上了一匹
　　　　　　栗色的快马颠过四吋宽的桥，将我自己的影子当作
　　　　　　个逆贼去追。天保佑你的五巧！汤姆好冷吓。O,
　　　　　　do, de, do, de, do, de. 天保佑你不受大风灾，不交晦
　　　　　　气星，不中邪气！对苦汤姆发发慈悲吧，可怜他给恶
　　　　　　鬼闹苦了。这下子我可就逮得住他了，这下子，还有
　　　　　　这下子，这下子。

　　　　　　　　　　　　　　　　〔风雨猖狂如故。〕

李　　　尔　什么，他女儿把他弄到了这样吗？——
　　　　　　你难道一点都不能留？要全给她们？

傻　　　子　不，他留下一张毯子，不然我们的脸全给丢光了。

李　　　尔　让浮在我们上空的，那些一窥见
　　　　　　人类的过错便马上降罚的瘟疹，
　　　　　　落在你女儿们的头上！

铿　　　德　大人，他没有女儿。

李　　　尔　该死，逆贼！除了他狠心的女儿们
　　　　　　再没有东西能磨他到这样不像人。
　　　　　　被遗弃的父亲对自己的身体这般
　　　　　　不存怜恤，可是已成了风气吗？

Judicious punishment! 'twas this flesh begot
Those pelican daughters.

Edgar *Pillicock sat on Pillicock — hill: —*
Halloo, halloo, loo loo!

Fool This cold night will turn us all to fools and madmen.

Edgar Take heed o' th' foul fiend; obey thy parents;
keep thy word justly; swear not; commit not with
man's sworn spouse; set not thy sweet heart on proud
array. Tom's a-cold.

Lear What hast thou been?

Edgar A serving-man, proud in heart and mind; that
curled my hair; wore gloves in my cap; served the
lust of my mistress' heart, and did the act of darkness
with her. swore as many oaths as I spake words, and
broke them in the sweet face of heaven. one that slept
in the contriving of lust, and waked to do it. wine
loved I deeply, dice dearly; and in woman out-
paramour'd the Turk. false of heart, light of ear,
bloody of hand; hog in sloth, fox in stealth, wolf in
greediness, dog in madness, lion in prey. Let not the
creaking of shoes nor the rustling of silks betray thy
poor heart to woman. keep thy foot out of brothel,
thy hand out of placket, thy pen from lender's book,
and defy the foul fiend. — *Still through the hawthorn
blows the cold wind.* says *suum, mun, nonny. Dol-
phin my boy, boy, sessa!* let him trot by.

> [*Storm still continues.*]

Lear Thou wert better in thy grave than to answer with
thy uncovered body this extremity of the skies. — Is
man no more than this? Consider him well. Thou o-
west the worm no silk, the beast no hide, the sheep
no wool, the cat no perfume. — Ha? here's three on's
are sophisticated. Thou art the thing itself; unaccom-
modated man is no more but such a poor, bare,
forked animal as thou art. — Off, off, you lendings!
— Come, unbutton here.

> [*Tears off his clothes.*]

Fool Pr'ythee, nuncle, be contented; 'tis a naughty night

这惩罚好不贤明！就是这身体
生出那班鹈鹕似的女儿们。

蔼　特　加　"小鸡鸡坐在小鸡鸡山上，"
Alow; alow, loo, loo!

傻　　　子　这冰冷的夜晚要把我们都弄成傻瓜和疯子了。

蔼　特　加　小心恶鬼；顺从你的爹妈；说话要守信用；不要赌咒；
莫去跟有老公的婆娘犯奸；别把你的宝贝心儿用在
衣裳显耀上面。汤姆好冷吓。

李　　　尔　你以前是做什么事的？

蔼　特　加　做过心高气傲的当差；把头发卷得鬈鬈的，帽子上佩
一副手套；侍候过东家太太心里的欲火，跟她干了亏
心的勾当。我赌的咒跟说的话一般多，青天白日下
又把它们一笔儿勾销。睡着时打算怎样淫乱，一醒
来就干。酒我爱得如同宝贝，骰子和性命一般；爱女
人要比土耳其人还厉害。心肠假，耳朵软，手段辣；
懒惰得像猪，阴险得像狐，贪得像狼，疯得像狗，猛得
像狮子。别让鞋子吱吱叫，绸衣窸窣响，逗得你为了
女人把灵魂儿颠倒。别让你的脚跨进窑子，你的手
摸进女人的裤子，你的名字落进放债人的簿子，另外
你还得跟恶鬼对抗。"冷风总是吹过那山楂枝"。说
"suum, mum, nonny. 多尔芬我的孩子，孩子唅，停
住！让他骑过去吧"。

［风雨猖狂如故。］

李　　　尔　你裸着身子在这样的狂风暴雨里头，还不如死了好
呢。人就不过是这个样儿吗？仔细端详端详他。你
不用蚕儿什么丝，不借畜牲什么皮，不少羊儿什么
毛，不欠猫儿什么香。吓？咱们这一伙儿三个都是
装孙子的。你才是真东西；原来不穿衣服的人不过
是你这样可怜的一个光溜溜的两脚动物。去，去，你
们这些装场面的废物！来，扣子解掉。

［撕去衣服。］

傻　　　子　请安静些吧，伯伯；这夜晚要泅水可太尴尬了。大空

to swim in. — Now a little fire in a wild fire were like an old lecher's heart, — a small spark, all the rest on's body cold. — Look, here comes a walking fire.

Edgar   This is the foul fiend Flibbertigibbet; he begins at curfew, and walks till the first cock; he gives the web and the pin, squints the eye, and makes the harelip; mildews the white wheat, and hurts the poor creature of earth.

> *Swithold footed thrice the old;*
> *He met the nightmare, and her nine-fold;*
> *Bid her alight*
> *And her troth plight,*
> *And aroint thee, witch, aroint thee!*

Kent   How fares your grace?

> [*Enter* Gloucester *with a torch.*]

Lear   What's he?

Kent   Who's there? What is't you seek?

Gloucester   What are you there? Your names?

Edgar   Poor Tom, that eats the swimming frog, the toad, the todpole, the wall-newt and the water; that in the fury of his heart, when the foul fiend rages, eats cow-dung for sallets; swallows the old rat and the ditch-dog; drinks the green mantle of the standing pool; who is whipped from tithing to tithing, and stocked, punished, and imprisoned; who hath had three suits to his back, six shirts to his body;

> *horse to ride, and weapons to wear; —*
> *But mice and rats, and such small deer,*
> *Have been Tom's food for seven long year.*

Beware my follower. — Peace, Smulkin! peace, thou fiend!

Gloucester   What, hath your grace no better company?

Edgar   The prince of darkness is a gentleman: Modo he's call'd, and Mahu.

Gloucester   Our flesh and blood, my lord, is grown so vile

地上一点小火好比是个老色鬼的心,只一小粒火星,他身上旁处都是冷的。瞧这儿来了杆会走路的火。

[葛洛斯忒手执火炬上。

蔼　特　加　这就是忽烈剖铁及白脱那恶鬼;一打了熄火钟他就开始,直到第一声鸡啼才走开;他叫人眼珠上长白翳,好眼变成斜眼,好嘴唇变成兔唇;他叫白麦的穗子长上霉,又伤害地上的小动物。

圣维妥在原野上巡行了三趟;

他碰见梦魇煞和她的九小魃;

叫了她下去,

要她发个誓,

去你的,雌妖魔,赶快走开去。

铿　　德　大人,你觉得怎么样?

李　　尔　他是什么?

铿　　德　谁在那儿?你找什么东西?

葛洛斯忒　你们是什么人?你们叫什么名字?

蔼　特　加　我叫苦汤姆,我吃水青蛙、癞蛤蟆、蛤蟆豆、壁虎和水蜥;恶鬼一发火我心里烦躁起来就得吞吃牛矢当拌生菜;我也吞吃老耗子和沟里的死狗;又喝死水池上浮着的绿苔;我在乡下从这一区给鞭打到那一区,上脚枷,吃刑罚,坐监牢;我背上有三套衣服,身上有七件衬衫;

胯下有马儿骑,身上有剑儿佩;

汤姆这七个年头来的饭和菜

是大小耗子和同样的小野味。

小心我这跟班的。——别闹,死殁尔禁! 别闹,你这魔鬼!

葛洛斯忒　什么,您大人没有好些的人作伴吗?

蔼　特　加　黑暗亲王是一位绅士;他名叫模涂,又叫马虎。

葛洛斯忒　大人,我们亲生的骨肉变成了

That it doth hate what gets it.

Edgar　Poor Tom's a-cold.

Gloucester　Go in with me; my duty cannot suffer
To obey in all your daughters' hard commands;
Though their injunction be to bar my doors,
And let this tyrannous night take hold upon you,
Yet have I ventur'd to come seek you out
And bring you where both fire and food is ready.

Lear　First let me talk with this philosopher. —
What is the cause of thunder?

Kent　Good my lord, take his offer; go into the house.

Lear　I'll talk a word with this same learned Theban. —
What is your study?

Edgar　How to prevent the fiend and to kill vermin.

Lear　Let me ask you one word in private.

Kent　Importune him once more to go, my lord;
His wits begin to unsettle.

Gloucester　　　　　　　　　Canst thou blame him?

　　　　　　　　　　　　　　　　[Storm continues.]

His daughters seek his death. ah, that good Kent!
He said it would be thus. poor banish'd man!
Thou say'st the king grows mad; I'll tell thee, friend,
I am almost mad myself. I had a son,
Now outlaw'd from my blood; he sought my life,
But lately, very late; I lov'd him, friend,
No father his son dearer; true to tell thee,
The grief hath craz'd my wits. What a night's this! —
I do beseech your grace, —

Lear　　　　　　　　　O, cry you mercy, sir. —
Noble philosopher, your company.

Edgar　Tom's a-cold.

　　　　　　　　这么坏,竟会对生他的人心存仇恨。

雷　特　加　苦汤姆好冷吓。

葛洛斯忒　同我屋里去,我不能为服从公主们
　　　　　　　残酷的命令,便弃去我对您的本责;
　　　　　　　她们的禁令虽要我关门下闩,
　　　　　　　尽这暴戾的夜分扼住您大人,
　　　　　　　但我依然要冒险出门来,寻您
　　　　　　　去到炉火和食品都备就的所在。

李　　尔　让我先跟这位哲学家说话。——
　　　　　　　打雷的原因是什么?

铿　　德　好主公,接受他这番供奉吧;屋里去。

李　　尔　我要跟这位博学的底皮斯人说句话。——
　　　　　　　你是研究什么的?

蔼　特　加　我研究怎样躲魔鬼和怎样杀虱子。

李　　尔　让我私下问你一句话。

铿　　德　请你再催他一声就走吧,大人;
　　　　　　　他神志开始在乱了。

葛洛斯忒　　　　　　　　　你能怪他吗?

　　　　　　　　　　　　　　　　　[风雨猖狂如故。]

　　　　　　　公主们巴他死。啊,那个好铿德!
　　　　　　　他说过会这样的,可怜他遭了流放!
　　　　　　　你说王上发疯了;我告你,朋友,
　　　　　　　我自己也差点发了疯。我有个儿子,
　　　　　　　如今已给我逐出;他谋害我的命,
　　　　　　　还是最近,很近呢;我爱他,朋友,
　　　　　　　再没有父亲更比我爱他的儿子了;
　　　　　　　实在告诉你,那阵子伤心弄得我
　　　　　　　神志全乱了。真是好一个晚上! ——
　　　　　　　我实在求王上,——

李　　尔　　　　　　　　喔,对不起,阁下。——尊贵的
　　　　　　　哲学家,咱们在一起。

蔼　特　加　汤姆好冷吓。

Gloucester In, fellow, there, into the hovel; keep thee warm.

Lear Come, let's in all.

Kent   This way, my lord.

Lear   With him;
I will keep still with my philosopher.

Kent Good my lord, soothe him; let him take the fellow.

Gloucester Take him you on.

Kent Sirrah, come on; go along with us.

Lear Come, good Athenian.

Gloucester No words, no words: hush.

Edgar *Child Rowland to the dark tower came,*
His word was still — Fie, foh, and fum,
I smell the blood of a British man.

                                          [*Exeunt.*]

SCENE V. *Gloucester's Castle.*

[*Enter* Cornwall *and* Edmund.]

Cornwall I will have my revenge ere I depart his house.

Edmund How, my lord, I may be censured, that nature thus
gives way to loyalty, something fears me to think of.

Cornwall I now perceive, it was not altogether your
brother's evil disposition made him seek his death,
but a provoking merit, set a-work by a reproveable
badness in himself.

Edmund How malicious is my fortune, that I must repent
to be just! This is the letter he spoke of, which approves him an intelligent party to the advantages of
France. O heavens! that this treason were not or not I
the detector!

Cornwall Go with me to the duchess.

Edmund If the matter of this paper be certain, you have
mighty business in hand.

Cornwall True or false, it hath made thee earl of Gloucester.

葛 洛 斯 忒	进去,家伙,这里,棚屋里去暖暖吧。
李　　尔	来吧,咱们都进去。
铿　　德	这里走,主上。
李　　尔	跟他去;我要跟我的哲学家在一起。
铿　　德	大人,顺了他吧;让他带着这人儿。
葛 洛 斯 忒	你带着他来。
铿　　德	得了,来吧,跟我们去。
李　　尔	来,好雅典人。
葛 洛 斯 忒	别说话,别说话! 莫做声。
蔼　特　加	"洛阑骑士来到暗塔前。 他老说着'fie,foh,fum,' 我嗅到一个不列颠人的血腥。"

〔同下。

第 五 景

〔葛洛斯忒堡邸中。〕
〔康华与蔼特孟上。

康　　华	我离开以前一定得报复。
蔼　特　孟	主上,我这般不顾父子的恩情,却一心报主,人家不知要怎样说法,想起了真有点害怕。
康　　华	我如今才知道,并非全是为了你哥哥本性凶恶所以要谋害他,只因他罪有应得,他自己那些可议的坏处激发得你哥哥那么样干的。
蔼　特　孟	我的命运好不恶毒,现在我这么公正了回头又得后悔! 这就是他说起的那封信,证明他是替法兰西当奸细的。天啊! 但愿他没有这个逆谋,或者发现的人不是我!
康　　华	跟我去见爵夫人。
蔼　特　孟	要是这信上的话是真的,您手头有的是大事情要办呢。
康　　华	不管真假,这件事已叫你当上了葛洛斯忒伯爵了。

Seek out where thy father is, that he may be ready for our apprehension.

Edmund [*Aside.*] If I find him comforting the king, it will stuff his suspicion more fully. —I will persever in my course of loyalty, though the conflict be sore between that and my blood.

Cornwall I will lay trust upon thee, and thou shalt find a dearer father in my love.

[*Exeunt.*]

SCENE VI. *A Chamber in a Farmhouse adjoining the Castle.*

[*Enter* Kent, Gloucester.]

Gloucester Here is better than the open air; take it thankfully. I will piece out the comfort with what addition I can; I will not be long from you.

Kent All the power of his wits have given way to his impatience. the gods reward your kindness!

[*Exit* Gloucester.]
[*Enter* LEAR, EDGAR, *and* FOOL.]

Edgar Fraretto calls me, and tells me Nero is an angler in the lake of darkness. —Pray, innocent, and beware the foul fiend.

Fool Pr'ythee, nuncle, tell me whether a madman be a gentleman or a yeoman.

Lear A king, a king!

Fool No, he's a yeoman that has a gentleman to his son; for he's a mad yeoman that sees his son a gentleman before him.

Lear To have a thousand with red burning spits
Come hissing in upon 'em, —

Edgar The foul fiend bites my back.

Fool He's mad that trusts in the tameness of a wolf, a horse's health, a boy's love, or a whore's oath.

Lear It shall be done; I will arraign them straight. —
[*To* Edgar.] Come, sit thou here, most learned justicer—
[*To the* Fool.] Thou, sapient sir, sit here. Now,

去寻找你父亲,我们好逮住他。

蔼　特　孟　我若找见了他在救助国王,便能加重他的嫌疑。我
还要继续尽忠,虽然忠诚和父子间的恩情冲突得使
我很痛苦。

康　　　华　我信托你,你也自会觉得我的爱宠比你父亲更可爱。

　　　　　　　　　　　　　　　　　　　　　　　　　　　［同下。

第　六　景

　　　　［毗连堡邸之佃舍内一室。］
　　　　［铿德与葛洛斯忒上。

葛洛斯忒　这里比露天要好些;安心待着吧。我去设法添几件
东西来,好让这里舒服些;我不久就回来。

铿　　　德　他所有的聪明才智完全让位给了狂怒。愿天神们报
答你的好心!　　　　　　　　　　　　　　　　［葛洛斯忒下。

　　　　　　［李尔,蔼特加,与傻子上。

蔼　特　加　弗拉忒阑多在叫我,他告诉我说尼罗在阴湖里钓水
蛙。——要祷告,天真儿,又得要留神那恶鬼。

傻　　　子　伯伯,请告诉我,一个疯子是一位绅士还是个平民
百姓。

李　　　尔　是个国王,是个国王!

傻　　　子　不,他自己是个平民,他儿子却是位绅士;为的是他
看见一位绅士儿子在他眼前,他就成了个疯子
平民。

李　　　尔　要有一千把烙得通红的铁叉
　　　　　　唑唑地刺进她们,——

蔼　特　加　恶鬼在咬我的背。

傻　　　子　谁相信一只狼没有野性,一只马没有毛病,一个孩子
的爱情,或一个窑姐赌的咒,谁就是个疯子。

李　　　尔　准得这么办;我马上来传讯她们。——
　　　　　　来,你请坐,学识精通的大法官。——
　　　　　　还有你,圣明的官长,这边请坐。——

you she-foxes! —

Edgar　Look, where he stands and glares! Want'st thou eyes at trial, madam?

> *Come o'er the bourn, Bessy, to me, —*

Fool　　　　*Her boat hath a leak,*
> *And she must not speak*
> *Why she dares not come over to thee.*

Edgar　The foul fiend haunts poor Tom in the voice of a nightingale. Hoppedance cries in Tom's belly for two white herring. Croak not, black angel; I have no food for thee.

Kent　How do you, sir? Stand you not so amaz'd.
Will you lie down and rest upon the cushions?

Lear　I'll see their trial first. —Bring in their evidence.
[*To* Edgar.] Thou, robed man of justice, take thy place; —
[*To the* Fool.] And thou, his yokefellow of equity,
Bench by his side: —[*To* Kent.] you are o' the commission,
Sit you too.

Edgar　Let us deal justly.

> *Sleepest or wakest thou, jolly shepherd?*
> *Thy sheep be in the corn;*
> *And for one blast of thy minikin mouth,*
> *Thy sheep shall take no harm.*

Purr! the cat is gray.

Lear　Arraign her first; 'tis Goneril. I here take my oath before this honourable assembly, she kicked the poor king her father.

Fool　Come hither, mistress. Is your name Goneril?

Lear　She cannot deny it.

Fool　Cry you mercy, I took you for a joint-stool.

Lear　And here's another, whose warp'd looks proclaim
What store her heart is made on. —Stop her there!
Arms, arms, sword, fire! Corruption in the place! —
False justicer, why hast thou let her 'scape?

来吧，你们这两只母狐狸。

蔼　特　加　瞧，他站在那儿睁着眼！娘娘，给当堂在审罪还要有
　　　　　　人瞅着你吗？

　　　　　　　　"过这小河来跟我白西"。

傻　　　子　　　　"她那船儿在漏水，
　　　　　　　　　她又不能向你说
　　　　　　　　为什么不敢过水来跟你。"

蔼　特　加　恶鬼装着夜莺鸟的歌声在烦扰苦汤姆。好拍当势在
　　　　　　汤姆肚里嚷着要吃两条鲜青鱼。不要阁阁阁地尽
　　　　　　叫，魔鬼；我没有东西给你吃。

铿　　　德　你觉得怎么样，大人？别呆呆地站着
　　　　　　可要躺下来靠在座垫上安息吗？

李　　　尔　我先要看她们的审判。——传进证人来。——
　　　　　　[对蔼特加]你这位长袍大服的法官请升座。——
　　　　　　[对傻子]还有你，你是他执法的同伴，也请
　　　　　　傍着他就位。——[对铿德]你也是陪审的人员，
　　　　　　也请坐下。

蔼　特　加　让我们公平裁判。

　　　　　　　　"你醒着还是在睡觉，牧羊儿？
　　　　　　　　　羊群都在麦陇上；
　　　　　　　　　只要你有样的小嘴吹一声，
　　　　　　　　　　羊群就平安无恙。"

　　　　　　拍尔！这猫是灰色的。

李　　　尔　先把她提上来；这是刚瑙烈。我当着廷上诸位宣誓，
　　　　　　她脚踢可怜的国王，她的父亲。

傻　　　子　走过来，女犯。你叫刚瑙烈吗？

李　　　尔　她赖不掉。

傻　　　子　对不起，我以为你是只折椅。

李　　　尔　这里还有个，她这副狰狞的面目
　　　　　　显得她的心用什么东西做。——拦住她！
　　　　　　武器，武器，快拿剑来，点上火！
　　　　　　贪赃舞弊！坏法官，你怎么放她逃？

Edgar Bless thy five wits!

Kent O pity! — Sir, where is the patience now
That you so oft have boasted to retain?

Edgar [*Aside.*] My tears begin to take his part so much
They'll mar my counterfeiting.

Lear The little dogs and all,
Tray, Blanch, and Sweet-heart, see, they bark at me.

Edgar Tom will throw his head at them. — Avaunt, you
   curs!

> Be thy mouth or black or white,
> Tooth that poisons if it bite;
> Mastiff, greyhound, mongrel grim,
> Hound or spaniel, brach or lym,
> Or bobtail tike or trundle-tail,
> Tom will make them weep and wail;
> For, with throwing thus my head,
> Dogs leap the hatch, and all are fled.

Do de, de, de. Sessa! Come, march to wakes and fairs
   and market-towns. Poor Tom, thy horn is dry.

Lear Then let them anatomize Regan; see what breeds a-
   bout her heart. Is there any cause in nature that
   makes these hard hearts? — [*To* Edgar.] You, sir, I
   entertain you for one of my hundred; only I do not
   like the fashion of your garments. you'll say they are
   Persian; but let them be changed.

Kent Now, good my lord, lie here and rest awhile.

Lear Make no noise, make no noise; draw the curtains;
So, so. We'll go to supper i' the morning.

Fool And I'll go to bed at noon.

[Re-enter Gloucester.]

Gloucester Come hither, friend; where is the king my master?

Kent Here, sir; but trouble him not, his wits are gone.

蔼 特 加	天保佑你的五巧！
铿　　德	啊，可怜！——大人，你从前常夸说 保持得有的那镇静，如今在哪里？
蔼 特 加	［旁白］我开始对他起了那样深的同情， 这眼泪就要妨碍我这番假装。
李　　尔	小狗们和旁的狗，屈蕾，小白，小宝贝，瞧，它们都在 对我咬。
蔼 特 加	让汤姆把帽子来扔它们。——滚开去，狗子们！ 　　　不管你是黑嘴巴，白嘴巴， 　　　咬人用的是不是毒的牙； 　　　大獒，灵猩，杂种的猛猁儿， 　　　猎狗或哈叭，警犬，花雌儿， 　　　卷尾的狗子或截尾的猫， 　　　汤姆准叫它哭了又去号； 　　　只要把我的帽子这样丢， 　　　它们便跳过了短门都逃走。 Do，de，de，de. 停住！来，去赶开教堂的守夜会，乡 村 的 市 集，和城镇的市场。苦汤姆，你的牛角 空了。
李　　尔	那么让他们把雷耿开膛破肚；看她心上生着什么东 西。天生这些硬心肠可有什么缘故没有？——［对 蔼特加］你，先生，也是我的一百个武士里的一个；不 过我不喜欢你这衣裳的式样。你会说这是波斯装； 可是把它换了吧。
铿　　德	好主公，躺在这里歇一会吧。
李　　尔	别做声，别做声，拉拢了帘幕；对了，对了。我们要在 早上吃晚饭呢。
傻　　子	我要在午上睡觉。

［葛洛斯忒重上。

葛 洛 斯 忒	过来，朋友；国王我主在哪里？
铿　　德	在这里，大人；且莫惊动他，他神志 完全迷乱了。

Gloucester Good friend, I pr'ythee, take him in thy arms;
I have o'erheard a plot of death upon him.
There is a litter ready; lay him in't,
And drive towards Dover, friend, where thou shalt meet
Both welcome and protection. Take up thy master.
If thou shouldst dally half an hour, his life,
With thine, and all that offer to defend him,
Stand in assured loss: take up, take up,
And follow me, that will to some provision
Give thee quick conduct.
Kent   Oppressed nature sleeps.
This rest might yet have balm'd thy broken sinews,
Which, if convenience will not allow,
Stand in hard cure. —Come, help to bear thy master;
[*To the* Fool.] Thou must not stay behind.
Gloucester   Come, come, away.
        [*Exeunt* Kent, Gloucester, *and* the Fool,
                        bearing off Lear.]

Edgar When we our betters see bearing our woes,
We scarcely think our miseries our foes.
Who alone suffers, suffers most i' the mind,
Leaving free things and happy shows behind.
But then the mind much sufferance doth o'erskip,
When grief hath mates, and bearing, fellowship.
How light and portable my pain seems now,
When that which makes me bend makes the king bow,
He childed as I fathered! Tom, away!
Mark the high noises; and thyself bewray
When false opinion, whose wrong thought defiles thee,
In thy just proof repeals and reconciles thee.
What will hap more to-night, safe 'scape the king!
Lurk, lurk.
                                    [*Exit.*]

葛洛斯忒　　　　　　　好朋友，请你抱着他；
我私下听到了一个要害他的奸谋。
我备得有一架床车；放他在车上，
赶往多浮城，朋友，那边你自会
遇到欢迎和保护。抬你的主公。
你若再作半点钟的迟延，他和你，
连同回护他的任何人，准都没有命。
抬起来，抬起来，跟我走，我马上领你
去到那备就的床车。

铿　　德　　　　　　　历尽了千重
磨难的身心如今已沉沉入睡。
这安休也许能抚苏你破碎的神经，
但若果事势不佳良，那就难治了。——
过来，来帮忙抬你的主公，[对傻子]你不能
退缩在后边。

葛洛斯忒　　　　　　　快来，快来，外面去。

　　　　　　　　　[铿德，葛洛斯忒，及傻子，舁李尔同下。

蔼　特　加　眼见到年高位重的和我们同病，
我们便不甚为自身的疾苦伤心。
最可悲莫过于孤身独自去忍受，
将有福者与开怀的乐事遗留在背后。
但若果忧愁有俦侣，受苦有同伴，
心中可就淡忘了许多的磨难。
那使我弯腰的痛楚使国王弓身，
我的便显得何等轻，何等好容忍：
我们父亲和儿子异曲而同工！
去吧，汤姆！注意那高处的来风，
只等诬蔑的讹传证明你恂良，
荣誉恢复后，你便能重现本相。
今晚上尽风云去变幻，愿国王逃掉。
躲着，躲着。　　　　　　　　　　　　[下。

SCENE VII. *Gloucester's Castle.*

[*Enter* Cornwall, Regan, Goneril, Edmund, *and* Servants.]

Cornwall　　Post speedily to my lord your husband; show
him this letter; the army of France is landed. — Seek
out the traitor Gloucester.

　　　　　　　　　　　　[*Exeunt some of the* Servants.]

Regan　　Hang him instantly.

Goneril　　Pluck out his eyes.

Cornwall　　Leave him to my displeasure. — Edmund, keep
you our sister company. the revenges we are bound to
take upon your traitorous father are not fit for your
beholding. Advise the duke where you are going, to a
most festinate preparation; we are bound to the like.
Our posts shall be swift and intelligent betwixt us.
Farewell, dear sister: — [*Enter* Oswald.] farewell,
my lord of Gloucester.

How now! Where's the king?

Oswald　　My lord of Gloucester hath convey'd him hence.
Some five or six and thirty of his knights,
Hot questrists after him, met him at gate;
Who, with some other of the lord's dependants,
Are gone with him towards Dover; where they boast
To have well-armed friends.

Cornwall　　　　　　　　　　Get horses for your mistress.

Goneril　　Farewell, sweet lord, and sister.

Cornwall　　Edmund, farewell.

　　　　　　　　[*Exeunt* Goneril, Edmund, *and* Oswald.]

　　　　　　　　Go seek the traitor Gloucester,
Pinion him like a thief, bring him before us.

　　　　　　　　　　　　[*Exeunt other* Servants.]

Though well we may not pass upon his life
Without the form of justice, yet our power
Shall do a courtesy to our wrath, which men
May blame, but not control. — Who's there? the traitor?

第 七 景

[葛洛斯忒之堡邸。]

[康华,雷耿,刚瑠烈,蔼特孟,及仆从上。]

康　　华　　[对刚瑠烈]快去见令夫君公爵去;给他看这封信;法
　　　　　　兰西军队已经上了岸。——把葛洛斯忒那逆贼找出
　　　　　　来。　　　　　　　　　　　　　　　[仆从数人下。

雷　　耿　　马上绞死他。

刚　瑠　烈　挖掉他的眼睛。

康　　华　　留给我来处治。——蔼特孟,你陪着我们姐姐走。
　　　　　　我们对你那谋叛的父亲的报复不配给你看见。你
　　　　　　到公爵那边,向他上议作速准备;我们也照样在准
　　　　　　备。两方的驿马得加快传递信息。——再会了,亲
　　　　　　爱的姐姐——再会,葛洛斯忒伯爵。——[奥士伐
　　　　　　上]怎么了,国王在哪里?

奥　士　伐　葛洛斯忒伯爵引他离了境。
　　　　　　有三十五六名他的武士正在
　　　　　　火急地寻他,恰跟他在城门前碰到;
　　　　　　他的挟着他和伯爵的另一班从人
　　　　　　向多浮进发,夸说有武装的朋友
　　　　　　在那边保护。

康　　华　　　　　　　　　替你主母去备马。

刚　瑠　烈　再会,亲爱的公爵和妹妹。

康　　华　　蔼特孟,再会。——[刚瑠烈,蔼特孟,与奥士伐
　　　　　　　　　　　　　同下。
　　　　　　　　　　　把那个逆贼找出来。
　　　　　　把他小偷似的反缚着膀子带来。[另有数仆从下。
　　　　　　虽然我们不能开秉公的审问
　　　　　　判处他死刑,但我们的权威自会
　　　　　　顺从我们的愤恨,世人只有去
　　　　　　非难,却无从来阻止。——那是谁? 那逆贼?

[*Enter* Gloucester, *brought in by two or three.*]

Regan Ingrateful fox! 'tis he.

Cornwall Bind fast his corky arms.

Gloucester What mean your graces?—Good my friends, consider

You are my guests; do me no foul play, friends.

Cornwall Bind him, I say.

[*Servants bind him.*]

Regan Hard, hard. —O filthy traitor!

Gloucester Unmerciful lady as you are, I'm none.

Cornwall To this chair bind him. — Villain, thou shalt
find, — [*Regan plucks his beard.*]

Gloucester By the kind gods, 'tis most ignobly done

To pluck me by the beard.

Regan So white, and such a traitor!

Gloucester Naughty lady,

These hairs which thou dost ravish from my chin

Will quicken, and accuse thee. I am your host;

With robber's hands my hospitable favours

You should not ruffle thus. What will you do?

Cornwall Come, sir, what letters had you late from France?

Regan Be simple-answer'd, for we know the truth.

Cornwall And what confederacy have you with the traitors

Late footed in the kingdom?

Regan To whose hands have you sent the lunatic king?

Speak.

Gloucester I have a letter guessingly set down,

Which came from one that's of a neutral heart,

And not from one oppos'd.

Cornwall Cunning.

Regan And false.

Cornwall Where hast thou sent the king?

Gloucester To Dover.

Regan Wherefore to Dover? Wast thou not charg'd at
peril, —

Cornwall Wherefore to Dover? Let him first answer that.

Gloucester I am tied to the stake, and I must stand the course.

Regan Wherefore to Dover?

〔二、三人挟葛洛斯忒上。

雷 耿	不知恩义的狐狸！是他。
康 华	把他那干瘪的臂膀缚紧了。
葛洛斯忒	您两位是什么意思？好朋友，要顾念 你们是我的客人；别害我，朋友们。
康 华	绑住他，我说。　　　　　　　　　　〔仆从捆绑他。
雷 耿	绑得紧，绑得紧。——臭贼！
葛洛斯忒	你这位忍心的爵夫人，我不是那个。
康 华	绑上这椅子。——坏蛋，你自会明白——
	〔雷耿抓他的胡须。
葛洛斯忒	我对仁蔼的天神们赌咒，你这么 扯掉我的须实在太下流。
雷 耿	这样白，却是这样一个逆贼！
葛洛斯忒	恶毒的夫人，你拉掉我颔下的这些须， 它们会活起来在神前将你控告。 我是东道主，你不该强盗般糟蹋我 殷勤款待你的容颜。你预备怎么样？
康 华	来，法兰西最近给了你什么信？
雷 耿	爽利些回答，因为我们已知道。
康 华	你跟最近偷进王国来的叛徒们 又有什么勾结？
雷 耿	你将发疯的国王送进了谁手里？ 你说。
葛洛斯忒	我有一封猜测情形的信函， 写信的乃是中立的，并不是对方，
康 华	真刁。
雷 耿	又假。
康 华	你送国王上哪里？
葛洛斯忒	上多浮。
雷 耿	为什么上多浮？不是说不准你——
康 华	为什么上多浮？——让他回答那句话。
葛洛斯忒	我已给系上了桩子，得对付这一场。
雷 耿	为什么上多浮？

Gloucester   Because I would not see thy cruel nails
Pluck out his poor old eyes, nor thy fierce sister
In his anointed flesh stick boarish fangs.
The sea, with such a storm as his bare head
In hell-black night endur'd, would have buoy'd up,
And quench'd the stelled fires; yet, poor old heart,
He holp the heavens to rain.
If wolves had at thy gate howl'd that stern time,
Thou shouldst have said, *Good porter, turn the key.*
All cruels else subscrib'd: — but I shall see
The winged vengeance overtake such children.

Cornwall   See't shalt thou never! — Fellows, hold the
chair! —
Upon these eyes of thine I'll set my foot.

Gloucester   He that will think to live till he be old,
Give me some help! — O cruel! — O you gods!

Regan   One side will mock another; the other too!

Cornwall   If you see vengeance, —

First Serv   Hold your hand, my lord!
I have serv'd you ever since I was a child;
But better service have I never done you
Than now to bid you hold.

Regan   How now, you dog!

First Serv   If you did wear a beard upon your chin,
I'd shake it on this quarrel. What do you mean?

Cornwall   My villain!

                         [*They draw and fight.*]

First Serv   Nay, then, come on, and take the chance of
anger.

                         [Cornwall *is wounded.*]

Regan   Give me thy sword—A peasant stand up thus?
   [*Snatches a sword, comes behind, and stabs him.*]

葛洛斯忒		为的是我不愿眼见你残酷的指爪

葛洛斯忒　　为的是我不愿眼见你残酷的指爪
抓出他可怜的老眼,我不愿眼见你
那凶狠的姐姐把她野猪似的长牙
刺进他香膏抹净了的圣洁的肌肤。
就是那海水,受了他光头赤顶
在地狱一般的黑夜里忍受的风暴,
也会涌上去泼息上边的星火;
可怜的老人啊,他却要上天下大些。
那样猖狂的风雨夜若果有豺狼
在你大门前悲嗥,你也该说道:
"好门子,开开门,可怜一切野兽吧,
任凭它们平时是怎样地残酷。"
但我会眼见到天罚飞来,降落在
这般的孩儿们头上。

康　　华　　　　　　　　你可决不会
见到! ——你们跟我按住这椅子! ——
让我用脚来踹掉你这双眼睛。

葛洛斯忒　谁想活到老年的快来救我! ——
嗄,真狠毒! 嗄,天神们!

雷　　耿　　那边的要笑话这边的,那只也踹掉。

康　　华　　你若见到了天罚——

仆　　甲　　　　　　　　住手,主公!
我自小侍候你到如今,可没有再比
我现在这要你住手更外尽忠了。

雷　　耿　　怎么的,你这狗子?

仆　　甲　　　　　　　你若是个男子,
为了这件事我也会向你挑战。——
你是什么意思?

康　　华　　　　　我的佃奴?　　　〔主仆拔剑相向。〕

仆　　甲　　得了,来打,冒冒义愤的险吧。　〔康华受伤。〕

雷　　耿　　你的剑给我。——贱人敢这样犯上?

　　　　　　　　　　　　　　　〔抽剑从背后刺他。〕

First Serv O, I am slain! — My lord, you have one eye left
To see some mischief on thim. O!   [*Dies.*]
Cornwall Lest it see more, prevent it. — Out, vile jelly!
Where is thy lustre now?
Gloucester All dark and comfortless. — Where's my son
  Edmund?
Edmund, enkindle all the sparks of nature,
To quit this horrid act.
Regan   Out, treacherous villain!
Thou call'st on him that hates thee: it was he
That made the overture of thy treasons to us;
Who is too good to pity thee.
Gloucester O my follies! Then Edgar was abus'd. —
Kind gods, forgive me that, and prosper him!
Regan Go thrust him out at gates, and let him smell
His way to Dover. — [*Exit* one with Glouster.]How is't,
  my lord? How look you?
Cornwall I have receiv'd a hurt: — follow me, lady. —
Turn out that eyeless villain; — throw this slave
Upon the dunghill. — Regan, I bleed apace;
Untimely comes this hurt. give me your arm.
          [*Exit* Cornwall, *led by* Regan.]
Second Serv I'll never care what wickedness I do,
If this man come to good.
Third Serv   If she live long,
And in the end meet the old course of death,
Women will all turn monsters.
Second Serv Let's follow the old earl, and get the Bedlam
To lead him where he would: his roguish madness
Allows itself to anything.
Third Serv Go thou. I'll fetch some flax and whites of eggs
To apply to his bleeding face. Now heaven help him!
                    [*Exeunt severally.*]

仆	甲	嘎，我给刺死了！——你还剩一只眼， 大人，能亲自见到他吃点亏。——嘎！　　［死去。］
康	华	别让它再见到什么。——烂掉贱肉冻！ 现在你眼光在哪里？
葛洛斯忒		一片漆黑，难道没有人来搭救？ 我儿子蔼特孟在哪里？——蔼特孟，燃起你骨肉的 至情，来报复这骇人的罪恶！
雷 耿		滚开，谋反的坏蛋！你叫他，他却恨你； 对我们透露你那个奸谋的就是他； 他是好人，不会来可怜你。
葛洛斯忒		啊，我笨到这样！蔼特加可冤了。 天神们，饶我吧，祝福他康宁无恙！
雷 耿		去把他推出大门外，让他嗅着路 到多浮。——［一仆引葛下。］怎么样，夫君？ 　　　　你怎么这样？
康 华		我受到一处剑伤，跟着我，夫人。—— 把那个没有眼睛的坏蛋赶出去； 扔他在粪堆上。——雷耿，我淌血淌得快； 这伤来得不巧。挽着我的臂。　　［雷耿扶康华下。
仆 乙		要是这人有什么好结果，不拘 怎样的坏事我都做。
仆 丙		要是她活得长， 到头来还能得一个好好的老死， 所有的女人全都会变成妖怪。
仆 乙		让我们跟着老伯爵一同出去， 去把那疯叫化找来，他想上那儿 就领他上那儿，那浮浪人什么都肯做。
仆 丙		你去。我去拿一点亚麻子和鸡蛋清 敷在他出血的脸上。但愿天救救他。　　［各自下。

ACT IV.

SCENE I. *The heath*.

[*Enter* Edgar.]

Edgar   Yet better thus, and known to be contemn'd,
Than still contemn'd and flatter'd. To be worst,
The lowest and most dejected thing of fortune,
Stands still in esperance, lives not in fear.
The lamentable change is from the best;
The worst returns to laughter. Welcome then,
Thou unsubstantial air that I embrace!
The wretch that thou hast blown unto the worst
Owes nothing to thy blasts. —But who comes here?

[*Enter* Gloucester, *led by an Old Man*.]

My father, poorly led? —World, world, O world!
But that thy strange mutations make us hate thee,
Life would not yield to age.

Old Man   O my good lord,
I have been your tenant, and your father's tenant,
These fourscore years.

Gloucester   Away, get thee away; good friend, be gone;
Thy comforts can do me no good at all;

第 四 幕

第 一 景

［荒原上。］

［蔼特加上。

蔼 特 加　但遭到鄙夷，而自己也明知如此，
总胜如逆受着包藏鄙夷的逢迎。
最卑微、最被命运所摧残的不幸者，
常在希望中存身，并无所怕惧。
可悲的变动乃是从高处往下掉；
坏到了尽头却只能重回笑境。
欢迎你，进我臂抱来的空虚的大气！
你刮起了狂风吹到绝处的可怜虫，
并不少欠你分毫的恩债。——谁来了？

　　　　　　　［一老人引葛洛斯忒上。

我父亲，叫化似的给领着？——世界啊，世界！
若不是你古怪的变幻使我们恨你，
人生许不会老去。

老　　　人　　　　　　我的好主公，
我当着您和您父亲治下的佃户
已经有八十年。

葛 洛 斯 忒　走开，走你的去吧；好朋友，去呀；
你给我的安慰对我全没有好处；

Thee they may hurt.

Old Man You cannot see your way.

Gloucester I have no way, and therefore want no eyes;
I stumbled when I saw: full oft 'tis seen
Our means secure us, and our mere defects
Prove our commodities. — O dear son Edgar,
The food of thy abused father's wrath,
Might I but live to see thee in my touch,
I'd say I had eyes again!

Old Man   How now! Who's there?

Edgar [*Aside.*] O gods! Who is't can say *I am at the worst*?
I am worse than e'er I was.

Old Man   'Tis poor mad Tom.

Edgar [*Aside.*] And worse I may be yet. The worst is not
So long as we can say *This is the worst*.

Old Man Fellow, where goest?

Gloucester   Is it a beggar-man?

Old Man Madman and beggar too.

Gloucester He has some reason, else he could not beg.
I' the last night's storm I such a fellow saw,
Which made me think a man a worm. my son
Came then into my mind, and yet my mind
Was then scarce friends with him. I have heard more since.
As flies to wanton boys are we to the gods;
They kill us for their sport.

Edgar [*Aside.*]   How should this be?
Bad is the trade that must play fool to sorrow,
Angering itself and others. — Bless thee, master!

他们还许会伤害你。

老　　　人　　　　　　　　　　你瞧不见路啊。

葛 洛 斯 忒　我没有路走，所以就不用眼睛；
眼明时我却摔了跤。我们常见到
人有了长处会变成疏懒放浪，
仅仅的缺陷倒反是福利的根源。——
啊，亲爱的蔼特加，我的儿，你无端
枉遭了你这被诳的父亲的狂怒，
只要我能在生前亲手接触到你，
我便好比恢复了眼睛的一样！

老　　　人　怎么！谁在那边？

蔼　特　加　　　　　　　　[旁白]啊，天神们，
谁能说"我已经到了恶运的尽头？"
我如今比往常更要糟。

老　　　人　　　　　　　　　　这是疯汤姆。

蔼　特　加　[旁白]我也许比现在还要糟，我们能说
"这是最糟不过"时还不算最糟呢。

老　　　人　人儿，上哪儿？

葛 洛 斯 忒　　　　　　　那是个叫花的不是？

老　　　人　又是疯子，又是叫花。

葛 洛 斯 忒　他并不完全疯，不然就不能去叫花。
昨夜在风暴里我见过这么一个人，
他使我想起了一个人只是一条虫。
那时候我就记念到蔼特加我的儿，
但当时我对他还并不怎样爱惜。
随后我又听到了一些个消息。
天神们对我们好比顽童对苍蝇，
把弄死我们当作玩。

蔼　特　加　　　　　　　[旁白]怎么会这样的？
最空劳无益莫过于假扮痴骏，
在伤心人前面去调侃解闷，惹得
自己和人家都不快。——保佑你，老爷！

Gloucester   Is that the naked fellow?

Old Man   Ay, my lord.

Gloucester   Then pr'ythee get thee gone. if for my sake
Thou wilt o'ertake us, hence a mile or twain
I' the way toward Dover, do it for ancient love;
And bring some covering for this naked soul,
Which I'll entreat to lead me.

Old Man   Alack, sir, he is mad.

Gloucester   'Tis the time's plague when madmen lead the
blind.
Do as I bid thee, or rather do thy pleasure;
Above the rest, be gone.

Old Man   I'll bring him the best 'parel that I have,
Come on't what will.

                                                  [*Exit.*]

Gloucester   Sirrah naked fellow.

Edgar   Poor Tom's a-cold. [*Aside.*] I cannot daub it further.

Gloucester   Come hither, fellow.

Edgar   [*Aside.*] And yet I must. —Bless thy sweet eyes,
they bleed.

Gloucester   Know'st thou the way to Dover?

Edgar   Both stile and gate, horseway and footpath. Poor
Tom hath been scared out of his good wits. bless
thee, good man's son, from the foul fiend! Five fiends
have been in poor Tom at once; of lust, as Obidicut;
Hobbididence, prince of dumbness; Mahu, of steal-
ing; Modo, of murder; Flibbertigibbet, of mopping
and mowing, — who since possesses chambermaids
and waiting women. So, bless thee, master!

Gloucester   Here, take this purse, thou whom the
heavens' plagues
Have humbled to all strokes: that I am wretched
Makes thee the happier. heavens, deal so still!
Let the superfluous and lust-dieted man,
That slaves your ordinance, that will not see

葛洛斯忒	他就是那赤裸的人吗？
老　　人	是的，主公。
葛洛斯忒	那么，请你就去吧。若为了多年 难舍的旧情你对我还有所顾念， 请在去多浮的路上赶我们一二哩； 带几件衣衫给这个赤身人掩体， 我要叫他领着路。
老　　人	哎呀，主公。 他是疯的啊。
葛洛斯忒	疯人领着瞎子走 乃是这年头的灾殃。听从我的话， 或随你去自便，但千万离了我去你的。
老　　人	我会拿给他我所有的最好的衣裳， 不管结果怎么样。　　　　　　　〔下。
葛洛斯忒	喂，光身的。
蔼特加	苦汤姆好冷吓。——〔旁白〕我不能再假装下去了。
葛洛斯忒	这里来，人儿，
蔼特加	〔旁白〕可是我不能不假装。—— 保佑你这可怜的眼睛，它们淌着血。
葛洛斯忒	你认识去多浮的路吗？
蔼特加	阶梯和城门，马路和走道，我全都认识。苦汤姆给人 吓掉了巧。好人的儿子，天保佑你不碰到恶鬼！苦 汤姆肚里一起来了五个鬼魔啦；淫欲魔奥被狄克脱； 噤口魔好拍当势；偷窃魔马虎；凶杀魔模涂；还有鬼 脸尖嘴魔忽烈剖铁及白脱；他后来又到手了不少的 小丫头和老妈子。因此上，天保佑你吧，老爷！
葛洛斯忒	拿去，收下这钱包，天降的灾殃 已使你对任何不幸都低头忍受； 我如遭了难正好给你些温存。 天神们，请永远这般安排！快让 富足有余和饕餮无厌者感受到 你们的灵威，他们藐视着神规，

Because he does not feel, feel your power quickly;
So distribution should undo excess
And each man have enough. Dost thou know Dover?

Edgar   Ay, master.

Gloucester   There is a cliff, whose high and bending head
Looks fearfully in the confined deep;
Bring me but to the very brim of it,
And I'll repair the misery thou dost bear
With something rich about me; from that place
I shall no leading need.

Edgar   Give me thy arm;
Poor Tom shall lead thee.

[*Exeunt.*]

SCENE II. *Before the* Duke *of* Albany's *Palace.*

[*Enter* Goneril *and* Edmund.]

Goneril   Welcome, my lord: I marvel our mild husband
Not met us on the way. —[*Enter* Oswald.] Now, where's
   your master?

Oswald   Madam, within; but never man so chang'd.
I told him of the army that was landed;
He smil'd at it. I told him you were coming;
His answer was, *The worse*; Of Gloucester's treachery
And of the loyal service of his son
When I inform'd him, then he call'd me sot,
And told me I had turn'd the wrong side out.
What most he should dislike seems pleasant to him;
What like, offensive.

Goneril   [*To* Edmund.] Then shall you go no further.
It is the cowish terror of his spirit,
That dares not undertake: he'll not feel wrongs,
Which tie him to an answer. Our wishes on the way

有眼不肯见，为的是全无感觉；
然后均衡的散播才夷平了过量，
人人能有个足数。你认识多浮吗？

蔼　特　加　认识的，老爷。

葛洛斯忒　那里有一座悬崖，高高低着头
俯视那有边沿的海面，真叫人骇怕；
你只用领我到那悬崖的尽头边上，
我自会把我身边的一点儿财宝
补偿你一身的穷苦；从那里起始
我就不用你领路。

蔼　特　加　　　　　　　　让我挽着你的手；
苦汤姆来带你去。　　　　　　　　［同下。

第　二　景

［亚尔白尼公爵府前。］
［刚瑠烈与蔼特孟上。

刚　瑠　烈　欢迎你，伯爵；我们那心软的夫君
我诧异为何不到路上来迎接。——［奥士伐上。］主
公呢？

奥　士　伐　在里边，夫人；无人像他那样地大变。
我对他告禀那上岸来的军队，他只笑。
我告他你正在回家，他说"才坏事"；
我提起葛洛斯忒和敌国私通，
又禀报他儿子怎样效忠勤主，
他叫我蠢才，又说我把正事说成倒。
依理不爱听的话他都像高兴听，
爱听的倒反要招怪。

刚　瑠　烈　　　　　　［对蔼特孟］那你就回步吧。
这都是他胆懦心惊之故，因而
不敢有施为；非还报不可的欺凌
他不愿去理会。我们在路上的愿望

May prove effects. Back, Edmund, to my brother;
Hasten his musters and conduct his powers.
I must change arms at home, and give the distaff
Into my husband's hands. This trusty servant
Shall pass between us; ere long you are like to hear,
If you dare venture in your own behalf,
A mistress's command. Wear this; spare speech;

> [*Giving a favour.*]

Decline your head. this kiss, if it durst speak,
Would stretch thy spirits up into the air.
Conceive, and fare thee well.

Edmund Yours in the ranks of death!

> [*Exit* Edmund.]

Goneril   My most dear Gloucester.
O, the difference of man and man!
To thee a woman's services are due.
My fool usurps my body.

Oswald   Madam, here comes my lord.

> [*Exit.*]

> [*Enter* Albany.]

Goneril I have been worth the whistle.

Albany   O Goneril!
You are not worth the dust which the rude wind
Blows in your face. I fear your disposition;
That nature which contemns it origin
Cannot be bordered certain in itself;
She that herself will sliver and disbranch
From her material sap, perforce must wither
And come to deadly use.

Goneril No more; the text is foolish.

Albany Wisdom and goodness to the vile seem vile;
Filths savour but themselves. What have you done?
Tigers, not daughters, what have you perform'd?
A father, and a gracious aged man,
Whose reverence even the head-lugg'd bear would lick,

　　　　也许会成事。蔼特孟，回到我妹夫前；
　　　　催促他的征募，你领着他的队伍。
　　　　我得在家中交换了他与我的武器，
　　　　把我的纺线杆递到他手里去掌管。
　　　　这可靠的仆人将在你我间来往；
　　　　你若敢为你自身去冒险，不久
　　　　也许会接到一位女将军的命令。
　　　　戴上了这个；不用说；低下头来。
　　　　这一吻，它若能言语，会使你的精神
　　　　高升到天上。听懂了我这话，再见。

蔼　特　孟　我誓死相报。

刚　瑠　烈　　　　　我至爱的葛洛斯忒！　　　〔蔼特孟下。
　　　　啊，人和人竟有这许多相差！
　　　　一个女人侍奉你才是该当。
　　　　那傻瓜不应将我的身体来霸占。

奥　士　伐　夫人，主公来了。　　　　　　　　　　〔下。
　　　　　　　　　　〔亚尔白尼上。

刚　瑠　烈　往常我还值得你吹一声哨子呢。

亚尔白尼　啊，刚瑠烈！你不值那疾风吹到你
　　　　脸上的尘沙。我为你的气质担忧；
　　　　鄙薄自己源流的天性就在它
　　　　自己的范畴里也万难保持不溃；
　　　　那枝桠脱离了供给它营养的树液，
　　　　准会枯槁而死，被采伐作柴薪。

刚　瑠　烈　不用多说了；你引的根本是蠢话。

亚尔白尼　智慧和善良在坏人眼里就变坏；
　　　　肮脏的只爱他们自己的癖好。
　　　　你们干的是什么？你们是猛虎，
　　　　不是女儿，你们做了些什么事？
　　　　他是你们的父亲，一位德性
　　　　洵良神灵庇护的老年人，就使
　　　　缆着头的一只熊也会对他致敬，

Most barbarous, most degenerate, have you madded.
Could my good brother suffer you to do it?
A man, a prince, by him so benefited!
If that the heavens do not their visible spirits
Send quickly down to tame these vile offences,
It will come,
Humanity must perforce prey on itself,
Like monsters of the deep.

Goneril   Milk-liver'd man!
That bear'st a cheek for blows, a head for wrongs;
Who hast not in thy brows an eye discerning
Thine honour from thy suffering; that not know'st
Fools do those villains pity who are punish'd
Ere they have done their mischief. Where's thy drum?
France spreads his banners in our noiseless land,
With plumed helm thy slayer begins threats,
Whiles thou, a moral fool, sitt'st still, and criest
Alack, why does he so?

Albany   See thyself, devil!
Proper deformity seems not in the fiend
So horrid as in woman.

Goneril   O vain fool!

Albany   Thou changed and self-cover'd thing, for shame,
Be-monster not thy feature. Were't my fitness
To let these hands obey my blood,
They are apt enough to dislocate and tear
Thy flesh and bones. howe'er thou art a fiend,
A woman's shape doth shield thee.

Goneril   Marry, your manhood now —

真残暴，真败类辱种！竟逼得他发狂。
我那位好襟弟可能让你们那样吗？
一个须眉的男子，一位受了他
不少恩惠的公侯！如果天神们
还不派遣他们的有形的神使
快来这下界惩创这顽凶极恶，
就会有一天，
人类准得要自相去残食强吞，
像海里的怪兽。

刚　瑙　烈　　　　　　　　獐肝鼠胆的男儿！
你有这脸皮专为捱人的拳打，
生就这脑袋乃为供人来凌虐；
你没有眼睛能判别受苦与荣遇，
你不知只有蠢人才会去怜恤
那未曾作恶先自受罚的恶徒们。
你的战鼓在哪里？法兰西在我们
声息全无的境内已展开了旗纛，
他戴着佩羽的战盔已开始威胁
你这份邦家，你这讲道的傻瓜
却坐着只高叫"啊呀，为什么他这样？"

亚尔白尼　魔鬼，去望望你自己！失形的怪相
只合魔鬼有，却不如呈现在女人
身上时可怕。

刚　瑙　烈　　　　　　　　啊，发呆的蠢才！

亚尔白尼　你这矫形藏丑的东西，羞死你，
别把你妖魔的本态毕露在脸上。
若使顺着血性去行事能无伤
我的身份，我准叫你全身骨架
脱尽榫，撕得你肌肤片片地飞。
可恨你虽是个恶魔，你这女身
却保了你的命。

刚　瑙　烈　　　　　　　算了，好一个大丈夫——

[Enter a Messenger. *]*

Albany   What news?

Messenger   O, my good lord, the Duke of Cornwall's dead,
Slain by his servant, going to put out
The other eye of Gloucester.

Albany   Gloucester's eyes!

Messenger   A servant that he bred, thrill'd with remorse,
Oppos'd against the act, bending his sword
To his great master; who, thereat enrag'd,
Flew on him, and amongst them fell'd him dead,
But not without that harmful stroke which since
Hath pluck'd him after.

Albany   This shows you are above,
You justicers, that these our nether crimes
So speedily can venge. — But, O poor Gloucester!
Lost he his other eye?

Messenger   Both, both, my lord. —
This letter, madam, craves a speedy answer;
'Tis from your sister.

Goneril   *[Aside.]*   One way I like this well;
But being widow, and my Gloucester with her,
May all the building in my fancy pluck
Upon my hateful life: another way,
The news is not so tart. — I'll read, and answer.

[Exit.]

Albany   Where was his son when they did take his eyes?

Messenger   Come with my lady hither.

Albany   He is not here.

Messenger   No, my good lord; I met him back again.

Albany   Knows he the wickedness?

Messenger   Ay, my good lord; 'Twas he inform'd against
   him,
And quit the house on purpose, that their punishment

         ［一信使上。

亚 尔 白 尼　有什么消息？

信　　　使　啊，大人，康华公爵过世了。
　　　　　　他正要弄瞎葛洛斯忒的第二只
　　　　　　眼睛时，被他自己的仆人所杀死。

亚 尔 白 尼　葛洛斯忒的眼睛！

信　　　使　　　　　　　　有一名他自己
　　　　　　所养大的家人，为哀怜所驱使，拔剑
　　　　　　对他的家主反抗他那番行动；
　　　　　　他怒从心起，便迎头将他击毙，
　　　　　　但自己也中了重伤的一击，随后
　　　　　　便因此丧生。

亚 尔 白 尼　　　　　　　这显得你们在上边，
　　　　　　公正的天神们，顷刻间能对我们
　　　　　　这下界的罪恶惩创得丝毫无爽。——
　　　　　　可是，啊，可怜的葛洛斯忒，他那
　　　　　　第二只眼睛也瞎了吗？

信　　　使　　　　　　　　全瞎了，大人。——
　　　　　　这封信，夫人，求您马上给回音，
　　　　　　这是二公主的。

刚 　瑙　烈　　　　　　［旁白］一方面我很高兴；
　　　　　　但成了寡妇，我那个又跟她在一起，
　　　　　　我想望中的全盘策划也许会倒下来，
　　　　　　要了我这条老命。那方面着想，
　　　　　　这消息可不坏。——我看了就写回信。　　　　［下。

亚 尔 白 尼　他们弄瞎他的时候他儿子在哪里？

信　　　使　跟夫人同来到这里的。

亚 尔 白 尼　　　　　　　　　他不在这里。

信　　　使　不错，大人；我路上碰见他回去。

亚 尔 白 尼　他知道了那行凶没有？

信　　　使　哎，大人；那是他告发了他的，
　　　　　　又故意离开了堡邸，好让他们

Might have the freer course.

Albany   Gloucester, I live
To thank thee for the love thou show'dst the king,
And to revenge thine eyes. —Come hither, friend;
Tell me what more thou know'st.

                                       [*Exeunt.*]

SCENE III. *The* French *camp near* Dover.

[*Enter* Kent *and a* Gentleman.]

Kent   Why the king of France is so suddenly gone back
      know you the reason?

Gent   Something he left imperfect in the state, which
      since his coming forth is thought of, which imports to
      the kingdom so much fear and danger that his person-
      al return was most required and necessary.

Kent   Who hath he left behind him general?

Gent   The Mareschal of France, Monsieur La Far.

Kent   Did your letters pierce the queen to any demonstra-
      tion of grief?

Gent   Ay, sir; she took them, read them in my presence,
And now and then an ample tear trill'd down
Her delicate cheek. it seem'd she was a queen
Over her passion; who, most rebel-like
Sought to be king o'er her.

Kent   O, then it mov'd her.

Gent   Not to a rage; patience and sorrow strove
Who should express her goodliest. You have seen
Sunshine and rain at once; her smiles and tears
Were like, a better day: those happy smilets
That play'd on her ripe lip seem'd not to know
What guests were in her eyes; which parted thence
As pearls from diamonds dropp'd. —In brief, sorrow

放开手去用刑罚。

亚尔白尼　　　　　　　　葛洛斯忒，

这辈子我总要谢你对国王的爱顾，

又替你那眼睛报仇。——这里来,朋友；

你还知道些什么也都告了我。　　　　　〔同下。

第　三　景

〔近多浮城之法兰西军营。〕

〔铿德与一近侍上。

铿　　德　法兰西国王忽然回去,你知道为什么缘故吗？

近　　侍　有一点事没有办妥,他出来过后才想起来,那可叫王
　　　　　国里担惊冒险得甚么似的,非他回去不成。

铿　　德　他留谁在这里当统帅？

近　　侍　法兰西的大元帅赖发将军。

铿　　德　你那封信可打动了王后,引得她有什么伤心的表
　　　　　示吗？

近　　侍　有的,阁下；她接下,当着我看了信,

不时有大点大点的眼泪滴下她

娇柔的脸颊。她好像是一位统制

那悲伤的女王,不过悲伤真倔强,

想当那驾驭她的君王。

铿　　德　　　　　　　　　　　　啊,她感动了。

近　　侍　可未曾动怒,镇静和悲伤争着要

表现她最高的德性。你见过阳光里

下雨吧；她一边微笑一边掉着泪,

要比单零的悲喜或忿怒透露着

更高超的德性；轻盈的浅笑游戏在

她红透的唇边,像茫然不晓她眼中

有何宾客在；那泪珠往下坠便比如

珍珠的坠子脱落了钻石穿的链。

总之,悲伤会变成最可爱的奇珍,

Would be a rarity most belov'd, if all
Could so become it.

Kent   Made she no verbal question?

Gent   Faith, once or twice she heav'd the name of *father*
Pantingly forth, as if it press'd her heart;
Cried *Sisters*! *sisters*! — *Shame of ladies*! *sisters*!
Kent! *father*! *sisters*! *What, i' the storm*? *i' the night*?
Let pity not be believ'd! — There she shook
The holy water from her heavenly eyes,
And clamour moisten'd: then away she started
To deal with grief alone.

Kent   It is the stars,
The stars above us, govern our conditions;
Else one self mate and mate could not beget
Such different issues. You spoke not with her since?

Gent   No.

Kent   Was this before the king return'd?

Gent   No, since.

Kent   Well, sir, the poor distressed Lear's i' the town;
Who sometime, in his better tune, remembers
What we are come about, and by no means
Will yield to see his daughter.

Gent   Why, good sir?

Kent   A sovereign shame so elbows him; his own unkind-
     ness,
That stripp'd her from his benediction, turn'd her
To foreign casualties, gave her dear rights
To his dog-hearted daughters; these things sting
His mind so venomously that burning shame
Detains him from Cordelia.

Gent   Alack, poor gentleman!

如果悲伤能使大家都像她
那样美妙。

铿　　德　　　　　　她没有对你说话吗？

近　　侍　　不错，她频频喘息里呼出一两声
　　　　　　"父亲"来，像是心中不禁那促迫；
　　　　　　她叫道"姐姐们！姐姐们！羞死当贵妇
　　　　　　当姐姐的人！铿德！父亲！姐姐们！
　　　　　　什么，在风雨中间？在夜晚？别让人
　　　　　　相信这世上还有哀怜存在！"
　　　　　　那妙绝的双睛早已被悲啼所潮润，
　　　　　　到这里她便倾注出一汪清泪；
　　　　　　随即走开去独自对付忧愁。

铿　　德　　这是星宿们，我们顶上的星宿们，
　　　　　　主宰着我们的情性；否则父母
　　　　　　全相同，不能生这般相差的儿女。
　　　　　　自后你没有跟她说过话？

近　　侍　　　　　　　　　　　　没有。

铿　　德　　这是在国王回去以前吗？

近　　侍　　　　　　　　　　不，在以后。

铿　　德　　好吧，阁下，这可怜遭难的李尔王
　　　　　　如今在城里；他偶然神志清明时
　　　　　　还记得我们是为什么来，可不肯
　　　　　　见他的女儿。

近　　侍　　　　　　为什么，动问老兄？

铿　　德　　一腔无上的惭愧挡着他；他自己
　　　　　　不存慈爱，对她已斫尽了亲恩，
　　　　　　使她去逆受异邦的风云变幻，
　　　　　　把她的名份反给了那两个狼心
　　　　　　狗肺的女儿，这种种刺得他入骨
　　　　　　伤心，如焚的羞惭使他不肯去
　　　　　　面见考黛莲。

近　　侍　　　　　　唉呀，可怜的老人家！

Kent Of Albany's and Cornwall's powers you heard not?

Gent 'Tis so; they are a-foot.

Kent Well, sir, I'll bring you to our master Lear,
And leave you to attend him. some dear cause
Will in concealment wrap me up awhile;
When I am known aright, you shall not grieve
Lending me this acquaintance. I pray you go
Along with me.

[Exeunt.]

SCENE IV. *The same. A Tent.*

[*Enter, with drum and colours*, Cordelia,
Physician, *and* Soldiers.]

Cordelia Alack, 'tis he. why, he was met even now
As mad as the vex'd sea; singing aloud;
Crown'd with rank fumiter and furrow weeds,
With harlocks, hemlock, nettles, cuckoo-flowers,
Darnel, and all the idle weeds that grow
In our sustaining corn. — A century send forth;
Search every acre in the high-grown field,
And bring him to our eye. [*Exit an* Officer.]
What can man's wisdom
In the restoring his bereaved sense?
He that helps him take all my outward worth.

Physician There is means, madam;
Our foster nurse of nature is repose,
The which he lacks; that to provoke in him,
Are many simples operative, whose power
Will close the eye of anguish.

Cordelia   All bless'd secrets,
All you unpublish'd virtues of the earth,

铿	德	你没有听说亚尔白尼和康华
		进兵的消息吗?
近	侍	是的,他们动员了。
铿	德	好吧,阁下,我带你看我们的主上去,
		留你在那边侍候他。为重大的原因
		我还得隐藏着一些时,等我透露出
		真名的那时候,你不愁空劳结识我
		这一场。请跟我同去吧。 〔同下。

第 四 景

〔布景同前。一帐幕内。〕
〔旗鼓前导,考黛莲、医师及众士卒上。

考 黛 莲	唉呀,是他。只刚才还有人见过他,
	癫狂得像激怒了的大海;高声歌唱着;
	又把丛生的玄胡索和田间的野草,
	所有那牛蒡,毒药芹,荨麻,假麦,
	杜鹃花,和养人的麦子里蔓芜的莠草,
	都采来编成了草冠戴在头上。——
	派一连士兵出去;去搜遍每一亩
	那麦子长得高高的田畴,找得他
	引到我们眼前来。〔一军官下。〕——人间的医药
	怎么样才能恢复他已丧的神志?
	谁若将他救治好,我身外的所有
	全给他作酬谢。
医 师	还有救方,娘娘;
	他无非欠少了安眠,那原是我们
	人身的养料,要使他堕入沉酣,
	却尽有许多灵验的药草,服用了
	便能把疾苦消弭。
考 黛 莲	这世间地上,
	凡是能赐人健康的秘草,你们

Spring with my tears! be aidant and remediate
In the good man's distress! — Seek, seek for him;
Lest his ungovern'd rage dissolve the life
That wants the means to lead it.

                [*Enter a* Messenger.]

Messenger   News, madam.
The British powers are marching hitherward.

Cordelia 'Tis known before; our preparation stands
In expectation of them. — O dear father,
It is thy business that I go about;
Therefore great France
My mourning and important tears hath pitied.
No blown ambition doth our arms incite,
But love, dear love, and our ag'd father's right;
Soon may I hear and see him!

                        [*Exeunt.*]

SCENE V. *Gloucester's Castle.*

             [*Enter* Regan *and* Oswald.]

Regan   But are my brother's powers set forth?
Oswald   Ay, madam.
Regan   Himself in person there?
Oswald   Madam, with much ado.
Your sister is the better soldier.
Regan   Lord Edmund spake not with your lord at home?
Oswald   No, madam.
Regan   What might import my sister's letter to him?
Oswald   I know not, lady.

一切效用尚未经宣明的灵药啊，
快跟我这双流的眼泪一同荣长！
请你们帮同治愈这好人的惨痛！
去寻求，去为他寻来，不然时生恐
那无从制止的狂怒，因没有理智
去引导，会断送他的命。

        ［一信使上。

信　　使	有消息，娘娘。

不列颠大军正在向此间推进。

考　黛　莲　知道了；我们准备着只等他们来。——
啊，亲爹，我此来原是为你的事；
因此法兰西大王
也不忍见我流伤心和哀求的眼泪。
我们这行军，非夸诞的野心所刺激；
乃是爱，衷心的挚爱，和老父的权益；
但愿马上听到他，看见他！　　　　　　［同下。

第　五　景

    ［葛洛斯忒之堡邸内。］
    ［雷耿与奥士伐上。

雷　　　耿　我姐的军队到底出动了没有？
奥　士　伐　出动了，夫人。
雷　　　耿　他亲自在那边指挥吗？
奥　士　伐　　　　　　　　　　夫人，可费了
好大的麻烦。你姐姐倒是位比他
更要强的军人。
雷　　　耿　蔼特孟伯爵没有到你主子家里
跟他说过话吗？
奥　士　伐　　　　　　　　　没有，夫人。
雷　　　耿　我姐姐给他的这信里可有什么事？
奥　士　伐　不知道，夫人。

Regan Faith, he is posted hence on serious matter.
It was great ignorance, Gloucester's eyes being out,
To let him live: where he arrives he moves
All hearts against us; Edmund, I think, is gone,
In pity of his misery, to despatch
His nighted life; moreover, to descry
The strength o' the enemy.

Oswald I must needs after him, madam, with my letter.

Regan Our troops set forth to-morrow; stay with us.
The ways are dangerous.

Oswald   I may not, madam:
My lady charg'd my duty in this business.

Regan Why should she write to Edmund? Might not you
Transport her purposes by word? Belike,
Something, — I know not what. I'll love thee much—
Let me unseal the letter.

Oswald   Madam, I had rather, —

Regan I know your lady does not love her husband;
I am sure of that: and at her late being here
She gave strange eyeliads and most speaking looks
To noble Edmund. I know you are of her bosom.

Oswald I, madam?

Regan I speak in understanding; you are, I know't.
Therefore I do advise you, take this note:
My lord is dead; Edmund and I have talk'd;
And more convenient is he for my hand
Than for your lady's; You may gather more.
If you do find him, pray you give him this;
And when your mistress hears thus much from you,
I pray desire her call her wisdom to her
So, fare you well.
If you do chance to hear of that blind traitor,
Preferment falls on him that cuts him off.

| 雷 | 耿 | 说实话,他赶忙离了这里有要事去。 |

雷　　　耿　说实话,他赶忙离了这里有要事去。
　　　　　　最糊涂莫过于葛洛斯忒瞎了眼
　　　　　　还容他活下去;他足迹所至离尽了
　　　　　　我们的人心;蔼特孟我想是去,
　　　　　　为可怜他受罪,去了结他永夜的余生;
　　　　　　另外也为去探视敌方的实力。
奥　士　伐　我定得赶上他,夫人,送他这封信。
雷　　　耿　我们的军队明天就开拔;你且
　　　　　　待在这里吧。路上很危险。
奥　士　伐　　　　　　　　　　　　　　我不能,
　　　　　　夫人。主妇责我办妥这事情。
雷　　　耿　为什么她得写信给蔼特孟? 你不能
　　　　　　替她传话不成? 看来是,有些事,——
　　　　　　我不知是什么。我会对你很好的,——
　　　　　　让我打开信看看。
奥　士　伐　　　　　　　　　　　夫人,我还是不——
雷　　　耿　我知道你主妇并不爱她的丈夫;
　　　　　　我深信她不爱;上回在这里她对
　　　　　　蔼特孟贵爵一叠连的秋波脉脉,
　　　　　　媚眼传言。我知道你是她心腹。
奥　士　伐　我,夫人?
雷　　　耿　我晓得所以说;你是她心腹;我知道。
　　　　　　所以让我告诉你,听我这句话:
　　　　　　我丈夫已然去世;蔼特孟和我
　　　　　　已有过商量;要嫁他我比你主妇
　　　　　　更加方便些;其余的任你去推想。
　　　　　　你若见到他,请你把这个交给他;
　　　　　　你主妇从你口里听到了如许时,
　　　　　　务必要请她识趣些,别痴心妄想。
　　　　　　好吧,再会。
　　　　　　要是你凑巧听到那瞎眼的逆贼时,
　　　　　　谁将他结果了,幸运便落在谁身上。

Oswald   Would I could meet him, madam! I should show
What party I do follow.
Regan   Fare thee well.

[*Exeunt.*]

SCENE VI. *Fields near* Dover.

[*Enter* Gloucester, *and* Edgar *dressed like a peasant.*]
Gloucester   When shall I come to the top of that same hill?
Edgar   You do climb up it now. look, how we labour.
Gloucester   Methinks the ground is even.
Edgar   Horrible steep.
Hark, do you hear the sea?
Gloucester   No, truly.
Edgar   Why, then, your other senses grow imperfect
By your eyes' anguish.
Gloucester   So may it be indeed;
Methinks thy voice is alter'd; and thou speak'st
In better phrase and matter than thou didst.
Edgar   You are much deceiv'd. in nothing am I chang'd
But in my garments.
Gloucester   Methinks you're better spoken.
Edgar   Come on, sir; here's the place. stand still. How
      fearful
And dizzy 'tis to cast one's eyes so low!
The crows and choughs that wing the midway air
Show scarce so gross as beetles. half way down
Hangs one that gathers samphire, dreadful trade!
Methinks he seems no bigger than his head.
The fishermen that walk upon the beach
Appear like mice; and yond tall anchoring bark,
Diminish'd to her cock; her cock a buoy
Almost too small for sight. the murmuring surge

奥 士 伐	但愿我能碰到他,夫人! 那时候 我自会表示我跟那方面走。
雷 耿	再会吧。　　　〔同下。

第 六 景

〔多浮城附近之田亩间。〕

〔蔼特加衣农夫服,导葛洛斯忒上。

葛 洛 斯 忒	我什么时候会到那山岩顶上?
蔼 特 加	你现在正在往上爬。瞧我们多辛苦。
葛 洛 斯 忒	我觉得地上是平的。
蔼 特 加	陡得可怕。 你听,可听见那海?
葛 洛 斯 忒	真的没有。
蔼 特 加	你别的官能,为了你眼睛的惨痛 也都变得不灵了。
葛 洛 斯 忒	也许真是的; 我觉得你口音改了,便是说话时 措辞和用意也比先前都好些。
蔼 特 加	你完全听错了。只除了我穿的衣服, 我毫无更改。
葛 洛 斯 忒	我觉得你说话好了些。
雷 特 加	来吧,老爷,这里就是了。站定着。 这么样低头下望真可怕得晕人! 老鸹和乌鸦展翅在下方的半空中 还不如甲虫一般大。采海茴香的人 空悬在崖半的中途,好惊心的行业! 我觉得他全身大小只及到他的头。 渔夫们行走在滩头像鼹鼠在匍匐; 那边抛着锚的那三桅的高舟缩成了 它尾后的小艇,那小艇成了个小得 几乎看不见的浮标。吟哦的海浪

That on the unnumber'd idle pebble chafes
Cannot be heard so high. — I'll look no more,
Lest my brain turn, and the deficient sight
Topple down headlong.

Gloucester　　　　　　Set me where you stand.

Edgar　Give me your hand. you are now within a foot
Of th' extreme verge. for all beneath the moon
Would I not leap upright.

Gloucester　　　　　　Let go my hand.
Here, friend, 's another purse; in it a jewel
Well worth a poor man's taking. fairies and gods
Prosper it with thee! Go thou further off;
Bid me farewell, and let me hear thee going.

Edgar　Now fare ye well, good sir.

　　　　　　　　　　　　　[*Seems to go.*]

Gloucester　　　　　　　　With all my heart.

Edgar　[*Aside.*] Why I do trifle thus with his despair
Is done to cure it.

Gloucester　[*Kneeling*]O you mighty gods!
This world I do renounce, and, in your sights,
Shake patiently my great affliction off;
If I could bear it longer, and not fall
To quarrel with your great opposeless wills,
My snuff and loathed part of nature should
Burn itself out. If Edgar live, O, bless him! —
Now, fellow, fare thee well.

Edgar　　　　　　　　Gone, sir; farewell. —

　　　　　　[Gloucester *leaps, and falls along.*]

[*Aside.*]And yet I know not how conceit may rob
The treasury of life when life itself
Yields to the theft. had he been where he thought,
By this had thought been past. — Alive or dead?
Ho you, sir! friend! Hear you, sir? — speak! —

在无数空劳的乱石间逞狂使暴，
但在这巉岩的高处却不能闻见。
我不想再望了，不然怕眼花头昏，
一失足会翻身滚落这万仞的危崖。

葛洛斯忒 让我站在你那里。

蔼 特 加 　　　　　　　把手伸给我。
现在你跟那边沿只相距一呎。
什么都可以，我可不愿往上跳。

葛洛斯忒 你放手。这里，朋友，还有个钱包；
这包里一颗宝石很值得穷苦人
到手。但愿神仙和天神们使你
得了它亨通顺遂！你走远一点；
跟我说过了再会，让我听你走。

蔼 特 加 再会了，善心的老爷。

葛洛斯忒 　　　　　　　我一心祝你好。

蔼 特 加 [旁白]我把他的绝望儿戏到如此，都为要
把它治好。

葛洛斯忒 　　[下跪]威力无边的天神们！
我要长辞这尘世，在你们眼前，
镇定着神魂，抖掉我这场奇祸；
我若能忍受得长久些，不跟你们那
不可抗的意志冲撞，这可恶的风烛
余生也总有那么一天会燃尽。
蔼特加若还活着，啊，祝福他！——
好吧，人儿，祝你好。

蔼 特 加 　　　　　　　我去了，老爷；再见。

　　　　　　　　　　　[葛洛斯忒仆地。]

[旁白]但生命既自愿被盗，我不知想象
会不会顺手把它那宝藏盗走。
他若去到了他想去的岩边，这下子
便会使得他永远不能去再想。
还活着没有？——喂！先生！朋友！

[*Aside.*] Thus might he pass indeed; yet he revives. —
What are you, sir?

Gloucester   Away, and let me die.

Edgar   Hadst thou been aught but gossamer, feathers, air,
So many fathom down precipitating,
Thou'dst shiver'd like an egg: but thou dost breathe;
Hast heavy substance; bleed'st not; speak'st; art sound.
Ten masts at each make not the altitude
Which thou hast perpendicularly fell;
Thy life is a miracle. — Speak yet again.

Gloucester   But have I fall'n, or no?

Edgar   From the dread summit of this chalky bourn!
Look up a-height; — the shrill-gorg'd lark so far
Cannot be seen or heard; do but look up.

Gloucester   Alack, I have no eyes. —
Is wretchedness depriv'd that benefit,
To end itself by death? 'Twas yet some comfort,
When misery could beguile the tyrant's rage
And frustrate his proud will.

Edgar   Give me your arm:
Up; so. How is't? Feel you your legs? You stand.

Gloucester   Too well, too well.

Edgar   This is above all strangeness.
Upon the crown o' the cliff, what thing was that
Which parted from you?

Gloucester   A poor unfortunate beggar.

Edgar   As I stood here below, methought his eyes
Were two full moons; he had a thousand noses,
Horns whelk'd and wav'd like the enridged sea.

听着,先生! 说话啊! ——[旁白]也许他果真
这么样死了;但还能苏醒过来。——
你是什么人,先生?

葛 洛 斯 忒　　　　　　　　　　走开,让我死。

蔼　特　加　只除非是空中的游丝,羽毛,或空气,
这么一呀又一呀地从高而降,
你怎样也得鸡卵般碎成万片;
可是你还能呼吸;有重量,有东西;
不流血,还会说话;又安全无恙。
首尾相衔接的十柱船桅,还不抵
你从高直掉下地来的这样高远;
你还活着真是个奇迹。再说句话。

葛 洛 斯 忒　但是我当真摔了没有?

蔼　特　加　从这可怕的白垩岩的边山绝顶上
掉下来! 向上望;那高歌的云雀远到
连这里不见又不闻;你只要向上望。

葛 洛 斯 忒　唉呀,我没有眼睛。
人到了悲惨的绝境时,难道用自尽
来解脱那悲惨的权利也不让享有?
但悲惨若能骗住了暴君的暴怒,
阻挠他骄强的意志,那倒也未始
不是慰人之处。

蔼　特　加　　　　　　　　　　把手臂伸给我。
起来;对了。怎么样? 还觉得你的腿?
倒还站得住。

葛 洛 斯 忒　　　　　　　站得太稳了,太稳了。

蔼　特　加　这事情实在太奇了。在山岩顶上
才跟你分手的是个什么东西?

葛 洛 斯 忒　那是一个穷苦不幸的乞丐。

蔼　特　加　我站在这下边,只见他双目炯炯,
像两轮满月;他有一千个鼻子,
头顶上高隆的觭角凹凸交错,

It was some fiend; therefore, thou happy father,
Think that the clearest gods, who make them honours
Of men's impossibility, have preserv'd thee.

Gloucester I do remember now. henceforth I'll bear
Affliction till it do cry out itself,
Enough, *enough*, and die. That thing you speak of,
I took it for a man; often 'twould say,
The fiend, *the fiend*; he led me to that place.

Edgar Bear free and patient thoughts. — But who comes
here?

[*Enter* Lear, *fantastically dressed up with flowers.*]
The safer sense will ne'er accommodate
His master thus.

Lear No, they cannot touch me for coining; I am the king
himself.

Edgar O thou side-piercing sight!

Lear Nature 's above art in that respect. — There's your
press money. That fellow handles his bow like a
crow-keeper. draw me a clothier's yard. — Look,
look, a mouse! Peace, peace; — this piece of toasted
cheese will do't. There's my gauntlet; I'll prove it on
a giant. — Bring up the brown bills. O, well flown,
bird! — i' the clout, i' the clout! hewgh! — Give the
word.

Edgar Sweet marjoram.

Lear Pass.

Gloucester I know that voice.

Lear Ha! Goneril with a white beard! — They flattered
me like a dog; and told me I had white hairs in my
beard ere the black ones were there. To say *ay* and *no*
to everything I said! — *Ay* and *no*, too, was no good
divinity. When the rain came to wet me once, and the
wind to make me chatter; when the thunder would
not peace at my bidding; there I found 'em, there I

好比是生峰的海面。那是个恶魔；
因此，你这位受神明护佑的老丈，
怀念着那班清明无比的神灵吧，
他们的光荣乃在把凡人无力
做到的做到，你全靠他们搭救。

葛洛斯忒 我现在记得了。我从此要忍受奇惨，
直到它自己叫"够了，够了"，然后死。
你说起的那东西，我当作人；它常说
"恶鬼，恶鬼"；它领我爬上那岩巅。

蔼 特 加 你得心神镇定些，自在些。——谁来了？

　　　　　　　　[李尔上，身上乱插野花。

神志清明的决不会这般装束。

李　　尔 不，他们不能碰我，说我私铸钱币。我自己就是
国王。

蔼 特 加 啊，这模样好不刺人的心肺！

李　　尔 在那件事情上造化可胜过了人为。——这是你们的
恩饷。——那家伙弯弓的模样活像个赶老鸹的草
人。——跟我放一支码箭出去。——瞧，瞧，一只小
耗子！别做声，别做声；这一块烤奶酪就行了。——
那是我的铁手套；待我用它来向一个巨人挑
战。——将长戟队带上前来。——啊，飞得好，鸟
儿！恰在靶眼上，恰在靶眼上！Hewgh！——叫
口令。

蔼 特 加 香薄荷。

李　　尔 过去。

葛洛斯忒 那声音我认得出来。

李　　尔 吓！刚瑙烈，——有一把白胡子！——以前他们狗
似的奉承我，告我说，我还没有黑胡子就跟长了白
胡子的一般通达事理。他们口口声声应答我"是"
和"不是"！那样的应答可也不是敬神之道。有一
回大雨湿透了我，风刮得我牙齿打磕；我叫停住了
打雷，雷声可不听我的话；那回子我就把他们看穿

smelt 'em out. Go to, they are not men o' their
words; they told me I was everything; 'tis a lie—I am
not ague-proof.

Gloucester   The trick of that voice I do well remember.
Is't not the king?

Lear   Ay, every inch a king:
When I do stare, see how the subject quakes.
I pardon that man's life. —What was thy cause? —
Adultery? —
Thou shalt not die; die for adultery? No;
The wren goes to't, and the small gilded fly
Does lecher in my sight.
Let copulation thrive; for Gloucester's bastard son
Was kinder to his father than my daughters
Got 'tween the lawful sheets.
To't, luxury, pell-mell! for I lack soldiers. —
Behold yond simpering dame,
Whose face between her forks presages snow,
That minces virtue, and does shake the head
To hear of pleasure's name, —
The fitchew nor the soiled horse goes to't
With a more riotous appetite.
Down from the waist they are centaurs,
Though women all above;
But to the girdle do the gods inherit,
Beneath is all the fiend's;
There's hell, there's darkness, There is the sulphurous
pit; burning, scalding, stench, consumption; fie, fie, fie!
pah, pah! Give me an ounce of civet, good apothecary, to
sweeten my imagination: there's money for thee.

Gloucester   O, let me kiss that hand!

Lear   Let me wipe it first; it smells of mortality.

了，看透了他们的本相。滚蛋，他们不是他们自称的
那种人；他们告诉我我高过一切；那是在撒谎，我还
免不掉打寒颤呢。

葛洛斯忒 那说话的音调我记得十分清楚。

可不是国王吗？

李　尔 　　　　　　　　对了，周身是国王。

我只要一瞪眼，那百姓便多么发抖。——

我饶赦了那个人的命。——你犯了什么罪？

是奸淫？

你不该死罪，为奸淫而死？用不到；

鹪鹩也在那里犯，细小的金苍蝇

就在我眼前宣淫。

让交媾尽管去盛行，葛洛斯忒的私生儿，

还比我合法的床褥间所生的女儿们，

对父亲要比较地亲爱。

去吧，淫乱，去胡干吧！因为我缺少兵。

瞧那边那装腔憨笑的婆娘，

她的脸显得她腿叉里有雪样的贞操，

她假装清贞洁白，一听见提起

寻欢作乐就摇头，——

野娼妇，或是放青的马，干起那营生来

不比她更外浪得滋味好。

从腰部以下她们简直是马怪，

虽然上身完全是女人；

到腰带为止她们归天神们所有，

下身全属于众鬼魔；

那儿是地狱，是黑暗，是硫磺的深坑，

在燃烧，在沸滚，恶臭，溃烂；嗽，嗽，嗽！呸，

呸！——给我一磅麝香；药铺里的大掌柜，把我的想

象弄香它，这儿有钱给你。

葛洛斯忒 啊，让我吻一吻那只手！

李　尔 先让我擦一下，那上面嗅得出尘凡的气息。

Gloucester   O ruin'd piece of nature! This great world
Shall so wear out to naught. — Dost thou know me?

Lear   I remember thine eyes well enough. Dost thou squiny at
me? No, do thy worst, blind Cupid; I'll not love. —
Read thou this challenge; mark but the penning of it.

Gloucester   Were all the letters suns, I could not see one.

Edgar   [*Aside.*]I would not take this from report; — it is,
And my heart breaks at it.

Lear   Read.

Gloucester   What, with the case of eyes?

Lear   O, ho, are you there with me? No eyes in your
head, nor no money in your purse? Your eyes are in a
heavy case, your purse in a light; yet you see how
this world goes.

Gloucester   I see it feelingly.

Lear   What, art mad? A man may see how the world goes
with no eyes. Look with thine ears; see how yond
justice rails upon yond simple thief. Hark, in thine
ear; change places, and, handy-dandy, which is the
justice, which is the thief? Thou hast seen a farmer's
dog bark at a beggar?

Gloucester   Ay, sir.

Lear   And the creature run from the cur? There thou mightst
behold the great image of authority; a dog's obeyed in
office. —
Thou rascal beadle, hold thy bloody hand!
Why dost thou lash that whore? Strip thine own back;
Thou hotly lust'st to use her in that kind
For which thou whipp'st her. The usurer hangs the cozener.
Through tatter'd clothes small vices do appear;
Robes and furr'd gowns hide all. Plate sin with gold,
And the strong lance of justice hurtless breaks;

葛 洛 斯 忒	啊,残毁不完的万民的楷模! 这广大的宇宙竟会这么破碎。—— 你认识我吗?
李 尔	你那双眼睛我很记得。你在瞟我不是? 不行,瞎眼 的小蔻璧,随你去捣多凶的乱;我可不会再去爱了。 你念念这封挑战书;只用仔细瞧它那笔法。
葛 洛 斯 忒	即使你字字是太阳,我也看不见。
蔼 特 加	〔旁白〕我不愿听信传闻;但果真是如此,我的心便不 免片片地在碎。
李 尔	你念。
葛 洛 斯 忒	什么,用我这眼眶念吗?
李 尔	啊哈,咱们成了一伙儿了吗? 你头上没有眼睛,钱 包里也没有钱,是不是? 你的眼睛只剩个框,你的 钱包轻得发慌;可是你还瞧得明白这世界是怎么一 回事。
葛 洛 斯 忒	我心里明白出来。
李 尔	什么,你疯了? 一个人没有眼睛也看得出这世界是 怎么回事。用你的耳朵去瞧;瞧那儿那法官对一个 笨家伙的小偷骂得多厉害。听着,听进去;换乱了 地位,混一混,你猜,哪一个是法官,哪一个是贼? 你可见过一个种地的养的狗对一个叫花的直咬吗?
葛 洛 斯 忒	见过,王上。
李 尔	那家伙可逃开那条狗? 那上面你可以瞧见那活龙活 现的所谓权力;一条狗当了权,人也得服从它—— 你这坏蛋的公差,停住了毒手! 你为什么要挥鞭毒打那娼家? 露出你自己的背来捱,热刺刺 你只想跟她干那桩好事,却又为 那事鞭打她。放印子钱的要绞死骗钱的。 大罪恶原来都在褴褛的衣衫里 显出来;重裘和宽袍掩盖着一切。 罪孽披上了金板铠,把法律的长枪

Arm it in rags, a pygmy's straw does pierce it.

None does offend, none. —I say none; I'll able 'em;

Take that of me, my friend, who have the power

To seal the accuser's lips. Get thee glass eyes,

And, like a scurvy politician, seem

To see the things thou dost not. —Now, now, now, now.

Pull off my boots; harder, harder, —so.

Edgar　[*Aside.*]O, matter and impertinency mix'd!

Reason, in madness!

Lear　If thou wilt weep my fortunes, take my eyes.

I know thee well enough; thy name is Gloucester.

Thou must be patient; we came crying hither.

Thou know'st, the first time that we smell the air,

We wawl and cry. —I will preach to thee; mark.

Gloucester　Alack, alack the day!

Lear　When we are born, we cry that we are come

To this great stage of fools. This' a good block:

It were a delicate stratagem to shoe

A troop of horse with felt. I'll put't in proof,

And when I have stol'n upon these sons-in-law,

Then kill, kill, kill, kill, kill, kill!

　　　　[*Enter a* Gentleman, *with* Attendants].

Gent　O, here he is; lay hand upon him. —Sir,

Your most dear daughter, —

Lear　No rescue? What, a prisoner? I am even

The natural fool of fortune. —Use me well;

戳断了也休想伤得它分毫；披上了
破衣片，矮房使一根柴草便穿透它。
没有人犯罪，没有人，我说，没有人；
有我来作保；信我这句话，朋友，
我自有权能去封闭告诉人的嘴。
你去装一副玻璃的眼珠，像一位
卑污的政客一般，假装看见你
不看见的东西。——好吧，好吧，好吧。
脱掉我的靴；用劲，用劲，对了。

蔼　特　加　　［旁白］清明的思路里纠缠着胡思乱想！
　　　　　　　　啊，疯癫里可又有理性！

李　　　尔　　你若要为我的命运哭泣，把我
　　　　　　　　这双眼睛拿去使。我们俩够熟的了；
　　　　　　　　你名叫葛洛斯忒。你得静下来；
　　　　　　　　我们当初都是哭着到这里来。
　　　　　　　　你知道，我们最初次嗅到这空气，
　　　　　　　　都呱呱地哭泣。我要对你传道；
　　　　　　　　你听着。

葛　洛　斯　忒　　　　　唉呀，唉呀，好惨啊！

李　　　尔　　我们初生时，我们哭的是自己
　　　　　　　　来到了这傻瓜们登场扮演的大戏台。
　　　　　　　　这是顶上好的毡帽：成队的马匹，
　　　　　　　　蹄底下都给钉上了毛毡的软底，
　　　　　　　　真是个神机妙策。我来试试看；
　　　　　　　　等我悄悄地赶上了这些女婿们，
　　　　　　　　就杀，杀，杀，杀，杀！
　　　　　　　　　　　　　　［一近侍率仆从数人上。

近　　　侍　　啊，他在这里；拉住他。——王上，
　　　　　　　　你的最亲爱的女儿——

李　　　尔　　没有人来救？什么，变成了囚犯？
　　　　　　　　我简直是生成的胚子要给命运
　　　　　　　　所提弄。好好待我吧；你们改天

You shall have ransom. Let me have surgeons;
I am cut to the brains.

Gent   You shall have anything.

Lear   No seconds? all myself?
Why, this would make a man a man of salt,
To use his eyes for garden water-pots,
Ay, and for laying Autumn's dust.

Gent   Good sir, —

Lear   I will die bravely, like a smug bridegroom. What!
I will be jovial. come, come, I am a king,
My masters, know you that?

Gent   You are a royal one, and we obey you.

Lear   Then there's life in't. Nay, an you get it, you shall
get it by running. *Sa, sa, sa, sa*!

> [*Exit running*. Attendants *follow*.]

Gent   A sight most pitiful in the meanest wretch,
Past speaking of in a king! — Thou hast one daughter,
Who redeems nature from the general curse
Which twain have brought her to.

Edgar   Hail, gentle sir.

Gent   Sir, speed you. What's your will?

Edgar   Do you hear aught, sir, of a battle toward?

Gent   Most sure and vulgar; every one hears that
Which can distinguish sound.

Edgar   But, by your favour,
How near's the other army?

Gent   Near and on speedy foot; the main descry
Stands on the hourly thought.

Edgar   I thank you, sir: that's all.

Gent   Though that the queen on special cause is here,

　　　　　　　　自会到手我这份赎身的买命钱。
　　　　　　　　跟我找几位外科医师来；我已给
　　　　　　　　切进了脑子里去。

近　　侍　　　　　　　　　　　你要什么都行。

李　　尔　　没有帮手吗？光我一个人？哦，
　　　　　　　　一个人的眼睛用作了浇花的水罐，
　　　　　　　　又用来洒落那秋风扬起的灰尘，
　　　　　　　　那人儿便会弄成一个泪人儿。

近　　侍　　大王在上，——

李　　尔　　我要死得勇敢，像一位衣裳
　　　　　　　　齐整的新郎。什么！我要很高兴。
　　　　　　　　算了，算了，我是一位国王，
　　　　　　　　我的主子们，你们知道了没有？

近　　侍　　您是位明哲的圣君，我们都奉命。

李　　尔　　那就还有一线希望。来吧，你们要抓它，可要跑得快
　　　　　　　　才抓得到。"沙，沙，沙，沙。"

　　　　　　　　　　　　　　　　　　　　　　　［急奔下，从者后随。

近　　侍　　最卑微的可怜虫降到了这般情景
　　　　　　　　也非常动人的怜悯，更何况是君王！
　　　　　　　　那两个女儿把你的身心坑进了
　　　　　　　　整个的人间地狱，多亏这一位
　　　　　　　　又把你重复济渡了回来。

蔼特加　　您好，大先生。

近　　侍　　　　　　　　　祝福你，老兄；什么事？

蔼特加　　先生，您可听说过快要打仗吗？

近　　侍　　听说之至，并且谁都知道；
　　　　　　　　只要辨得出声音的，谁都听说过。

蔼特加　　要劳驾动问，对方的军队多近了？

近　　侍　　很近了，且正在疾进，那大军快随时
　　　　　　　　都能瞭望到。

蔼特加　　　　　　　　　多谢您，先生；这就够了。

近　　侍　　虽然王后因特别的原因在这里，

Her army is mov'd on.

Edgar   I thank you, sir.

[*Exit* Gentleman.]

Gloucester   You ever-gentle gods, take my breath from me;
Let not my worser spirit tempt me again
To die before you please!

Edgar   Well pray you, father.

Gloucester   Now, good sir, what are you?

Edgar   A most poor man, made tame to fortune's blows;
Who, by the art of known and feeling sorrows,
Am pregnant to good pity. Give me your hand,
I'll lead you to some biding.

Gloucester   Hearty thanks:
The bounty and the benison of heaven
To boot, and boot!

[*Enter* Oswald.]

Oswald   A proclaim'd prize! Most happy!
That eyeless head of thine was first fram'd flesh
To raise my fortunes. — Thou old unhappy traitor,
Briefly thyself remember; — the sword is out
That must destroy thee.

Gloucester   Now let thy friendly hand
Put strength enough to it.

[Edgar *interposes.*]

Oswald   Wherefore, bold peasant,
Dar'st thou support a publish'd traitor? Hence!
Lest that the infection of his fortune take
Like hold on thee. Let go his arm.

Edgar   Chill not let go, zir, without vurther 'casion.

Oswald   Let go, slave, or thou diest!

Edgar   Good gentleman, go your gait, and let poor voke
pass. An chud ha' bin zwaggered out of my life,
'twould not ha' bin zo long as 'tis by a vortnight.
Nay, come not near the old man; keep out, che vore
ye, or ise try whether your costard or my bat be the
harder; chill be plain with you.

她的兵可开上前去了。

葛 特 加　　　　　　　　　　　劳您驾，先生。

[近侍下。

葛 洛 斯 忒　常存恻隐的天神们，停止我的呼吸；
　　　　　别让附在我身上的恶精灵，在你们
　　　　　愿我去世前，重复引诱我自尽！

葛 特 加　祷告得好，老丈。

葛 洛 斯 忒　这位仁善的君子，你是什么人？

葛 特 加　一个最可怜的人，在命运的打击下
　　　　　安身而立命；我知道而心感过悲哀，
　　　　　故此就敏于怜恤。把手伸给我，
　　　　　我领你到一所安身的地方去。

葛 洛 斯 忒　　　　　　　　　　　真感谢；
　　　　　但愿天恩和天福多多临照你。

[奥士伐上。

奥 士 伐　正是那公告悬缉的正凶！好运气！
　　　　　你那个没有眼睛的脑袋生就了
　　　　　要使我交运。——种祸生殃的老贼，
　　　　　快记起你过往的罪孽向天祈祷；
　　　　　那准要杀死你的宝剑已拔出鞘来。

葛 洛 斯 忒　让你那友好的手臂用够了力量。　　[葛特加劝阻。

奥 士 伐　好胆大的村夫，你怎敢公然扶助
　　　　　这一名广布周知的逆贼？滚开去！
　　　　　不然那大祸蔓延时，你同他会同遭
　　　　　不幸。放开他的臂膀。

葛 特 加　老先生，没有旁的缘故咱可不能放开。

奥 士 伐　放掉，奴才，不然你就得死！

葛 特 加　好先生，走您自个儿的道，让咱们苦人儿过去。咱要
　　　　　随便让人吓唬住了，就不用等到今儿，咱两礼拜以前
　　　　　就该让吓坏了。别走上这老儿身边来；走开点儿，咱
　　　　　跟您说一声吧，不然咱就来试试，您那脑瓜儿硬还是
　　　　　咱的棍儿硬；咱可不跟您客气。

Oswald Out, dunghill!   [*They fight.*]

Edgar Chill pick your teeth, zir. Come; No matter vor
   your foins.

Oswald Slave, thou hast slain me. villain, take my purse;
If ever thou wilt thrive, bury my body;
And give the letters which thou find'st about me
To Edmund Earl of Gloucester; seek him out
Upon the British party. O, untimely death!
Death!   [*Dies.*]

Edgar I know thee well; a serviceable villain,
As duteous to the vices of thy mistress
As badness would desire.

Gloucester   What, is he dead?

Edgar Sit you down, father; rest you. —
Let's see these pockets; the letters that he speaks of
May be my friends. — He's dead; I am only sorry
He had no other death's-man. Let us see.
Leave, gentle wax; and, manners, blame us not.
To know our enemies' minds, we'd rip their hearts;
Their papers is more lawful.

[*Reads.*] *Let our reciprocal vows be remembered. You
   have many opportunities to cut him off: if your will
   want not, time and place will be fruitfully of-
   fered. There is nothing done if he return the con-
   queror: then am I the prisoner, and his bed my gaol;
   from the loathed warmth whereof deliver me, and
   supply the place for your labour.*

        Your wife, so I would say affectionate servant,
                                    Goneril.

O indistinguish'd space of woman's will!
A plot upon her virtuous husband's life;
And the exchange my brother! — Here in the sands
Thee I'll rake up, the post unsanctified
Of murderous lechers: and in the mature time

奥 士 伐	滚蛋,臭东西!	[二人交剑。]
蔼 特 加	小子,咱来搂你;来;咱不怕你刺人。	
奥 士 伐	奴才,你把我刺死了。把钱包拿去;	
	你若要有一天能发迹,非得埋了我;	
	你把在我身边找到的一封信	
	去交给葛洛斯忒伯爵蔼特孟;	
	你往英吉利军中去找他。唉,	
	死得真不是时候!死!	[死去。]
蔼 特 加	我很知道你;你是个跑快腿的坏蛋,	
	对你那主妇的凶邪险恶真是	
	顺从到万分地如意。	
葛 洛 斯 忒	什么,他死了吗?	
蔼 特 加	坐下来,老丈;歇一会。——	
	我们来看他的口袋;他说起的那封信	
	也许与我有益。他死了;我只在	
	可惜没有刽子手来执法。我来看。	
	让我来打开你,封蜡;礼貌啊,别见怪。	
	要明晓仇家的主意,我们划破	
	他们的心;拆开一封信更合法。	

[读信]别忘了我们间交宣的誓约。你有许多机会斩除他;只要不缺少决心,时间和地点自会俯拾即是。他若凯旋而回,就没法办了;那时候我是个囚犯,他的床是我的监狱;所以你得从那可恶的淫热里救我出来,就替代了他,作为你那番辛勤的酬谢。

你的——但愿能说是妻——恋慕的

情人,　　　　　　　　　　刚瑙烈。

	女人的欲海啊,浩瀚得渺无边限!
	想谋害那么个德行淘良的丈夫,
	掉换品,竟是我的兄弟!——在这沙地里,
	待我来掩埋你这个奔波于淫妇
	奸夫间的奸邪的信使;等时机成熟,
	我就向那位险遭毒手的公爷,

With this ungracious paper strike the sight
Of the death-practis'd duke. for him 'tis well
That of thy death and business I can tell.
Gloucester   The king is mad. how stiff is my vile sense,
That I stand up, and have ingenious feeling
Of my huge sorrows! Better I were distract;
So should my thoughts be sever'd from my griefs,
And woes by wrong imaginations lose
The knowledge of themselves.
Edgar   Give me your hand;

                       [*A drum afar off.*]

Far off, methinks I hear the beaten drum;
Come, father, I'll bestow you with a friend.

                               [*Exeunt.*]

SCENE VII. *A Tent in the* French *Camp.*

[*Enter* Cordelia, Kent. *and* Physician.]

Cordelia   O thou good Kent, how shall I live and work
To match thy goodness? My life will be too short,
And every measure fail me.
Kent   To be acknowledg'd, madam, is o'erpaid.
All my reports go with the modest truth,
Nor more nor clipp'd, but so.
Cordelia   Be better suited;
These weeds are memories of those worser hours;
I pr'ythee, put them off.
Kent   Pardon, dear madam;
Yet to be known shortens my made intent;
My boon I make it that you know me not
Till time and I think meet.
Cordelia   Then be't so, my good lord. [*To the* Physi-
      cian.] How, does the king?
Physician   Madam, sleeps still.
Cordelia   O you kind gods,
Cure this great breach in his abused nature!
The untun'd and jarring senses, O, wind up

揭发这封可鄙的信。幸而我能
告诉他你死了,你干的又是什么事。

葛 洛 斯 忒 王上发了疯。我这份可恶的理性
却如此矫强,我还能危然兀立着,
神思清醒地深感到自己的悲怆!
我不如也错乱了精神,不再去想念
哀愁,迷惘里虽痛苦也不自知觉。

蔼 特 加 让我挽着手;我听到远方的军鼓声;[远远闻鼓声。]
来吧,老丈,我替你去找个朋友。　　　　[同下。

第 七 景

[法军中一帐幕外。]
[考黛莲、铿德、近侍及医师上。

考 黛 莲 忠良的铿德啊,怎么样我才能偿清
你那番仁善? 只愁我生命太短促,
黾勉也无用。

铿 德 蒙娘娘嘉奖已然是过分的恩酬。
我所有的陈禀都和真情相吻合,
不增添,也未经截短,不爽分毫。

考 黛 莲 请你去改穿好些的衣裳;这服装
只是那不幸时的留念;把它换了吧。

铿 德 请恕我,我敬爱的娘娘;现在就显露
真相,便和我既定的计划相妨;
我认为时机未到时,且请莫认我,
我就把这隐秘当作娘娘的恩典。

考 黛 莲 就依你的话,贤卿。——王上怎样了?

医 师 还睡着,娘娘。

考 黛 莲 啊,慈蔼的天神们,
请救治他惨遭酷虐的心头这巨创!
这位被孩儿们逼迫成疯的父亲,
啊,你们务必要丝丝理整他

Of this child-changed father!

Physician   So please your majesty
That we may wake the king? he hath slept long.

Cordelia Be govern'd by your knowledge, and proceed
I' the sway of your own will. Is he array'd?

Gent Ay, madam. In the heaviness of sleep
We put fresh garments on him.

Physician Be by, good madam, when we do awake him;
I doubt not of his temperance.

Cordelia   Very well.

Physician Please you draw near. — Louder the music
    there!

Cordelia O my dear father, Restoration hang
Thy medicine on my lips, and let this kiss
Repair those violent harms that my two sisters
Have in thy reverence made!

Kent   Kind and dear princess!

Cordelia Had you not been their father, these white flakes
Had challeng'd pity of them. Was this a face
To be oppos'd against the warring winds?
To stand against the deep dread-bolted thunder?
In the most terrible and nimble stroke
Of quick cross lightning? to watch, poor perdu!
With this thin helm? Mine enemy's dog,
Though he had bit me, should have stood that night
Against my fire; and wast thou fain, poor father,
To hovel thee with swine and rogues forlorn,
In short and musty straw? Alack, alack!
'Tis wonder that thy life and wits at once
Had not concluded all. — He wakes; speak to him.

Physician Madam, do you; 'tis fittest.

Cordelia How does my royal lord? How fares your majesty?

轧轳不成调的神志!

医　　师　　　　　　　　　　陛下要不要
我们弄醒老王上?他睡得够久了。

考　黛　莲　运用你医理上的识见,随意去办。——
他换上衣服没有?

近　　侍　　　　　　　　　换好了,娘娘;
他正在沉睡中,我们替他更了衣。

医　　师　我们弄他醒来时请娘娘在旁;
我信他举止已经安静。

考　黛　莲　　　　　　　　　　很好。

　　　　　　　　[仆从以抬椅舁李尔上。

医　　师　请您走近些。——那边的音乐响一点!

考　黛　莲　亲爱的父亲啊,让康复将起病的灵药
挂在我唇边,让我这一吻医愈了
我两位姐姐对父王横施的这暴创!

铿　　德　好一位温良亲挚的公主娘!

考　黛　莲　即使你不是她们的亲爹,这苍苍的白发
也该叫她们不忍。难道这是个
任凭交恶的狂飙去吹打的脸庞?
任它跟满载惊人霹雳的弘雷
相对峙?像一名敢死军,头戴着轻盔,
守在那最可怕的急电的飞金乱窜,
和迅雷的猛击之中?找仇人的狗,
纵然它咬了我,那晚上我也要让它
在炉前歇宿;你却是否宁愿,
可怜的父亲,跟猪豚和无归的浮浪者
去同处,在泥污和烂草之间存身?
唉呀,唉呀!奇怪的是你的生命
竟没有和灵明同时完结。——他醒了;
你跟他说话。

医　　师　　　　　　　娘娘,您说最好。

考　黛　莲　父王怎么样?陛下贵体如何?

Lear You do me wrong to take me out o' the grave;
Thou art a soul in bliss; but I am bound
Upon a wheel of fire, that mine own tears
Do scald like molten lead.

Cordelia   Sir, do you know me?

Lear You are a spirit, I know; when did you die?

Cordelia Still, still, far wide!

Physician He's scarce awake; let him alone awhile.

Lear Where have I been? Where am I?—Fair daylight?
I am mightily abus'd. I should e'en die with pity,
To see another thus. I know not what to say.
I will not swear these are my hands. let's see;
I feel this pin prick. Would I were assur'd
Of my condition!

Cordelia   O, look upon me, sir,
And hold your hands in benediction o'er me.
No, sir, you must not kneel.

Lear   Pray, do not mock me:
I am a very foolish fond old man,
Fourscore and upward, not an hour more nor less;
And, to deal plainly,
I fear I am not in my perfect mind.
Methinks I should know you, and know this man;
Yet I am doubtful; for I am mainly ignorant
What place this is, and all the skill I have
Remembers not these garments; nor I know not
Where I did lodge last night. Do not laugh at me;
For, as I am a man, I think this lady
To be my child Cordelia.

Cordelia   And so I am. I am.

Lear Be your tears wet? yes, faith. I pray, weep not:
If you have poison for me, I will drink it.

李	尔	你不该将我从墓中拖出来受罪;
		你超登了极乐;我却被绑在火轮上,
		甚至我自己的热泪也熔铅似的在烫我。
考 黛 莲		父亲,你认识我吗?
李	尔	你是个鬼魂,我知道,何时死的?
考 黛 莲		依旧,依旧,迷糊得很呢!
医	师	他还不很醒;等一会再跟他说话。
李	尔	我到了什么地方?现在在哪里?
		这么大晴天?我太给骗得懵懂了。
		我见了旁人这样,也兀自会替他
		可怜得要死。我不知要说什么话。
		我不敢赌咒这是我的手。等我看;
		我感觉到这一下针刺。但愿我能
		明知自己的处境!

考　黛　莲　　　　　　　　　　父亲啊,望着我,
　　　　请伸手放在我头上为我祝福。
　　　　别那样,父亲,切莫跪下来。

李　　　尔　　　　　　　　　　　　请你
　　　　别开我的玩笑;我是个极痴愚的老人,
　　　　年纪在八十以上,不多也不少;
　　　　要说老实话,
　　　　我怕我神志有点儿不很灵清。
　　　　想起来我该认识你,也认识这人儿;
　　　　可是我犹豫难决;因为我全不知
　　　　这是什么地方,我使尽心机
　　　　也不能记起这些衣袍,也不知
　　　　我昨夜在哪里宿歇。别把我取笑;
　　　　这事情很分明,我想这位贵夫人
　　　　是我的孩儿考黛莲。

考　黛　莲　　　　　　　　　　我确是,我确是。

李　　　尔　你在流泪吗?不错,你在哭。请别哭。
　　　　你若有毒药给我喝,我也会喝下。

I know you do not love me; for your sisters
Have, as I do remember, done me wrong;
You have some cause, they have not.

Cordelia   No cause, no cause.

Lear   Am I in France?

Kent   In your own kingdom, sir.

Lear   Do not abuse me.

Physician   Be comforted, good madam; the great rage,
You see, is kill'd in him; and yet it is danger
To make him even o'er the time he has lost.
Desire him to go in; trouble him no more
Till further settling.

Cordelia   Will't please your highness walk?

Lear   You must bear with me. Pray you now, forget and
forgive: I am old and foolish.

> [*Exeunt all but* Kent *and* Gentleman.]

Gent   Holds it true, sir, that the Duke of Cornwall was
so slain?

Kent   Most certain, sir.

Gent   Who is conductor of his people?

Kent   As 'tis said, the bastard son of Gloucester.

Gent   They say Edgar, his banished son, is with the Earl
of Kent in Germany.

Kent   Report is changeable. 'Tis time to look about; the
powers of the kingdom approach apace.

Gent   The arbitrement is like to be bloody. Fare you
well, sir.

> [*Exit.*]

Kent   My point and period will be throughly wrought,
Or well or ill, as this day's battle's fought.

> [*Exit.*]

我知道你并不爱我;因为,我记得,
你两个姐姐都把我虐待过;她们
全没有原因,你却有。

考　黛　莲　　　　　　　没有,没有。

李　　　尔　我是在法兰西吗?

铿　　　德　　　　　　在您的本国,王上。

李　　　尔　不要哄我。

医　　　师　娘娘可以安心了,失心的疯癫
已在他胸中过去;但如果要使他
把他经临的后影和前尘贯串得
丝丝入扣,那可就还很危险。
要他里边去;等他更显得安静前,
且莫再打扰他。

考　黛　莲　王上高兴离开这里吗?

李　　　尔　你可要耐着我一点才好。我如今要请你忘怀和宽
恕;我老昏了。

〔除铿德与近侍外余众尽下。

近　　　侍　真的吗,阁下,说是康华公爵让人弄死了?

铿　　　德　一点不错,阁下。

近　　　侍　现在是谁统带着他的部下?

铿　　　德　听说是葛洛斯忒的野儿子。

近　　　侍　他们说他那个给逐出的儿子蔼特加跟着铿德伯爵在
德意志呢。

铿　　　德　传闻可没有准。我们这该仔细些了;王国的军队说
话就赶到。

近　　　侍　这场决战许会大大地流血。再见了,阁下。　　〔下。

铿　　　德　我殷勤护主的愿望能不能成功,
全系在今天这场决战的胜败中。　　　　　　〔下。

ACT V.

SCENE I. The British
Camp near Dover.

[*Enter, with drum and colours,*
Edmund, Regan, Gentleman and Soldiers.]

Edmund   Know of the duke if his last purpose hold,
Or whether since he is advis'd by aught
To change the course. he's full of alteration
And self-reproving. bring his constant pleasure.
                    [*To an* Gentleman, *who goes out.*]

Regan   Our sister's man is certainly miscarried.

Edmund   Tis to be doubted, madam.

Regan   Now, sweet lord,
You know the goodness I intend upon you;
Tell me, — but truly, — but then speak the truth,
Do you not love my sister?

Edmund   In honour'd love.

Regan   But have you never found my brother's way
To the forfended place?

Edmund   That thought abuses you.

Regan   I am doubtful that you have been conjunct
And bosom'd with her, as far as we call hers.

Edmund   No, by mine honour, madam.

Regan   I never shall endure her: dear my lord,

第 五 幕

第 一 景

［近多浮城之不列颠军营。］
［旗鼓前导，蔼特孟、雷耿、数近侍及众士卒上。

蔼 特 孟　去探听公爵最后的定计与否
还有效，往后可经过什么事劝阻
又更改了方针没有。他变换无常，
总自相矛盾。问明他下定的决心来。

　　　　　　　　　　　　　　［对一近侍语此，近侍即下。

雷 　 耿　大姐的那家臣准是遭逢了不测。
蔼 特 孟　恐怕是如此，夫人。
雷 　 耿　　　　　　　　　可爱的贤卿，
告诉我，——只要说真话，——可得说真话，
你不爱我姐姐吗？
蔼 特 孟　　　　　　　　我爱她得光明磊落。
雷 　 耿　难道你从未踏上我姐夫的路径
到过那禁地吗？
蔼 特 孟　　　　　　　　那你就转错了念头。
雷 　 耿　我怕你同她已结下不解的私情，
她已把一身所有全给了你。
雷 特 孟　把我的信誉打赌，没有过，夫人。
雷 　 耿　我决不容许她对你那么样亲昵。

Be not familiar with her.

Edmund Fear me not. —

She and the duke her husband!

[*Enter*, *with drum and colours*, Albany,
Goneril, *and* Soldiers.]

Goneril [*Aside.*] I had rather lose the battle than that sister
Should loosen him and me.

Albany Our very loving sister, well be-met. —
Sir, this I heard: the king is come to his daughter,
With others whom the rigour of our state
Forc'd to cry out. Where I could not be honest,
I never yet was valiant: for this business,
It toucheth us, as France invades our land,
Not bolds the king, with others whom, I fear,
Most just and heavy causes make oppose.

Edmund Sir, you speak nobly.

Regan Why is this reason'd?

Goneril Combine together 'gainst the enemy;
For these domestic and particular broils
Are not the question here.

Albany Let's, then, determine
With the ancient of war on our proceeding.

Edmund I shall attend you presently at your tent.

Regan Sister, you'll go with us?

Goneril No.

Regan 'Tis most convenient; pray you, go with us.

Goneril [*Aside.*] O, ho, I know the riddle. — I will go.

[*As they are going out*, *enter* Edgar *disguised.*]

Edgar If e'er your grace had speech with man so poor,
Hear me one word.

Albany I'll overtake you. —

亲爱的贤卿,莫跟她相好。

蔼 特 孟	别担心。——

她和她丈夫来了!

〔旗鼓前导,亚尔白尼、刚瑙烈及众士卒上。

刚 瑙 烈　〔旁白〕我宁愿战事失利,不甘心那妹子
　　　　　将我们两人拆散。

亚尔白尼　亲爱的二妹,我们相遇得正好。——
　　　　　伯爵,听说是这样:父王投奔了
　　　　　他小女,还有忍不住我邦的暴政,
　　　　　不禁疾首高呼的百姓们,也都已
　　　　　跟着他同去。我问心不能无愧时,
　　　　　还从未心生过奋勇;但这事能使我
　　　　　关怀,都因为法兰西遣兵来犯境,
　　　　　却不因他推戴了王上,又连结
　　　　　叛民们,至于他们的兴兵,我怕是
　　　　　义正而辞严,正自有重大的缘由。

蔼 特 孟　公爷这话伟大。

雷　　耿　　　　　　为什么讲这个?

刚 瑙 烈　联合了起来共同和敌人对抗;
　　　　　这些国内的私争都不是邻兵
　　　　　压境的原因。

亚尔白尼　　　　　那就让我们去向
　　　　　我军的宿将们共商行军的进止。

蔼 特 孟　我去了马上就回到你帐中候命。

雷　　耿　大姊,你跟我们一块儿去吗?

刚 瑙 烈　不。

雷　　耿　那样最合式;你同我们去吧。

刚 瑙 烈　〔旁白〕啊哈,我可猜透了这个谜。——我就去。

〔众拟下时,蔼特加乔装上。

蔼 特 加　若是公爷同我这样的穷苦人
　　　　　曾有过交谈,且请听我一句话。

亚尔白尼　回头我来赶上你。——

[Exeunt all but Albany *and* Edgar. *]*

Speak.

Edgar Before you fight the battle, ope this letter.
If you have victory, let the trumpet sound
For him that brought it; wretched though I seem,
I can produce a champion that will prove
What is avouched there. If you miscarry,
Your business of the world hath so an end,
And machination ceases. Fortune love you!

Albany Stay till I have read the letter.

Edgar   I was forbid it.
When time shall serve, let but the herald cry,
And I'll appear again.

Albany Why, fare thee well. I will o'erlook thy paper.

[Exit Edgar. *]*

[Re-enter Edmund. *]*

Edmund The enemy's in view; draw up your powers.
Here is the guess of their true strength and forces
By diligent discovery; — but your haste
Is now urg'd on you.

Albany   We will greet the time.

[Exit.]

Edmund To both these sisters have I sworn my love;
Each jealous of the other, as the stung
Are of the adder. Which of them shall I take?
Both? one? or neither? Neither can be enjoy'd,
If both remain alive. to take the widow
Exasperates, makes mad her sister Goneril;
And hardly shall I carry out my side,
Her husband being alive. Now, then, we'll use
His countenance for the battle; which being done,
Let her who would be rid of him devise
His speedy taking off. As for the mercy
Which he intends to Lear and to Cordelia, —
The battle done, and they within our power,

〔除亚尔白尼及蔼特加，余众尽下。

你说吧。

蔼　特　加　在开战之前，请开缄一读这封信。
　　　　　　你如果战胜，叫军号传呼我来到；
　　　　　　我虽然外观鄙贱，但我能给你
　　　　　　看一名拥护这信里的言辞的战士。
　　　　　　若万一不幸，你也就料清了世务，
　　　　　　阴谋便自然终止。祝你幸运！

亚尔白尼　待一会，等我看完信。

蔼　特　加　　　　　　　　　我不能等待。
　　　　　　到时候，只要让令官高呼挑战，
　　　　　　我自会再来。

亚尔白尼　好吧，再见。我准定看你这封信。　〔蔼特加下。

　　　　　　　　　　〔蔼特孟重上。

蔼　特　孟　敌军已在望；扎定你队伍的阵势。
　　　　　　根据勤报，我这里记着有他们
　　　　　　实力的约数；如今可不容你再有
　　　　　　倏忽的从容。

亚尔白尼　　　　　　　我就去预备应变。　　〔下。

蔼　特　孟　我对这两姐妹都曾起誓过说爱好；
　　　　　　她们交互猜忌，好比见杯弓
　　　　　　就疑心蛇影。二人中我何从何去？
　　　　　　都要？要一个？都不要？两人都活着，
　　　　　　就一个也享受不到。要了那寡妇，
　　　　　　会激得她姐姐刚瑙烈恼怒成疯；
　　　　　　至于我同她，因为她丈夫还在，
　　　　　　也暂难成事。如今我们且利用
　　　　　　他那份声威来应战；等战事一停，
　　　　　　她本想把他去掉，就让她去设法
　　　　　　快将他除去。至于他存心要顾怜
　　　　　　李尔和考黛莲，——战事一经停当，
　　　　　　他们在我们掌中，便休想得赦；

Shall never see his pardon; for my state
Stands on me to defend, not to debate.

[Exit.]

SCENE II. *A field between the two Camps.*

[Alarum within. Enter, with drum and colours, Lear,
Cordelia, and Soldiers, over the stage; and exeunt.]
[Enter Edgar and Gloucester.]

Edgar   Here, father, take the shadow of this tree
For your good host; pray that the right may thrive;
If ever I return to you again,
I'll bring you comfort.
Gloucester   Grace go with you, sir!

[Exit Edgar].

[Alarum and retreat within. R-enter Edgar.]

Edgar   Away, old man; give me thy hand; away!
King Lear hath lost, he and his daughter ta'en.
Give me thy hand; come on!
Gloucester   No further, sir; a man may rot even here.
Edgar   What, in ill thoughts again? Men must endure
Their going hence, even as their coming hither;
Ripeness is all. come on.
Gloucester   And that's true too.

[Exeunt.]

SCENE III. *The* British *Camp near* Dover.

[Enter, in conquest, with drum and colours, Edmund;
Lear and Cordelia, as prisoners; Captain, Soldiers, &c.]
Edmund   Some officers take them away; good guard
Until their greater pleasures first be known

再说我自身眼前的处境,那只要
防护得周全,不用去疑难自扰。〔下。

第 二 景

〔介于两军间的一片旷野。〕
〔内作进军之号鸣。旗鼓前导,李尔、考黛莲及众士
卒上,过台面,下。

〔蔼特加与葛洛斯忒上。

蔼 特 加　　耽在这里吧,老丈,就把这树荫
　　　　　　当作寓主人;祝福有道者战胜;
　　　　　　只要我回得来,自会带宽慰给你。

葛 洛 斯 忒　愿神灵护佑你安全!　　　　　　　〔蔼特加下。
　　　　　　　　　　　　〔内作进军及退军之号鸣。蔼特加重上。

蔼 特 加　　快走,老人,让我搀着你,快走!
　　　　　　李尔王败了,他们父女俩遭了擒。
　　　　　　伸手给我;来吧。

葛 洛 斯 忒　　　　　　　　　不用再走远了,
　　　　　　老兄,我在这里死也是一样。

蔼 特 加　　什么,又往坏里想了?人去世
　　　　　　得跟投生同样地听其自然;
　　　　　　等成熟就是了。来吧。

葛 洛 斯 忒　　　　　　　　　这话也对。　　　　〔同下。

第 三 景

〔近多浮城之不列颠军中。〕
〔旗鼓前导,蔼特孟凯旋上,李尔与考黛莲被虏;队
长及众士卒随上。

蔼 特 孟　　要几名公差把他们带走;好好
　　　　　　看管起来,且等掌握重权者

That are to censure them.

Cordelia   We are not the first
Who with best meaning have incurr'd the worst.
For thee, oppressed king, am I cast down;
Myself could else out-frown false fortune's frown.
Shall we not see these daughters and these sisters?

Lear No, no, no, no. Come, let's away to prison:
We two alone will sing like birds i' the cage.
When thou dost ask me blessing, I'll kneel down
And ask of thee forgiveness. so we'll live,
And pray, and sing, and tell old tales, and laugh
At gilded butterflies, and hear poor rogues
Talk of court news; and we'll talk with them too,
Who loses and who wins, who's in, who's out;
And take upon's the mystery of things,
As if we were God's spies. and we'll wear out,
In a wall'd prison, packs and sects of great ones
That ebb and flow by the moon.

Edmund   Take them away.

Lear Upon such sacrifices, my Cordelia,
The gods themselves throw incense. Have I caught thee?
He that parts us shall bring a brand from heaven,
And fire us hence like foxes. Wipe thine eyes;
The goodyears shall devour them, flesh and fell,
Ere they shall make us weep; we'll see 'em starve first.
Come.

              [*Exeunt* Lear *and* Cordelia, *guarded.*]

Edmund Come hither, captain; hark.

判定要如何处置。

考　黛　莲　　　　　　　自来用意
善良招祸深，原不从我们开端。
为了你，蒙难的父王，我忧心如捣，
不为你，我自能藐视命运的颦眉。
我们不见见这些女儿和姐姐吗？

李　　尔　不要，不要，不要，不要。来吧，
让我们跑进牢里去；我们父女俩，
要像笼鸟一般，孤零零唱着歌。
你要我祝福的当儿，我会跪下去
恳请你饶恕。我们要这么过着活，
要祷告，要唱歌，叙述些陈年的故事，
笑话一般金红银碧的朝官们，
听那些可怜的东西说朝中的闻见；
我们也要和他们风生谈笑，
议论那个输，那个赢，谁当权，谁失势，
还要自承去参透万象的玄机，
仿佛上帝派我们来充当的密探。
我们要耐守在高墙的监里，直等到
那般跟月亮的盈亏而升降的公卿
徒党们都云散烟消。

蔼　特　孟　　　　　　　　　把他们带走。

李　　尔　在这样的牺牲上面，我的考黛莲，
就是天神们也要投奠些香花。
我拉住你没有？谁若要把我们离散，
除非从天上取下一炷火炬来，
将我们，像洞里的狐狸，熏出这人间。
揩干了眼泪；他们要我们哭泣，
可自会有恶毒的邪魔先把他们
遍体的肌肤都吞噬；我们先看了
他们死掉。来。　　　　　　[李尔及考黛莲被押下。

蔼　特　孟　你过来，队长，听着。

Take thou this note; go follow them to prison.
One step I have advanc'd thee; if thou dost
As this instructs thee, thou dost make thy way
To noble fortunes; know thou this, that men
Are as the time is: to be tender-minded
Does not become a sword; thy great employment
Will not bear question; either say thou'lt do't,
Or thrive by other means.

Captain   I'll do't, my lord.

Edmund   About it; and write happy when thou hast done.
Mark, — I say, instantly; and carry it so
As I have set it down.

Captain   I cannot draw a cart, nor eat dried oats;
If it be man's work, I'll do't.

[*Exit.*]

[*Flourish. Enter* Albany, Goneril,
Regan, Captain, Soldieys.]

Albany   Sir, you have show'd to-day your valiant strain,
And fortune led you well; you have the captives
Who were the opposites of this day's strife.
We do require them of you, so to use them
As we shall find their merits and our safety
May equally determine.

Edmund   Sir, I thought it fit
To send the old and miserable king
To some retention and appointed guard;
Whose age has charms in it, whose title more,
To pluck the common bosom on his side,
And turn our impress'd lances in our eyes
Which do command them. With him I sent the queen.
My reason all the same; and they are ready
To-morrow, or at further space, to appear
Where you shall hold your session. At this time
We sweat and bleed; the friend hath lost his friend;
And the best quarrels, in the heat, are curs'd

收下这张文件；跟他们监里去。
我已经提升你一级；你若奉行
这里边的训令，就上了荣华的大道；
你要明白，人得听时势去推移；
靡软的心肠不配作军人；你这件
重大的使命不容你说话；你先说
你准定办到，不然就另去高就吧。

队　　长　我准定办到，大人。

蔼　特　孟　　　　　　　　就动手；完了事
你就能自庆幸运，听我说，——马上干；
依我的指令去照办。

队　　长　我不能拉一辆大车，也不能吞干麦；
只要是人做的工作，我准能做到。　　　　[下。
　　　　　　　　[号声大作。亚尔白尼、刚瑙烈、雷耿、
　　　　　　　　队长及众士卒同上。

亚尔白尼　伯爵，你今天显示了你天性的骁勇，
又多亏命运将你好好地指引；
今天这战事的敌人已被你虏到。
我要你交出他们，等我们来决定，
按他们应得的罪名，也为我们
自己的安全之计，该如何处治。

蔼　特　孟　公爷，我认为那年老不幸的国王
该将他送交看管的专人去监守；
他那样的高年，更重要是他那名位，
都能吸引民心哀怜拥戴他，
反叫我们用饷银招募来的士兵
倒戈刺进我们发令者的眼里来。
法兰西王后我送她同去；至于
为什么理由，说不定都一样；他们
明天或往后，准备你升庭去审问。
如今我们流着汗，流着血；亲友们
战死在疆场；须知最有道的争端，

By those that feel their sharpness.
The question of Cordelia and her father
Requires a fitter place.

Albany   Sir, by your patience,
I hold you but a subject of this war,
Not as a brother.

Regan   That's as we list to grace him.
Methinks our pleasure might have been demanded,
Ere you had spoke so far. He led our powers,
Bore the commission of my place and person;
The which immediacy may well stand up
And call itself your brother.

Goneril   Not so hot;
In his own grace he doth exalt himself,
More than in your addition.

Regan   In my rights
By me invested, he compeers the best.

Goneril   That were the most if he should husband you.

Regan   Jesters do oft prove prophets.

Goneril   Holla, holla!
That eye that told you so look'd but asquint.

Regan   Lady, I am not well; else I should answer
From a full-flowing stomach. —General,
Take thou my soldiers, prisoners, patrimony;
Dispose of them, of me; the walls are thine.
Witness the world that I create thee here
My lord and master.

Goneril   Mean you to enjoy him?

Albany   The let-alone lies not in your good will.

Edmund   Nor in thine, lord.

Albany   Half-blooded fellow, yes.

Regan   [*To* Edmund.] Let the drum strike, and prove my
    title thine.

参与者，就是正在热血奔腾时，
遭逢了惨痛，也无有不把它诅咒。
怎么样判处考黛莲和她的父亲，
要另找相宜的所在。

亚尔白尼　　　　　　　　　阁下，对不起，
这番战争里我把你只当是下属，
不当作同僚。

雷　　耿　　　　　　那得看我们要怎样
借重他。我想你话未出口，该先问
我们的意向。他带着我们的队伍，
又身负我们自身和权位的委托；
他掌握的权能和我这么样近似，
也就无妨自号是你的同僚。

刚　瑙　烈　不用这般暴躁；他自身的光荣
抬高他他自己胜如你给他的虚衔。

雷　　耿　经我授与了我自己的权能名位，
他便能跟任何位重权高者相抗。

亚尔白尼　他当了你丈夫，至多也不过这样。

雷　　耿　开玩笑的常变成了先知。

刚　瑙　烈　　　　　　　　啊哈，啊哈！
对你这样说的那眼睛有点歪斜。

雷　　耿　爵夫人，我身子不很好受；不然时，
我该当大怒着用恶声相报。——将军，
把我的军队，俘虏，承产，都收下；
将他们，将我完全去自由支配。
让大家来作证，我在这里使你
作我的夫君。

刚　瑙　烈　　　　　你想占有他是不是？

亚尔白尼　准不准许可不必由你来决定。

蔼　特　孟　也不必由你，公爵。

亚尔白尼　　　　　　　混血儿，得由我。

雷　　耿　[对蔼特孟]传令击鼓，证明我给了你名衔。

Albany Stay yet; hear reason. —Edmund, I arrest thee
On capital treason; and, in thine arrest,

[*pointing to* Goneril]

This gilded serpent, —For your claim, fair sister,
I bar it in the interest of my wife;
'Tis she is subcontracted to this lord,
And I, her husband, contradict your bans.
If you will marry, make your loves to me;
My lady is bespoke.

Goneril   An interlude!

Albany Thou art arm'd, Gloucester; let the trumpet
    sound.

If none appear to prove upon thy person
Thy heinous, manifest, and many treasons,
There is my pledge; I'll prove it on thy heart,
Ere I taste bread, thou art in nothing less
Than I have here proclaim'd thee.

Regan   Sick, O, sick!

Goneril [*Aside.*] If not, I'll ne'er trust medicine.

Edmund There's my exchange. what in the world he is
That names me traitor, villain-like he lies.
Call by thy trumpet; he that dares approach,
On him, on you, who not? I will maintain
My truth and honour firmly.

Albany A herald, ho!

Edmund   A herald, ho, a herald!

Albany Trust to thy single virtue; for thy soldiers,
All levied in my name, have in my name
Took their discharge.

Regan   My sickness grows upon me!

Albany She is not well. —Convey her to my tent.

亚尔白尼	等一下；听我说。——蔼特孟，我将你逮捕，
	罪名是谋叛；和你同时逮捕的[指刚瑙烈]
	是这条五彩的花蛇。——美貌的姨妹，
	为了我妻子的利权起见，我取消
	你对他的所有权，她早跟这位伯爵
	有重婚的密约在先，我是她丈夫，
	我反对你这要和他成婚的预告。
	你若是要婚嫁，不如向我来求爱；
	我妻子早跟他订了婚。
刚 瑙 烈	好一出趣剧！
亚尔白尼	你身上佩的是武装，葛洛斯忒；
	让号声去吹放。如果没有人证明
	极恶的，显然的，和多数的逆图丛聚在
	你一人身上，这便是我给你的担保。
	我自会在餐前从你这心头证实
	我这里宣告你的罪名分毫不假。
雷 耿	病了啊，我病了！
刚 瑙 烈	[旁白]要不然，我决不再信
	毒药的灵效。
蔼 特 孟	那是我给你的交换品。
	这世上不论谁对我以逆贼相称，
	便撒了个无耻的大谎。快吹送军号；
	谁敢上前来挑衅，我对他，对你，——
	对谁不都一样？——自会决心去
	保持我忠贞的声誉。
亚尔白尼	传令官，喂！
蔼 特 孟	传令官，喂，传令官！
亚尔白尼	信赖你个人的勇敢；因为你的兵，
	征募来原都用我的名义，也都已
	用我的名义遣散。
雷 耿	我病得厉害了！
亚尔白尼	她病了。——送她到我的帐幕里去。

[Exit Regan, *led.]*

[Enter a Herald.*]*

Come hither, herald. — Let the trumpet sound, —
And read out this.

Officer   Sound, trumpet!

[A trumpet sounds.]

Herald   *[Reads.]* *If any man of quality or degree within the lists of the army will maintain upon Edmund,
supposed Earl of Gloucester, that he is a manifold
traitor, let him appear by the third sound of the
trumpet. He is bold in his defence.*

Edmund   Sound!   *[First trumpet.]*
Herald   Again!   *[Second trumpet.]*
Herald   Again!   *[Third trumpet.]*

[Third trumpet. Trumpet answers within.
Enter Edgar, *armed, preceded by a trumpet.]*

Albany   Ask him his purposes, why he appears
Upon this call o' the trumpet.

Herald   What are you?
Your name, your quality? and why you answer
This present summons?

Edgar   Know, my name is lost;
By treason's tooth bare-gnawn and canker-bit.
Yet am I noble as the adversary
I come to cope.

Albany   Which is that adversary?

Edgar   What's he that speaks for Edmund Earl of
    Gloucester?

Edmund   Himself: — what say'st thou to him?

Edgar   Draw thy sword,
That, if my speech offend a noble heart,
Thy arm may do thee justice: here is mine.
Behold, it is the privilege of mine honours,
My oath, and my profession. I protest, —
Maugre thy strength, youth, place, and eminence,
Despite thy victor sword and fire-new fortune,

　　　　　　　　　　　　　　　　　[雷耿被扶下。

　　　　　　　　　　　[一传令官上。

　　这里来,传令官,——就让号声去吹放,——把这个
　　去宣读。

队　　　长　吹号!　　　　　　　　　　　　　[号声作。]

传　令　官　[高诵]号令本部军中,若有不论哪一位出身高贵的
　　　　　　将士,认为这僭号葛洛斯忒伯爵的蔼特孟是个叛逆
　　　　　　多端的反贼,就让他在第三次号声时出头挑战;蔼特
　　　　　　孟是勇于自卫的。

蔼　特　孟　吹号!　　　　　　　　　　　　　[第一遍号。]

传　令　官　再吹号!　　　　　　　　　　　　[第二遍号。]

传　令　官　三吹号!　　　　　　　　　　　　[第三遍号。]

　　　　　　　　　　　　　　　　　[幕后有号声响应。]

　　　　[号声第三遍时蔼特加武装上场,一军号手前导。

亚尔白尼　问他来这里的目的,为何在这阵
　　　　　　号声里来到。

传　令　官　　　　　　　你是谁? 报出姓名
　　　　　　身份来。为什么你应答这声召唤?

蔼　特　加　我没有名字;奸谋的毒齿已把它
　　　　　　咬光蚀尽;但我来会战的那对手,
　　　　　　我出身的高贵却并不让他分毫。

亚尔白尼　那对手是谁?

蔼　特　加　　　　　　　他名叫蔼特孟,僭号称
　　　　　　葛洛斯忒伯爵,谁替他来答话?

蔼　特　孟　他亲自答话。你对他有什么话说?

蔼　特　加　拔出剑来,若果我言语冲撞的
　　　　　　是一副高贵的心肠,你能用武器
　　　　　　主张你自己的公道;这是我的剑:
　　　　　　你看,我向你挑战乃是我荣誉,
　　　　　　信誓,和武士的职业给我的特权:
　　　　　　我声言,——尽你去力壮年青权位高,
　　　　　　听你有战胜的余威和簇新的幸运,

Thy valour and thy heart, — thou art a traitor,
False to thy gods, thy brother, and thy father,
Conspirant 'gainst this high illustrious prince,
And, from the extremest upward of thy head
To the descent and dust beneath thy foot,
A most toad-spotted traitor. Say thou 'No,'
This sword, this arm, and my best spirits are bent
To prove upon thy heart, whereto I speak,
Thou liest.

Edmund   In wisdom I should ask thy name;
But since thy outside looks so fair and warlike,
And that thy tongue some say of breeding breathes,
What safe and nicely I might well delay
By rule of knighthood, I disdain and spurn.
Back do I toss those treasons to thy head;
With the hell-hated lie o'erwhelm thy heart;
Which, — for they yet glance by and scarcely bruise,
This sword of mine shall give them instant way,
Where they shall rest for ever. — Trumpets, speak!

> [*Alarums. They fight.* Edmund *falls.*]

Albany   Save him, save him!

Goneril   This is mere practice, Gloucester;
By the law of arms thou wast not bound to answer
An unknown opposite; thou art not vanquish'd,
But cozen'd and beguil'd.

Albany   Shut your mouth, dame,
Or with this paper shall I stop it. — Hold, sir;
Thou worse than any name, read thine own evil. —
No tearing, lady; I perceive you know it.

> [*Gives the letter to* Edmund.]

Goneril   Say if I do, — the laws are mine, not thine:
Who can arraign me for't?

任凭你多么凶，多么勇，——你是个逆贼，
对天神不真诚，对父兄信义全无，
想危害这一位尊荣显耀的明公，
从你头顶的最高尖直到你脚下
最低处的尘埃，整是个毒点污斑
生满身的贼子。只消你说声"不是"，
这剑，这臂膀，连同我登高的英勇，
准会在你那心窝里证明我这话：
你撒谎。

蔼　特　孟　　　　　聪明些我该问明你是谁，
但既然你外表有这般勇武英俊，
言语间还显示几分优良的教养，
我便不屑去顾虑武士风的成规，
谋安全，拘细礼，拒绝对你应战。
我把那叛乱不义罪掷还你头上去；
叫地狱般可恶的巨谎摧毁你的心，
又只因它们擦过了不曾留什么
伤痕，我这剑便马上会替它们开路，
让它们永远留在你心中。——吹号！

　　　　　　〔警号频传。二人剑斗。蔼特孟倒地。〕

亚尔白尼　饶了他，饶了他！
刚　瑙　烈　　　　　葛洛斯忒，这是奸谋，
按着决斗的规条你毋须去应答
一个不知名的对手；你不曾战败，
只受了人诳骗。
亚尔白尼　　　　　闭住你的嘴，女人，
不然，我就把这封信停止你开口。——
接住，你这狗贱贼；再没有名称
能形容你的坏，去看你自己的孽迹。——
别撕，夫人；我看你知道这封信。
刚　瑙　烈　就说我知道，法律在我掌握中，
不由你分配。谁能将我来问罪？　　　　　　〔下。

Albany   Most monstrous! O! —
Know'st thou this paper?

Edmund   Ask me not what I know.

              [*Exit.*]

Albany Go after her; she's desperate; govern her.

Edmund What, you have charg'd me with, that have I done;
And more, much more; the time will bring it out.
'Tis past, and so am I. — But what art thou
That hast this fortune on me? If thou'rt noble,
I do forgive thee.

Edgar   Let's exchange charity.
I am no less in blood than thou art, Edmund;
If more, the more thou hast wrong'd me.
My name is Edgar, and thy father's son.
The gods are just, and of our pleasant vices
Make instruments to plague us.
The dark and vicious place where thee he got
Cost him his eyes.

Edmund   Thou hast spoken right; 'tis true;
The wheel is come full circle; I am here.

Albany Methought thy very gait did prophesy
A royal nobleness. I must embrace thee;
Let sorrow split my heart, if ever I
Did hate thee or thy father!

Edgar   Worthy prince, I know't.

Albany Where have you hid yourself?
How have you known the miseries of your father?

Edgar By nursing them, my lord. — List a brief tale; —
And when 'tis told, O that my heart would burst! —
The bloody proclamation to escape
That follow'd me so near, — O, our lives' sweetness!
That with the pain of death we'd hourly die

亚尔白尼	真骇人听闻！啊！——你知道这信吗？
蔼　特孟	别问我知道些什么。 〔下。
亚尔白尼	赶上她；她要亡命胡干了；止住她。
蔼　特孟	你们所责我的罪状我确曾犯过；
	还不止，多得多；到时候自然会分晓。
	这一切都已成前尘，我也完了事。——
	可是你是谁，加给我这部命运？
	果真你系出名门，我便能原谅。
蔼　特加	让我们交相怜爱吧。蔼特孟，我身家
	不比你低微；若说我出身比你好，
	你将我这般伤害就加罪几分。
	我就是蔼特加，你父亲的儿子。
	天神们最是公平，把我们寻欢
	作乐的非行利用来将我们惩创。
	父亲在他那黑暗的胡为里生了你，
	也丢了他眼睛一双。
蔼　特孟	你说得不错；
	真是的，命运的轮盘满转了回来；
	我如今在这里生受。
亚尔白尼	我当初就见你
	步履间预示出身世的尊严华贵。
	我得拥抱你，我若对你们父子
	曾有过仇恨，让悲哀裂破我的心！
蔼　特加	可敬的公爷，我知道。
亚尔白尼	你一向在哪里
	躲避？怎么知道了你父亲的惨祸？
蔼　特加	看护了那疾苦我所以知道，公爷。
	请听我略叙些经临；等我话尽时，
	啊，但愿这颗心会顿时爆裂！
	为逃避追得我紧紧的那凶残的文告，——
	啊，最叫人醉心的莫过于生命！
	我们怎样也不甘心把一死来了事，

Rather than die at once! — taught me to shift
Into a madman's rags, to assume a semblance
That very dogs disdain'd; and in this habit
Met I my father with his bleeding rings,
Their precious stones new lost; became his guide,
Led him, begg'd for him, sav'd him from despair;
Never, — O fault! — reveal'd myself unto him,
Until some half hour past, when I was arm'd;
Not sure, though hoping of this good success,
I ask'd his blessing, and from first to last
Told him my pilgrimage; but his flaw'd heart,
Alack, too weak the conflict to support!
'Twixt two extremes of passion, joy and grief,
Burst smilingly.

Edmund   This speech of yours hath mov'd me,
And shall perchance do good: but speak you on;
You look as you had something more to say.

Albany If there be more, more woeful, hold it in;
For I am almost ready to dissolve,
Hearing of this.

Edgar   This would have seem'd a period
To such as love not sorrow; but another,
To amplify too much, would make much more,
And top extremity.
Whilst I was big in clamour, came there a man,
Who, having seen me in my worst estate,
Shunn'd my abhorr'd society; but then, finding
Who 'twas that so endur'd, with his strong arms
He fastened on my neck, and bellow'd out
As he'd burst heaven; threw him on my father;
Told the most piteous tale of Lear and him
That ever ear receiv'd; which in recounting

宁肯去随时忍受那临终的惨痛！——
我换上了疯人的褴褛，装一副外表
连狗子都鄙弃；然后遇见我父亲，
血涔涔的镶框，正新丧了那双瑰宝；
我为他当向导，领着他，替他乞食，
绝望里救了他回来；可是我从未，
——啊，真不该！——直到半点钟以前，
佩戴了武装，才向他，显露我自己；
我当时不敢说，虽然希望，结局好，
于是先请他为我祝了福，然后
细告他我们那长行的经过；唉，他那
有裂痕的心儿，太微弱，可不能支撑！
在极乐和深悲的两情冲激中，微微
一笑便碎了。

蔼 特 孟 你这番言语感动了我，
也许有几分善果；你且接着
往下说；看来你话还不曾说尽。

亚尔白尼 如果还有话，更加要伤心，停住吧，
我听你诉叙，几乎要化成热泪了。

蔼 特 加 不爱悲哀的到这里总以为该完结；
可不知祸患不单行，悲痛上还有
悲痛要添加，多的会更多，有分叫
如今这伤心的绝顶上增一层忉怛。
我正在大声号哭时，来了一个人，
他见我身处可鄙的穷途末路中，
本想要回避；但一见那是谁遭逢到
这般的不幸，他就伸长了双臂，
将我齐颈子搂紧，高声叫嚷得
仿佛要震破天空；又去拥抱我父亲；
又说起他自己和李尔，从无人耳听过
那样可怜的故事；正细诉遭遇时，
他那阵悲哀更变得高峭欲绝了，

His grief grew puissant, and the strings of life
Began to crack. twice then the trumpets sounded,
And there I left him tranc'd.

Albany   But who was this?

Edgar Kent, sir, the banish'd Kent; who in disguise
Follow'd his enemy king and did him service
Improper for a slave.

  [*Enter* a Gentleman *hastily, with a bloody knife.*]

Gent Help, help! O, help!

Edgar   What kind of help?

Albany   Speak, man!

Edgar What means that bloody knife?

Gent   'Tis hot, it smokes!
It came even from the heart of—O! she's dead!

Albany Who dead? speak, man!

Gent Your lady, sir, your lady! and her sister
By her is poisoned; she hath confess'd it.

Edmund I was contracted to them both: all three
Now marry in an instant.

Edgar   Here comes Kent.

Albany Produce their bodies, be they alive or dead.

        [*Exit* Gentleman.]

This judgement of the heavens, that makes us tremble,
Touches us not with pity.

     [*Enter* Kent.]

     —O, is this he?
The time will not allow the compliment
That very manners urges.

Kent   I am come
To bid my king and master aye good night.
Is he not here?

Albany   Great thing of us forgot!
Speak, Edmund, where's the king? and where's Cordelia?
Seest thou this object, Kent?

   [*The bodies of* Goneril *and* Regan *are brought in.*]

Kent Alack, why thus?

生命的弦丝便开始脱裂。那时节
有两通号报，我离他在那边晕去。

亚尔白尼　这是谁？

蔼　特　加　　　　是铿德，公爷，被放逐的铿德；
化了装他跟在仇视他的那君王左右，
供他作就是奴婢也不堪任的驱使。

　　　　　　　　　　　［一近侍手执血刃上。

近　　侍　救人啊，救人，救人！

蔼　特　加　　　　　怎么样救法？

亚尔白尼　你说吧，喂！

蔼　特　加　　　　这血刃是什么意思？

近　　侍　滚热的，还冒着烟！ 这是从她
心里头拔出来的——啊，她已经死了！

亚尔白尼　谁死了？ 说啊，你这人！

近　　侍　您夫人，公爷，是您的夫人！ 她妹妹
让她给药死了；这是她自己承认的。

蔼　特　孟　我跟她们俩都订得有婚约，现在
三个人正同时婚嫁。

蔼　特　加　　　　　铿德来了。

亚尔白尼　不用管她们死或活，把尸身抬出来。　　　［近侍下。
天神们这番谴罪好不叫我们
胆战心惊，但引不起我们的怜悯。

　　　　　　　　　　［铿德上。

啊，这是他吗？ 这样的时会可不容
我们去细讲礼貌上应有的客套。

铿　　德　我来和我的王上和主公永诀。
他不在这里吗？

亚尔白尼　　　　大事情我们忘掉了。
蔼特孟，王上在哪里？ 考黛莲在哪里？ ——
你看见这情景没有，铿德？

　　　　　　　　［刚瑙烈及雷耿之尸身被异上。

铿　　德　唉呀，为什么这样？

Edmund　　　　　Yet Edmund was belov'd.
The one the other poisoned for my sake,
And after slew herself.

Albany　Even so. — Cover their faces.

Edmund　I pant for life; some good I mean to do,
Despite of mine own nature. Quickly send, —
Be brief in it, — to the castle! for my writ
Is on the life of Lear and on Cordelia.
Nay, send in time!

Albany　　　　　Run, run, O, run!

Edgar　To who, my lord? — Who has the office? send
Thy token of reprieve.

Edmund　Well thought on. take my sword,
Give it the Captain.

Albany　　　　　Haste thee for thy life!

　　　　　　　　　　　　　　　　[*Exit* Edgar.]

Edmund　He hath commission from thy wife and me
To hang Cordelia in the prison, and
To lay the blame upon her own despair,
That she fordid herself.

Albany　The gods defend her! — Bear him hence awhile.

　　　　　　　　　　　　　　[Edmund *is borne off*.]

　　[*Re-enter* Lear, *with* Cordelia *dead in his arms*;
　　　　　Edgar, Captain, *and others following*.]

Lear　Howl, howl, howl! — O, you are men of stone.
Had I your tongues and eyes, I'ld use them so
That heaven's vault should crack! She's gone for ever!
I know when one is dead, and when one lives.
She's dead as earth! Lend me a looking glass;
If that her breath will mist or stain the stone,
Why, then she lives!

Kent　　　　　Is this the promis'd end?

Edgar　Or image of that horror?

Albany　　　　　　　　　Fall, and cease!

蔼　特　孟	只因都爱了 蔼特孟；这一个为了我先将那一个 使毒药弄死，随后她又自杀。
亚尔白尼	说得不错。——把她们的脸盖住。
蔼　特　孟	我口吐着生命的残喘，我决心背着我 天生的本性，在未死前稍微行点善。—— 快派人，赶快去，到堡里！因为我下了 命令叫把李尔和考黛莲都处死。 嗳，要趁早！
亚尔白尼	快跑，快跑啊，快跑！
蔼　特　加	去找谁，公爷？——那值班管事的是谁？ 给我一个免刑的凭证。
蔼　特　孟	想得周全。拿我这把剑去， 把它交给那队长。
亚尔白尼	拼命赶快去！　　　　〔蔼特加下。
蔼　特　孟	他有你妻子和我的命令，叫当监 绞死了考黛莲，只推说她自尽是为 绝望过度。
亚尔白尼	天神们护佑她！——把他暂时抬开。 　　　　　　　　　　　〔蔼特孟被舁下。 〔李尔抱考黛莲之尸身重上，蔼特加、队长及余人 随上。
李　　　尔	快哀号，快哀号，快哀号！啊，你们是铁石人！ 我有了你们的那些舌头和眼睛， 便要用它们来号哭得天崩地陷！ 她一去不来了！我知道怎样时人活着， 怎样时已经死。她死得跟泥土一般！ 借一面镜子给我，要是她呼吸 沾雾了镜面，哈，那她还有命！
铿　　　德	难道这就是世界的末日到了？
蔼　特　加	还许是那恐怖未来前的象兆？
亚尔白尼	倒下来，

Lear This feather stirs! she lives! If it be so,
It is a chance which does redeem all sorrows
That ever I have felt.

Kent   O my good master! [*Kneeling.*]

Lear Pr'ythee, away!

Edgar   'Tis noble Kent, your friend.

Lear A plague upon you, murderers, traitors all!
I might have sav'd her; now she's gone for ever! —
Cordelia, Cordelia! stay a little. Ha!
What is't thou say'st? — Her voice was ever soft,
Gentle, and low, — an excellent thing in woman. —
I kill'd the slave that was a-hanging thee.

Officer 'Tis true, my lords, he did.

Lear   Did I not, fellow?
I have seen the day, with my good biting falchion
I would have made them skip. I am old now,
And these same crosses spoil me. — Who are you?
Mine eyes are not o' the best; I'll tell you straight.

Kent If fortune brag of two she lov'd and hated,
One of them we behold.

Lear This is a dull sight. — Are you not Kent?

Kent   The same,
Your servant Kent. — Where is your servant Caius?

Lear He's a good fellow, I can tell you that;
He'll strike, and quickly too. he's dead and rotten.

Kent No, my good lord; I am the very man, —

Lear I'll see that straight.

Kent That from your first of difference and decay
Have follow'd your sad steps. —

　　　　　　　终止这伤心的惨事。

李　　　尔　　　　　　　　　这羽毛还在动！
　　　　　　　她还没有死！要是她果真还活着，
　　　　　　　便算我幸运，可以赎尽偿清
　　　　　　　我从来所受的悲痛。

铿　　　德　　　　　　　　　我的好主公啊！　　　〔跪下。

李　　　尔　请你走开去！

蔼　特　加　　　　　　　这是你的朋友铿德。

李　　　尔　满都去遭瘟，你们那班逆贼
　　　　　　　和杀人的凶犯！我还许救得她回来！
　　　　　　　如今她可一去不回了！——考黛莲，
　　　　　　　考黛莲！耽一会。哈！你说什么？——
　　　　　　　她声音永远是轻软，温柔，低低的，
　　　　　　　那在女人家是个优良的德性。——
　　　　　　　我已经把那绞死你的奴才杀死。

队　　　长　不错，大人们，他杀了。

李　　　尔　　　　　　　　可不是吗，人儿？
　　　　　　　我有过那日子，用一把锋利的偃月刀
　　　　　　　能叫他们吓得跳。如今我老了，
　　　　　　　这种种磨难累得我不中用。——你是谁？
　　　　　　　我眼睛不怎么顶好；等我来马上说。

铿　　　德　若是命运神夸说她先宠而后恨过
　　　　　　　两个人，你同我各人眼中有一个。

李　　　尔　我眼光好暗啊。——你不是铿德吗？

铿　　　德　　　　　　　　　　　　　正是，
　　　　　　　你臣仆铿德。你仆人凯优斯在哪里？

李　　　尔　我跟你说吧，他是个好人；他会打，
　　　　　　　并且打得快。他已经死掉，烂掉了。

铿　　　德　没有死，我的好主公，我就是那人——

李　　　尔　让我就来认认。

铿　　　德　自从你初次转进了命运的坎坷，
　　　　　　　一直跟你到如今——

Lear   You are welcome hither.

Kent   Nor no man else. All's cheerless, dark, and dead-
     ly. —

Your eldest daughters have fordone themselves,
And desperately are dead.

Lear   Ay, so I think.

Albany   He knows not what he says, and vain is it
That we present us to him.

Edgar   Very bootless.

          [*Enter a* Captain.]

Captain   Edmund is dead, my lord.

Albany   That's but a trifle here. —
You lords and noble friends, know our intent:
What comfort to this great decay may come
Shall be applied. for us, we will resign,
During the life of this old majesty,
To him our absolute power. —[*to* Edgar *and Kent*] you to
     your rights;
With boot, and such addition as your honours
Have more than merited. —All friends shall taste
The wages of their virtue, and all foes
The cup of their deservings. —O, see, see!

Lear   And my poor fool is hang'd! No, no, no life!
Why should a dog, a horse, a rat, have life,
And thou no breath at all? Thou'lt come no more,
Never, never, never, never, never! —
Pray you undo this button. thank you, sir. —
Do you see this? Look on her, —look, —her lips, —
Look there, look there! —

                      [*He dies.*]

Edgar   He faints! —My lord, my lord! —

Kent   Break, heart; I pr'ythee break!

李　　　尔　　　　　　　　　欢迎你这里来。

铿　　　德　除了我再没有旁人。满目的凄凉，
　　　　　阴惨惨，死沉沉。你两位长公主她们，
　　　　　都是去自寻的死路，死得没有救。

李　　　尔　哦，我也这么想。

亚尔白尼　　　　　　　　　他说什么话，
　　　　　连他自己都不知道，我们要他
　　　　　认识我们更不成。

蔼　特　加　　　　　　　　　一点都不行。
　　　　　　　　　　　［一队长上。

队　　　长　大人，蔼特孟死了。

亚尔白尼　　　　　　　　那无关紧要。——
　　　　　亲贵友好们，请明白我们的意思：
　　　　　这大祸该怎样善后就怎样去善后。
　　　　　至于我们自己，已决心辞了任，
　　　　　在这位老王上生前，把君权让给他
　　　　　收回自用。——［对蔼特加及铿德］你们，各自
　　　　　　　去复了位；
　　　　　另外还有些酬功，但那可偿不清
　　　　　你们那片精忠。一切的亲者
　　　　　都得尝自己那美德的报酬，仇者
　　　　　喝一樽应受的惩创。——啊呀，你们看！

李　　　尔　我这可怜的小宝贝给他们绞死了！
　　　　　没有，没有，没有了命！为什么
　　　　　一条狗，一匹马，一只老鼠要有命，
　　　　　你却没有一息气？你不会回来了，
　　　　　决不会，决不会，决不会，决不会，决不会！——
　　　　　请你解开这扣子。多谢你，阁下。
　　　　　你看见这个吗？看她，——看着，——她嘴唇——
　　　　　看那里！——看那里！　　　　　　　　　［死去。］

蔼　特　加　　　　　　　　晕过去了。——王上，王上！

铿　　　德　快碎啊，我的心，快碎掉！

Edgar   Look up, my lord.

Kent   Vex not his ghost. O, let him pass! he hates him
That would upon the rack of this rough world
Stretch him out longer.

Edgar   He is gone indeed.

Kent   The wonder is he hath endur'd so long;
He but usurp'd his life.

Albany   Bear them from hence. — Our present business
Is general woe. — [*To* Kent *and* Edgar.] Friends of my
      soul, you twain
Rule in this realm and the gor'd state sustain.

Kent   I have a journey, sir, shortly to go;
My master calls me, — I must not say no.

Edgar   The weight of this sad time we must obey,
Speak what we feel, not what we ought to say.
The oldest have borne most. we that are young
Shall never see so much, nor live so long.

                    [*Exeunt, with a dead march.*]

蔼 特 加	
	王上,向上看。

铿　　德　别打扰他的魂。啊,让他去了吧!
谁把他在这具刑架上,这强韧的人间,
多架些时候,准会遭他的痛恨。

蔼　特　加　他真的去了。

铿　　德　　　　　　　奇怪的乃是他竟会
支持得这么久;他只是强据着生命。

亚 尔 白 尼　把他们抬走。——我们目今的事务
是要上下一体地去同伸哀悼。——
〔对铿德及蔼特加〕朋友们,这一片邦疆由
　　　　你们两位
来主宰,请你们来支持这分崩共残碎。

铿　　德　公爷,我不久就要别离这尘世;
我主公叫我去,我不能向他推辞。

蔼　特　加　我们得逆来忍受着这伤心的重担;
有话说不出,只能道心中的悲痛。
最老的遭逢得最多。我们年少的
决不会身经如许,还活得这样老。

〔同下,奏丧亡进行曲。

图书在版编目（CIP）数据

李尔王/[英]莎士比亚著;孙大雨译.
—上海:上海三联书店,2018.
ISBN 978-7-5426-6173-9

Ⅰ.①李… Ⅱ.①莎… ②孙… Ⅲ.①悲剧—剧本—
英国—中世纪 Ⅳ.①I561.33

中国版本图书馆 CIP 数据核字(2017)第 320865 号

李尔王（中英文双语对照）

著　　者　[英]威廉·莎士比亚
译　　者　孙大雨

责任编辑　钱震华
装帧设计　陈益平

出版发行　上海三联书店
　　　　　(201199)中国上海市都市路 4855 号
印　　刷　上海昌鑫龙印务有限公司

版　　次　2018 年 4 月第 1 版
印　　次　2018 年 4 月第 1 次印刷
开　　本　890×1240　1/32
字　　数　240 千字
印　　张　8.25
书　　号　ISBN 978-7-5426-6173-9/I·1360
定　　价　30.00 元